NEST OF THIEVES

Jules Adrienn

The characters and events in this book are fictitious. Any similarity to real persons, living or dead, places, or events is coincidental and not intended by the author.

Nest of Thieves

ISBN: (ebook) 978-1-964636-31-3
(print) 978-1-964636-32-0

Inkspell Publishing
207 Moonglow Circle #101
Murrells Inlet, SC 29576

Edited By Toni Kelley
Cover art By Emily's World By Design

DEDICATION

To all the writers working to create their best story—remember that perseverance is your ace in the hole. To all the readers who have taken the time to point out my gifts and my flaws—thank you for helping me persevere.

Now let's get this party started…

CHAPTER ONE

Conor Monroe ran up the hill toward the chain link fence but couldn't hold the pace. He slowed to catch his breath. Once he and Sully cleared the fence, they'd be home free. He tightened his grip on the black metal cash box under his arm and looked back. Sully met his gaze, his face black with grease paint.

"C'mon! We're almost there!" Conor yelled, pushing back into a sprint.

He looked ahead at the silhouette of the fence stamped against the clear night sky. A quick look back at Sully told the story. The two security guards chasing them were twenty—maybe twenty-five—yards back. And the off-duty cop with the beer belly was totally out of the picture, watching their escape with binoculars from the stadium's ticket booth. The problem was the empty dog leashes hanging from the cop's hand. Everything hinged on when the cop had released his Rottweilers. That and how fast those black and tan monsters could run. He and Sully had to get over that fence. Fast.

Adrenaline dumped into his system. The night sky peeled open, turning bright as his pupils dilated. He bore down, ignoring the trouble whirling around him.

The impossible weight of each step.

The acid burn in his thighs and lungs.

The shouts of the security guards screaming for him to stop.

He tossed the cash box over the fence, scrambled up it, and then vaulted the barbed wire. His feet hit the sidewalk. He rolled. Back on his feet, he grabbed the fence. The two security guards hadn't made up much distance. Sully was going to make it. Then Conor's heart sank as he watched the Rottweilers fly by the security guards with fantastic speed. They closed on Sully in great, muscled strides. Sully looked back, caught sight of the dogs, and stumbled. Conor shook the fence and yelled, "Run!"

In a dead run, Sully threw his cash box over the fence. Conor heard the box hit the sidewalk behind him, change pinging on the concrete. The fence rattled as Sully slammed into it. Gasping for air, he said, "I…can't…climb."

Conor pushed nose-to-nose with him. "The dogs are coming! Move!"

Sully scrambled up the fence, but the lead Rottweiler was a stride away, ready to leap. Conor shook the fence and screamed at the dog.

The Rottweiler threw himself at Conor. Slobber flew into Conor's eye as the dog hit the fence and clamped down on the chain link.

Conor backed up, blinking to clear his vision. A blurry image of Sully perched on top of the barbed wire came into focus. Sully leaped. Conor watched him plummet and hit the ground with a thud.

Sully lay face-down in the grass. He wasn't moving. Conor held his breath. He couldn't leave Sully. But he couldn't stand here and let the guards catch him either.

Sully moaned and pushed off the ground.

Conor exhaled. *Thank God.*

The fence shook with a jackpot rattle as the second Rottweiler and both security guards slammed into it. Conor helped Sully up and then turned toward the fence. The guards obviously spent a lot of time in the weight room. One was goateed, bald, and a couple inches shy of six feet.

The other was well over six feet and probably turned sideways to fit through doors. Conor decided the bald guy was the scarier of the two. His neck was a pillar of muscle, and his vein-wrapped arms stretched the sleeves of his blue golf shirt embroidered with "Armco Security."

Eyes bulging, the bald guy shook the fence. "You guys are dead!"

Conor grabbed Sully by the shoulder and pulled him away from the fence. Sully pointed back at the guard. "Yeah? Come over here and we'll see who's dead, you motherfu—"

Conor clapped a hand over Sully's mouth and whispered, "Shhh. You want them to pick you out of a lineup? Let's go before they get over the fence."

Sully glanced at the guards and mumbled, "It'll be tomorrow before those muscleheads get over it."

Conor pointed at Sully's cash box on the sidewalk. The lid was broken open. Change was spilled everywhere along with a few bills.

Sully nodded and got down on a knee, shoving the money back into the box. Conor turned, looking for his box. It stood on end in a mud puddle. He picked it up, wiped off the mud, and shoved it under his arm. A gust of wind blew a few loose tens and twenties from Sully's broken box around his feet. He picked up the bills, stuffing them in his pocket. Behind him, the fence rattled. Conor looked back.

The bald security guard was halfway up the fence. His monster of a partner crouched below him, straining to push him higher.

Sully tapped Conor's shoulder. Cash box in hand, Sully dipped his head toward the quiet neighborhood of split-levels and colonials across the street. Conor nodded, following Sully in a run across the street.

Four blocks deep into the neighborhood, Conor cut through the backyard of a big, white house with two-story pillars bracing the front porch. He pushed through a hedge at the back end of the property, walking out into a parking lot with Sully close behind. A Ford Bronco idled next to a handicapped parking sign. Conor opened the front passenger door.

Fitz stared at him from the driver's seat. "Did I hear dogs barking?"

Conor slid into the front passenger seat, breathing hard. "They were doing more than barking."

"One nearly tore a piece outta me," said Sully, slamming his door shut. "Just drive. Security might still be on our ass."

Fitz put the Bronco in drive and pulled out of the parking lot. He eased into traffic behind a red pickup and glanced over at Conor. "How much we get?"

Conor opened the glove compartment, grabbed a rag, and wiped the greasepaint off his face. Then he opened the lid on his cash box, shut it, and put it on the floorboard between his feet.

"What's wrong?" asked Fitz.

Conor held up his shaking hand. "Just give me a minute, okay?"

Fitz looked back at Sully, glanced at Conor, and then reached under his seat. He pulled a can of beer from under the seat, passed it back to Sully, and then pulled out another can and tossed it in Conor's lap. "There's gotta be a better way than this," he said, easing into a turn lane.

"For what?" asked Conor, cracking open his beer.

"Just saying," said Fitz, turning left onto a busy street lined with strip malls on either side. "Too much risk, not enough reward."

"We probably got around five grand," said Sully. "That ain't bad. Plus, those security guards got lucky. If they hadn't been—"

"I agree with Fitz," said Conor. He turned in his seat to face Sully. "We almost got caught."

Sully returned his gaze, looking serious as he took a sip of his beer, seemingly deep in thought. "But you know what, Conor?" he said.

"What?"

Sully smiled. "We didn't."

Conor couldn't help it. Sully's big, goofy smile set him off. He started laughing. A little at first, and then a lot, with both Sully and Fitz joining in. He shook his beer, spraying it and laughing until he could barely breathe. Sully reached over the back seat, hugging him. Fitz wrapped his hand on the back of Conor's neck, joining in the group hug while he drove.

It took a minute before everyone calmed down. Conor wiped his eyes, shook his head, and took a deep, cleansing breath. He looked over at Fitz, and then back at Sully. These guys were family. In a town like Brannigan, that mattered. Without people to back you up, you were nothing. And they'd done pretty good for themselves, all things considered. With the economy the way it was—no real work to speak of for guys without a degree—he, Sully, and Fitz had carved out a niche.

A little part-time work here and there as auto mechanics, supplemented by an occasional robbery or theft. But to make it all work, they stuck to a set of rules.

No jobs that gathered attention.

And no jobs where civilians could get hurt.

Up until now, those rules had put them in a pretty good place. They were able to pay their bills, they stayed under the radar, and they had enough cash to have fun. The problem was that it was becoming increasingly clear that Fitz was right. The rules, by design, added up to, "Too much risk for too little reward." But what was the alternative?

"Hey, you guys want to go to the Red Fox and celebrate?" said Sully.

"I'm in," said Fitz.

Conor nodded. "Sure, but only if your sister's not there."

Sully sighed. "You can't keep ducking her. You gotta talk to her and work it out or break it off for good."

"Not today," said Conor.

"Fine," mumbled Sully. "But you have no idea what your bullshit puts me through. I gotta live with her."

"Move out of your mom's house and that wouldn't be a problem," said Fitz.

Conor held in a laugh. There was no need to torment Sully—his sister, Mona, already did that on a regular basis. She was huge trouble. A black-haired, hourglass-figured beauty from the depths of hell who probably had the bodies of all her previous boyfriends buried in her backyard. Conor knew she was a problem the first day he'd met her when they were five years old. But somehow, someway, he still managed to get caught in her web. It had been exciting while it lasted. The girl was hot. Like surface of the sun hot. But it went south fast, just the way he knew it would, with Mona becoming more and more demanding. She actually started talking marriage after two weeks. Conor looked out his window, watching the streets of Brannigan zip by. Marriage. That was the last thing he needed. And it wasn't going to happen any time soon, especially with Mona.

"Just drop me off at home. You guys have fun without me," said Conor. He looked over at Fitz. "And feel free to come up with any ideas about planning something big."

Fitz looked over. "You serious?"

Conor shrugged. "Maybe."

Fitz tilted down his rear-view mirror to eyeball Sully. "What do you think?"

Sully took a moment, then said, "I think we're fine, but we can talk."

The brakes squealed as Fitz pulled to the curb next to Conor's apartment complex.

"I'll see you guys later for my split on this job," said Conor. He opened his door, stepped out on the street, and then leaned back into the SUV. "And let me know if you come up with any ideas."

Sully eyed him. "We can do that—if you talk to Mona."

"I'll take care of it," said Conor. He stepped out of the Bronco, shut the door, and walked toward his apartment complex, waving as the Bronco slipped into the night.

CHAPTER TWO

Fitz tapped his cigarette on an ashtray and looked over the bar. The Red Fox was dead. A few lowlifes nursed their drinks, but except for Mona and her crew of divas— who left in a huff when Conor didn't show—it was a quiet night. That was a good thing as far as Fitz was concerned. It gave him and Sully a chance to talk over the next job, which turned into lots of ideas for penny-ante heists, but nothing with a big payout. He stubbed out his cigarette and looked around. Old timers everywhere. His gaze drifted across the front of the bar. Two old men playing cards caught his attention. He glanced at Sully, holding a red plastic cup of beer. Reaching for the pack of Marlboros in front of Sully, Fitz pulled out a cigarette and lit it. Smoke drifted into his eye. He blinked, and then leaned across the table toward Sully.

"Hey," he said. "Isn't that Duck and Artie playing cards up front?"

Sully wiped beer off his chin. He craned his neck for a look. "Yeah. So what?"

"I'd bet my left nut that if anyone knows about a big job, it's those two."

"How you figure?"

Fitz sucked in a lungful of smoke and stared at the two men. Duck had been a union rep at Swan Manufacturing back in the day. Word was he barely did a lick of work, but somehow managed to get a big payout when the plant moved overseas. What he did now was anyone's guess. But he drove a nice car, had a big house, and was never short on cash. Artie was less conspicuous—just an old bald guy who smoked, drank, and kept a seat warm at the Fox. But there had been rumors for years. Whispers about the two of them doing more than playing cards and sipping rum and cokes. The truly deluded swore they ran the criminal underworld. Fitz wasn't about to give them that much credit, but there was something not right about them. Like they stayed too far under the radar for it to be real.

Fitz turned his attention back to Sully. "You know what people say. Maybe it's true."

Sully rolled his eyes. "Maybe twenty years ago they stole somebody's wallet. Look at them. They can barely breathe."

Fitz stubbed his cigarette. He stood up and drank the rest of his beer. "Well, I'm gonna get a beer and take a seat up front. Maybe I'll hear something interesting."

"And what am I supposed to do?" said Sully.

Fitz shrugged. "I don't know. Watch the game. Hit on a girl or something. I'll be back after one beer."

As he walked down the length of the bar, Fitz watched Duck lift a cigarette to his mouth. The old man's head was covered in a lion's mane of thick, white hair, the same color and style he'd worn for the past twenty years. His pal Artie had a head that shined like a newly waxed car except for the thin gray fringe of hair that wrapped around his ears and the back of his head. It was funny how both of them never seemed to age. They were old and had always been old. Fitz slipped into a seat at the end of the bar. He ordered a draft. His back faced the old men who sat maybe eight feet behind him. The bartender filled a mug and handed it over. Fitz sipped the beer and leaned back.

At first, all he heard was the shuffling of cards, slurping of drinks, and an occasional curse word. It took him a minute before he heard their murmur of conversation. They tried to keep it between themselves, but their old ears betrayed them, forcing them to whisper loud enough for him to hear. A continual low banter. Apparently, they'd already heard about the theft of the cash boxes at the football game. That pricked Fitz's radar. There was no way that information had gone public yet. Either they'd heard about it from someone who'd watched it go down, or they were told about it from a friend inside the police department. Either way, it confirmed that the talk was at least a little bit true—Duck and Artie were somehow connected. Fitz could barely wait to go back and tell Sully. Not like the old geezers had whispered the combination to Fort Knox, but still, it would be fun to gossip. He lifted his mug to drain it, eager to talk to Sully, and then lowered his beer, focusing his attention. The mumbled whispers of the two old men had moved to a new subject. Something that didn't sound real—couldn't be real.

The more Fitz listened, the more his whole body tightened. His heart pounded. When they'd finished, he forced himself to sip his beer and stay put. It wouldn't look right if he jumped up right after hearing that. He made a show of finishing his beer and watching the game on the flat screen over the bar. Then he got up, put a couple bucks on the bar, and walked calmly toward Sully.

A girl with long blonde hair and piercings in her nose and bottom lip sat next to Sully. Sully had his hand on her leg while he whispered in her ear, oblivious to everything around him. Fitz tapped Sully on the shoulder.

"We need to talk," he said.

The girl turned. "We're busy."

Fitz looked at Sully, glanced back at Duck and Artie, and then stared at Sully with raised eyebrows.

Sully didn't look happy, but he lifted his hand from the girl's leg and reached for his wallet. "Go get me a drink," he said, handing her a twenty. "I'll be right over."

The girl took the money, flashed a look of displeasure at Fitz, and then headed for the bar.

Fitz took a seat. He tapped a cigarette out of the pack on the table. His hand shook while he lit it.

"You're not going to believe this," he said, exhaling a cloud of smoke.

"What?" whispered Sully.

"I think I got something," said Fitz. He glanced around, his whispers coming out in curls of smoke. "It's big. But we have to move fast. Real fast."

Sully leaned closer. "What is it?"

Fitz reached out, grabbed Sully by the back of the neck, and pulled him close.

CHAPTER THREE

Conor pulled his keys out as he ran up the stairs to his apartment. He flipped through the keys as he got to the second floor. Rounding a corner into the hallway, he walked straight into someone.

"Damn. Sorry," he said, picking up the key ring the person had dropped. He smiled. A girl with dark, shoulder-length hair looked back at him with big brown eyes. Even with no makeup and dressed in the blue, nondescript work clothes of a janitorial, delivery, or warehouse worker, she looked great. Except for the angry scar on her cheek. Healed, but still pink, as if it happened not too long ago.

"That was my fault," she said, taking her keys from his hand. "Wasn't paying attention. I'm all out of whack—just got switched to day shift."

Conor smiled. "You live here?"

He watched her play with her keys, avoiding eye contact, keeping her head turned to hide her scar.

She glanced up, and then held her hand out. "I'm your next-door neighbor, Julia."

Conor frowned. "You're my what?"

Julia managed half a smile, her hand still outstretched. She glanced at her hand. "You gonna leave me hanging?"

He shook her hand, feeling his face grow hot. "Sorry. I'm Conor. So, how long—"

"Have I lived next door? A little over a month." She

pulled her hand away and turned toward the stairwell. "Nice to finally meet you, Conor. See you around."

"Wait," Conor said, waiting for Julia to turn back toward him before adding, "You've lived here over a month?"

That pulled a big smile out of her. And what a smile. Her whole face seemed to light up. "Yeah," she said. "Right next door. I waved a few times, but you always seemed to be in a rush."

Conor smiled sheepishly. A good-looking girl… No. A s*moking-hot girl* moved in next door and he was too busy to notice. That sounded about right. His mouth went on auto pilot.

"Listen, I been kinda occupied lately. I'm really sorry. I'm not that kinda guy. I'd never—"

When she laughed, it knocked all the embarrassment out of him. "It's fine," she said. "No harm done."

Conor smiled, embarrassed, then said, "If you need anything, I owe you. Just say the word."

Her smile flattened. She played with her keys for a moment, lost in thought, and then looked up, and said, "Uh, yeah. Sure," and turned away.

He reached out and touched her arm. "Is something wrong?"

She looked down the hall at the doors to their apartments. "It's nothing. I just got home and—I don't know—I have a weird feeling that someone's in my apartment."

"Really?"

Julia nodded.

"Why would you think someone's in your apartment?"

"I don't know. I just do," she said.

Conor peered down the hall toward her apartment. Her answer didn't make sense. But if taking a look made her feel better, why not? "Let me check it out," he said. "It's the least I can do after being such a jerk."

Telling her to stay in the hall, Conor unlocked her door and walked into her apartment. It was sparse. White curtains on the windows. A vase of dried sunflowers on the kitchen counter. He walked into the living room. Above the couch, a painting of a dark-haired girl sitting on a sand dune looking out over the ocean caught his attention. The scene was painted in a hazy blur. It seemed distant—beautiful, but a little sad. The signature caught his attention.

Julia Terranova.

He glanced toward the open front door, seeing Julia in profile.

This girl was full of surprises.

The rest of the apartment was more of the same—clean and simple. Some decorative clamshell soaps were in the bathroom. Art books were stacked on the floor next to her twin bed. A crease of light blue sheets peeked out beneath the bed's white comforter. An easel and a small table arranged with a palette, paints, and brushes were set up in the corner of her bedroom under the only window. The canvas was blank. The only hint of disorder was a small pile of clothes near her closet. He walked over and looked at the T-shirt, crumpled Lycra shorts, and worn running shoes.

He walked back to the front door.

"No one's here," he said as he entered the hall.

She stepped by him into her apartment. "Thanks. I appreciate it."

He stuck his foot in the jamb as she tried to close the door. "Hey, Julia?"

Her face appeared in the crack.

"You're going to need these," he said, holding her keys.

He dropped them in her outstretched hand. Before she could close the door, he blurted, "You doing anything tomorrow?"

The door swung open a bit and her face brightened. "Nope. I'm off work. Why?"

"Do you want me to show you around?"

"Sure."

He stepped away and then looked back with a smile. "I'll come over around noon. Okay?"

She nodded and then pulled her door shut. He heard her say, "Thanks for checking my apartment. See you tomorrow," from behind the closed door.

Staring at the closed door, he exhaled the breath he'd been holding, and then walked the five feet that separated his door from hers, jangling his keys, in disbelief that a girl like Julia had lived next door to him for over a month, and he hadn't even noticed. He unlocked his door, stepped inside, threw his keys on his kitchen counter, and turned to stare at the wall separating his apartment from Julia's.

Life was full of surprises. Sometimes they were even good.

* * *

He was almost asleep when his cell buzzed. The mattress creaked as he grabbed his phone from his nightstand. It was Sully.

"Yeah?" he said, sitting up in bed.

"We gotta talk," said Sully.

"About what?"

"About going big."

"Oh—really? Let's hear it."

"No. In person. You, me, and Fitz."

Conor looked at the radio clock on his nightstand.

"Uh, it's a little late. How 'bout tomorrow?"

"It would be better now," said Sully. "This can't wait."

"I'm beat. Can I call you in the morning?"

Sully huffed, "Fine." Then he added, "And don't forget to talk to Mona. When I saw her at the Fox, she got bitchy as hell when I told her you weren't coming," before he ended the call.

Conor put his cell on his nightstand. It glowed a moment before going black. He lay back in his bed, wondering what Sully and Fitz had cooked up. Probably nothing. It was even money they'd gone to the Red Fox, got drunk, and came up with some half-wit idea that would land them all in jail.

When morning came, they'd forget all about it.

He closed his eyes and settled in under the covers.

If nothing else, it would be fun to hear what they had cooked up . Those two were his brothers, and like any family, they all shared dreams—even if some of them were good for nothing but a laugh.

CHAPTER FOUR

Neither Sully nor Fitz answered when Conor called the next morning, which was fine. They clearly got wrecked last night. Sully wouldn't have called, yammering away about "going big," unless they went on a bender and conjured up something stupid like robbing a bank. Whatever their plan was, it could wait. Conor had more important matters to attend to.

Like riding a hot girl around town on the back of his motorcycle in a few hours.

* * *

He could tell Julia hadn't ridden on a motorcycle before. She had her arms locked around his chest in a death grip. He swerved every now and then to get a scream out of her. It took a while, but she finally relaxed after he'd shown her most of the town. Her hands circled his waist while her chin rested on his shoulder. He could feel her body pressed against him from behind, and her breath in his ear as she said, "I'm hungry."

Conor nodded. He pulled into what looked to be a greasy-spoon diner. Julia raised an eyebrow and gave a 'What the hell is this?' expression as she got off the bike. He held out his hand. The parking lot was empty. And even though it was hard to see through the scum that coated the windows, it was clear that no diners were inside. Conor ignored her expression, took her hand, and led her to the front door. He nodded at the old man sitting in a booth near the door, smoking a cigar and reading a newspaper. A small television was set up in the middle of the dining area, tuned to a soccer match. The old man folded his paper and shuffled behind the counter. Conor ordered two hot dogs. When Julia started whispering, asking the normal question of where in God's name he'd taken her, he shushed her. He didn't want to embarrass Rollo, the old man who owned the place.

Rollo was infamous for staying in business with no visible customers. The rumor was his diner was run by criminals. Conor knew better. Yes, Rollo had the unfortunate luck of opening a restaurant in a crappy location, but he'd figured out really quick that survival required a flexible business plan. Selling Lotto tickets did the trick. His customer base lived in the surrounding neighborhood of crumbling homes, holding onto the belief that they could change the course of their miserable lives with one lucky ticket. As a result, Rollo had a daily influx of customers who were in and out in under a minute—giving his restaurant the appearance of a dead zone to most people. But the law-abiding citizens that shunned Rollo's were missing out on a basic truth.

The man cooked a mean dog.

Conor finished his all-beef hot dog slathered in coleslaw, onions, and cheese, drank his soda, and watched Julia finish her meal. He dumped their trash and stacked their food trays on top of the garbage can on the way out, and then gave Rollo a wave. Julia put a hand on her stomach as she walked next to him.

"That was great," she said. "How come no one eats here?"

Conor got on his motorcycle and waited for her to slide in behind him.

"I don't know," he said. "But I do know you're gonna like the next place even more."

Conor rode out of town on Route 13. Businesses dotted the roadside for the first couple of miles. Conor reached back, held Julia's thigh, and raced down the open road. Then they passed the interstate and the countryside opened up.

He parked next to the bridge by the Gorman-Rupp valve plant, hopped off the bike, and led Julia to the river.

Julia stuck tight to him as he led the way down a steep bank and stepped into the river. The rocks were slippery with algae in the midsummer heat. She held his hand and walked alongside him, splashing through the water toward a bridge that crossed the river. They entered the darkness under the bridge. The air stunk of mildew. Julia waved away the buzz of mosquitoes as she followed Conor.

"Where are you taking me?" she said, splashing through the ankle-high water.

"Trust me. It'll be worth it," he said, pulling her along.

The water got deeper as they walked out from under the bridge—nearly knee-high. Conor looked back at Julia, squeezed her hand, and nodded at a calm pool of water in front of them, dappled with bright sunlight and bordered by willow trees on the right side of the riverbank.

"It's beautiful," she said.

He pulled her toward a sandy beach on the left side of the pool. Once there, he took his boots off and sat with his feet in the cool water. Julia joined him.

"Now do you forgive me?" said Conor.

"For what?"

"Ignoring my new neighbor for a month."

Julia laughed. "Maybe. Let me think about it."

He picked up a rock and threw it into the water. Ripples bloomed over the surface.

Julia glanced at him. "So, what's your story?"

He threw another rock. "My story? Uh, I grew up here. Live here. Work here. It's a pretty boring story."

"Parents?"

"Yeah. A dad. My mom left when I was nine." He eyed her. "But my dad's no prize either. He's a drunk. Lives on the street."

"Sorry. I didn't mean to—"

Conor waved. "Ah, it's nothing. I used to think it made me look bad. But I'm over it. He can live on the street all he wants—it's better than having him live with me."

"I guess that's true," she said. "What about your work?"

"I work at an auto repair shop, when I can." He sighed and turned to face her. "And I do other stuff. But what about you? Why'd you move here?"

She met his gaze and smiled. The scar across her cheek puckered, pink and jagged. "Okay. Here's me," she said. "My mom had me when she was seventeen. I don't know who my dad is. Never had many friends, and I barely ever saw my mom. She was always working some shitty job."

"How 'bout that? I work shitty jobs too," Conor said with a big smile. "What kind does she do?"

"You mean, 'did she do,' said Julia. "Her hand got messed up working at a factory. It was bad for a while. Then she got hooked on Oxy and OD'd before I graduated."

Conor lifted a rock on the edge of the water with his foot and pushed it over with a splash. "Man, that sucks. What did you do?"

"A teacher talked me into finishing high school. Said I was too smart to stop. So, I lived with a foster family for a couple years, graduated, then I started working my own shitty jobs. And voilà, here I am."

"Yeah," said Conor. "Here you are."

An awkward silence held for a bit. Conor dug his feet under the sand. He looked out over the stream, watching flashes of sunlight sparkle. "So, what about dreams?"

"What about 'em?"

"Do you have any?"

"Every night," she said.

"No. I mean like dreams for your life," he said, feeling her turn to stare at him.

"I don't know. Why?"

He shrugged. "You just seem like you would." He turned to meet her gaze.

"Is that a pick-up line?"

"No."

She looked away. "No one's ever asked me that before." She leaned back, bracing her hands in the sand. "I'll think about it and let you know."

He leaned back, moving his hand next to hers, just close enough to touch. "Promise?" he said, staring at her profile. He watched her glance down at his hand. She hooked her pinkie finger over his, lifted her gaze, smiled, and said, "I pinkie swear." A drop of sweat trailed over her scar. Her eyes were so big he felt like he could dive into them. "I'm gonna hold you to that," he said, reaching up to wipe the sweat away from her scar.

Her smile fell. She pulled away, covering the scar on her cheek.

"Sorry," he said, straightening.

She blushed. "No, I'm sorry. Sorry that I'm so ugly."

"It doesn't make you ugly," he said. "Just different."

"Yeah. Ugly different."

He reached over, pulled her hand off her scar, and touched it. "It makes you look dangerous—in a good way."

She grinned. "That's me. Dangerous. The dangerous janitor."

"Janitor?"

She nodded. "Yeah. I work at Sacred Heart Cathedral. I clean the school. And—"

He watched her struggle to talk for a moment before she continued.

"And—I can't believe I'm telling you this—the reason I have this ugly scar is my ex-boyfriend. He did it."

Conor wanted to say something. How he'd go find the guy and show him what happened to men who put hands on a woman. How she didn't deserve to be with someone who would do such a thing. But he barely knew her. They'd just met. The problem was, he had a feeling about her. A connection he couldn't make sense of. Even so, it didn't give him the right to act like he was her knight in shining armor. All they really shared, so far, were broken families. That wasn't enough to jump in with a lot of big talk. So, he decided to do the next best thing. Listen.

"My ex is a piece of work," she continued. "He's why I felt like someone was in my apartment yesterday. He has no idea where I am—there's no way he could—but I keep thinking he's looking for me. That he's going to hurt me again."

Conor couldn't stop himself. He put his hand on her bare knee. "That won't happen."

"How do you know?" she said.

"I just do," he replied.

"You'll have to do better than that."

He smiled. "Well, you know those really thin walls between our apartments? If you even whisper my name, I'll be over in two seconds."

She looked at his hand on her knee, and then shifted her gaze to his face. "I appreciate that."

Conor stood. He held out his hand. "Enough of this depressing shit. Let's go swimming."

She grabbed his hand and stood. Brushing sand off her legs, she said, "I don't want to get my clothes all wet."

"C'mon," he said, pulling off his T-shirt.

"I can't," she said, smiling. "I don't know how to swim."

Conor tossed his shirt in the sand. "I can teach you."

"Maybe later," she said, raising her hands and taking a step back.

Conor pulled her in by her waist. She shrieked as he lifted her. He carried her into the clear, deep pool, her feet kicking and splashing water. A red-winged blackbird flew out of a willow across the river, escaping the commotion.

"Not too far out," she screamed.

Chest deep in the pool, he relaxed his grip on her. She hooked her arms around his neck and leaned her head back, dunking her hair. Then she shook her head, spraying water over Conor's face. "How do you like that?" she whispered.

He grabbed her thighs, pulling her against him. Her legs circled his waist.

"You're not very nice," he said, sliding his hands up her thighs. He leaned in to kiss her. She tilted her head back, out of reach, then leaned forward, pressing her lips against his.

He held the kiss as he carried her across the pool into the shallows under the willows. She sighed, unwrapped her legs from around his waist, and stood in the ankle-deep water.

"Water feels good, right?" he said, brushing her hair out of her face.

She stripped off her shirt and hung it on a willow branch hanging over the water. A strap on her black sports bra hung loose over a shoulder.

He reached for her.

She put a hand on his chest, pulled the strap back over her shoulder, and then ran a finger down Conor's stomach to his shorts. She tugged the waistband.

Conor walked to the bank, hopping on one leg to pull off his shorts. By the time he turned around in his underwear, she was twenty feet away, swimming toward the other side of the river.

"I thought you couldn't swim," he yelled.

She rolled to her back and waved. "I'll wait for you at your motorcycle," she said. "And don't forget my shirt."

He splashed water in her direction, shook his head, and laughed. He liked this girl. He really did.

* * *

It was still light when he pulled into his apartment's parking lot.

He parked his bike and followed Julia toward the stairwell. Walking behind her was like having a front row seat at the best show in town.

He followed her up the stairs and down their hallway.

"You want to come in?" she said, stopping at her apartment. "I think I have a couple beers."

Conor looked down at his wet clothes. "I gotta take a shower."

"Me too," she said. "How long will it take you?"

"How long you need?"

"Come back over in fifteen," she said, closing her door.

* * *

It took Conor five minutes to jump in the shower, wash up, brush his teeth, and then pull on a pair of jeans. He pumped out a set of fifty push-ups before putting on a black T-shirt and a pair of old wrestling shoes. His hand was on his doorknob when his cell vibrated. He pulled it out.

Shit.

It was a text from Mona. And there were three calls from Sully. Even Fitz left a message, which wasn't like him. He'd call them later. Mona was first in line. She'd been waiting for over a week to talk to him. He'd told her they were done last time he saw her, but he knew it wouldn't take. It was time to put their relationship to bed for good. After he finished with her, he'd call Sully and Fitz.

He pocketed his cell and took a long inhale, mentally preparing himself for battle with Mona. She was at Ricky's Pub, a restaurant that catered to people who drank ten-dollar beers and fifteen-dollar cocktails—the best place in town to break up with her. Being in a place like Ricky's would keep her from throwing a bottle at his head.

He knocked on Julia's door. If she was up for it, he'd come back after talking to Mona. He knocked again and put his mouth against the door jamb. "Julia, you in there?"

It was faint, but he heard a floorboard creak in her apartment. Her voice was soft. "I'm not feeling well."

"You need anything? An aspirin or something?" he asked.

"I'll be fine. I…I gotta get some sleep."

Conor put his hand on the doorknob, then looked at his watch. This was actually working out perfect. Now he could meet with Mona and Julia wouldn't even know he was bailing on her. He backed away from the door. "I'll check in later to see how you're doing," he said. "Get some sleep. We'll get together when you feel better."

Hearing a soft, "Thanks," he stared at her door. The possibility that he'd done something to piss Julia off crossed his mind. She seemed okay with their kiss at the river, but women were weird. He looked at his watch, calculating if he had time to go in and talk to her. No, Mona wouldn't wait. He walked down the hall and headed downstairs, running over his list of to-dos in his mind.

In less than fifteen minutes, he'd be talking to Mona.

Then he'd call Sully and Fitz to see why they were blowing up his phone.

And then he'd come back and check in with Julia to make sure she was okay.

It was all gonna work out just fine.

CHAPTER FIVE

The hand gripping Julia's bare shoulder kept her quiet. She wished the front door wasn't locked. If she screamed, it would take a while for Conor to break the door down, and, based on past experience, it would be a stretch of pain for her. She trembled. The hand on her shoulder pulled her toward the living room. She clutched her bath towel against her chest as she walked, feeling the cold linoleum kitchen tile under her feet turn to soft carpet as she stepped into her living room. A shove knocked her forward. She fell on the couch, the bath towel riding up her hips.

"Cover yourself," said James, pacing in front of her coffee table. "You can strip for your boyfriend later."

"I don't have a boyfriend," said Julia, adjusting the towel. Knees together, she looked at her ex, James. "Can I get dressed?"

"I wish you could," said James, pulling the coffee table away from the couch. "But I found out what happens when I'm nice, so the answer is no."

She watched him sit on the table then scoot it forward until his knees were an inch from hers. He placed a clammy hand on her knee, then slid his hand up her thigh. The smell of his stale sweat filled her head.

"I paid a lot of money to find you, so now you're going to sit there and listen to me," he said, his voice booming.

"Do you understand?"

She nodded, wishing she hadn't jumped out of the shower and opened the door when he'd knocked. Just ten more seconds and it would've been Conor. How bad could a person's luck be? She looked down, willing her hands to stop trembling. His voice scared the shit out of her, which was funny because it was what had attracted her to him.

The first time she'd heard him, voice echoing through the halls she mopped at Massey High School, she'd thought his volume made him important. It had taken one date in a dark corner booth of a French restaurant—nearly an hour's drive from Massey—to understand that he talked loudly because he thought loud equaled important. He bellowed that whole night, ordering the waitress around in a voice that everyone in the restaurant could hear. She had a feeling right then that he was a narcissistic ass, but she'd ignored her intuition. A month later she'd seen enough to know he was an arrogant pig, but she'd decided to stick it out, convinced that the lifestyle he'd lavished on her was worth the sacrifice. It had been a bad bargain, and it had given loud-mouthed James Stockton—upstanding citizen and superintendent of Woodlands Public Schools—time to roll out his whole bag of tricks. She winced, feeling the scar on her cheek. Yeah, he'd really enjoyed showing her he was boss in more ways than one. She flinched as he slapped her thigh.

"People look up to me," he said. "I've been asked more than once to run for state office. Then there's you. No family. No prospects. Cleaning toilets for a living. You don't leave a man like me. How do you think that makes me feel?"

"I don't know."

He gripped her thigh. "I said *listen*. I didn't say talk. You need to learn how to listen. Understand?"

"Yes. I—"

The slap came out of nowhere. Her head snapped to the side. She went limp for a moment. Stars flashed and popped in a field of black. His voice surrounded her.

"That's disgusting. Get your towel on. I'm not going to sit here and have you flash your tits at me. If I'd known you were a whore, I never would have had you in my bed."

The room spun. She fought to keep her head up. She wrapped the towel around her.

"Now let's start again. And this time, listen."

She nodded.

"See? You don't have to interrupt me. That's not so hard, is it?"

She shook her head and smiled. Her mouth was so dry that her lips stuck to her teeth.

"Here's the thing," he said. "I gave you everything, and you repaid me by sneaking away. Maybe I got a little rough, but that was your fault. A girl from your background needs to know her place."

She nodded, her cheeks aching from holding the smile.

He stroked her hair, then stood and paced. "I shouldn't tell you this, but you scared me."

She rubbed the numb spot where he'd slapped her, tensing as his voice sharpened.

"I thought you were going to talk to somebody. Can you imagine how embarrassing that would have been? To admit I'd been seeing you? And in the condition you were in, people would've gotten all kinds of crazy ideas. But everyone knows a girl like you will lie to take advantage of someone like me. You would've been laughed out of town. The problem is you left without telling me what you were going to do. You have no idea what that did to me. It was hell on me. Absolute hell."

The words at this point didn't mean a thing to Julia. She'd been around James long enough to know his body language. And she could see he was at a tipping point. Puffing his chest out. Banging a fist on his thigh. Breathing through an open mouth. She pulled the towel around herself as tightly as possible. Unless she did something, it was going to happen again.

"I'm sorry," she whispered.

James stopped pacing. "What did you say?"

"I said I'm sorry."

"Look at me when you talk."

Julia twisted a handful of towel against her chest and looked at James. "You deserve better," she said. "I'm not good enough for you."

She inhaled quickly as he stepped toward her and grabbed her by the ears, sticking his face close to hers. "That's my choice to make, not yours. And by the time I'm done, you'll be good enough, whether you like it or not. But, like everything else, it's going to be up to me to make it happen."

He gave her ears a twist before straightening. Hands on hips, he loomed over her. She wanted to rub her burning ears, but she kept still while he talked.

"First off, you're staying in Brannigan. No one knows you're here, so no one can get in my business. I'll visit—might be every night for a while—and teach you how to treat a man. And you'll learn how to be a proper, traditional woman. One who takes care of her man, cooks for him, cleans for him. And handles his physical needs."

She watched him hook his thumbs into his chinos under the overhang of his belly.

"But there's a problem," he said. "You ran. And you might think you can do it again."

She shook her head, mouthing, "No."

"And there's also the notion of payback," he continued. "You have no idea what you put me through. My stomach was in knots, thinking how you'd blabber some wild story of how I assaulted you before I could find you and get your head right."

"Please," she whispered.

"So, here's what we're going to do," he said, undoing his belt. "You sit there and take what I give you. Some of it will feel good and some won't, but you brought it on yourself. It'll give you something to remember if you ever think about running again."

Julia listened to the soft clink of the buckle being undone and the slip of leather through belt loops as he pulled his belt free. James was as tall as Conor, but much heavier, and his hand was huge and doughy as he wrapped the belt around his palm. She looked at the front door, twisting the towel in her lap, wishing that Conor would break in and beat James to a pulp.

"We'll start with something you'll like and move on from there," said James, unzipping his pants.

She inhaled sharply as he grabbed her hair and pulled her forward, fumbling with his boxers. She looked at the door.

"Stop fighting. You're just making it harder," he said, yanking her hair.

Pain shot down her neck as he twisted her head. The belt buckle in his hand cut into her scalp as he held her, forcing her to watch him pull down his boxers. They fell to his ankles. He grabbed her head with both hands. She tried to pull away, but he was too strong.

As James wrestled to hold her head still, she let go of the towel and arched back. James stepped forward, spreading his legs for balance. She punched him in the crotch.

He let out a strangled moan and dropped his belt on the couch. Then he collapsed on her, blotting out light, sound, and air. She could feel his belt buckle under the back of her neck. She tried to breathe and got nothing. She bucked and shrieked. His dead weight muffled her scream. Panic rose through her. She dug her left hand behind her head, grabbed the belt, and pulled. The buckle cut the back of her neck as she yanked the belt free. Her lungs screamed for air. She whipped the belt as hard as she could, feeling the solid whack of the buckle hit James' back. Again and again and again…

Blackness descended.

Then air rushed into her lungs.

At first, she couldn't move. She stared at the ceiling, her chest rising and falling. The urge to lie there naked and do nothing but breathe was overwhelming. Every part of her body felt heavier than she could ever imagine. She turned her head. James rocked on his side on the floor, holding his groin.

In an instant she was on her feet. She swung the belt and caught the buckle in her free hand. The sound was slight. A mere clink. James opened his eyes.

She jumped on his chest, looped the belt around his neck, and then pressed all her weight down. His face turned bright red as the belt tightened. Her body shook. A thread of her saliva fell on James' chin as she stared into his eyes. He clawed at her back, then got a grip on her right elbow. The belt began to slip from her hand as he pulled. She clamped her thighs on his chest and lowered her face to his, shaking from the strain.

His eyes dimmed. His grip on her elbow loosened. His pupils dilated. He went slack.

She unlooped the belt from his neck, looked at the ceiling, and breathed deeply, taking her time before coming to a decision. Raising her right hand, she slapped him. It took three more loud, stinging slaps before he inhaled his first shuddering breath. Then she got off his chest and walked into the kitchen.

She came back holding cooking shears. James groaned. She kept an eye on him as she unplugged the floor lamp next to the couch and cut off its electrical cord. A drop of blood fell from her nose to the carpet. She cut the cord in half. Another drop of blood fell on the carpet. She kept her gaze on James and held up the two lengths of electrical cord.

The blood would have to be cleaned up later.

There was work to do.

CHAPTER SIX

Conor walked into Ricky's Pub. A loud hum of conversation mixed with the clinks of silverware and an undertone of soft music. He walked past the hostess and scanned the restaurant, looking for Mona. The place was packed. Candles flickered on tables set in neat rows down the center of the room. Recessed blue lighting glowed behind the bar. He caught sight of a woman with long, flowing, black hair sitting at the bar with a drink in her hand. It was Mona. Had to be. No one else in town had hair like hers—so black it looked blue.

He walked toward her. Her hair spilled over her bronze shoulders in soft waves. Her black dress was a second skin. A black, strappy stiletto dangled on the end of her foot, her calf muscle flexing as she kept time with a bass-heavy beat playing under the murmur of the room. It wasn't until he was right behind her that he noticed the guys sitting alongside her. Derek Ryder and Johnny Tong. Local guys. Not big on thinking, but a handful for anyone who wasn't careful. Derek fought in the MMA circuit. Johnny Tong used to be a pretty good—and pretty brutal—boxer.

Derek sat to the left of Mona. He was the more conversational of the two, holding eye contact with Mona while he told her she should forget about whoever was supposed to meet her and join them for dinner.

The barmaid walked over, stopped in front of Mona, and lifted her chin at Conor.

"Can I get you something?"

He nodded. "Whatever lager you have on tap."

Mona turned and gave him a withering look while the barmaid went to fill a glass. "You are so fucking late." Derek and Johnny stared at Conor. He ignored them and put his hand on Mona's shoulder. "I got your text and came right over. How's that late?"

The barmaid put a frosted pint in front of Mona. Conor reached between Mona and Derek, handing the barmaid his credit card. He could feel Derek eyeing him as he said, "Run a tab." Derek pushed his stool back into Conor's legs. Conor stepped away, giving Derek room to stand. Derek stared at Conor as he laid his hand on Mona's shoulder, slid a piece of paper onto the bar next to her drink, and said, "I'll catch you later, Beautiful." Then he looked at Johnny and nodded.

Conor watched them walk away before taking a seat next to Mona. He waited a few beats before looking back. The two men edged by tables toward the back of the dining room. Derek stared back at him as he sat down at a table next to a man in a suit and tie, a perfect haircut, and designer eyeglasses. Turning back to Mona, Conor lifted his glass and clinked it against Mona's before taking a sip.

"What's up with frick and frack?" he said.

"You could've texted me to let me know you were coming," said Mona.

The pint was as cold as ice. Conor set the glass down. "I thought it would be better to just get over here."

Mona's face darkened. She turned away and touched the piece of paper next to her drink. Conor could see the phone number on it before she shoved it in her purse. Derek Ryder was hot on Mona. That would've pissed Conor off a few weeks ago when he'd first started seeing her. Not now.

"I waited for you at the Red Fox last night. And you never showed. All I do is wait for you," said Mona.

He looked into her slate black eyes. "You know, you should watch who you talk to."

"What's that supposed to mean?"

Conor glanced back at the table with Derek, Johnny, and the man in the suit. "See that guy Derek and Johnny are sitting with? He's Barry Cline."

"So?"

He flicked the edge of his pint glass and it pinged. "So, he just got out of prison—again. And he'll probably be back there real soon, with your new friends."

"They're not my friends," said Mona. "And you're no angel, so don't act like you're better than them."

"Look," he said. "I'm not here to argue about who's better than who or get a history lesson in why I'm such an asshole. I came to tell you—*again*—that it's over. We'll still see each other because I'm friends with Sully, but we're done. We aren't good together." He waited a beat for her to reply. She turned away and lifted her glass to take a drink, a cue he'd seen before. She wasn't going to say a word. She was going to build up a head of steam in silence. And then she was going to blow. But who cared? She needed to get this through her beautiful, thick head. He laid a hand on her shoulder. "Mona, we can either do this like adults, or like two-year-olds. It doesn't matter what you say or do, I'm not your boyfriend. We're not getting back together. That's it. You understand?"

Mona stood. She touched his arm. "I have to pee. Wait until I get back and then we'll talk—like grownups."

Conor watched her walk toward the restrooms in the back hall. The buzz of the room flowed over him—a low roar of talking, clattering silverware, and laughter. She didn't get it. She still thought she had her hooks in him. He stood and walked the length of the bar, a dead spot in the noise that swirled through the dinner crowd. A waiter brushed by, holding a silver platter with a bottle of Maker's Mark. He watched him walk toward the table where Barry Cline sat with Derek and Johnny.

Conor looked away from the table of criminals. Whatever they were up to wasn't his problem, Mona was. Why couldn't she let this end? Everything had to be drama with her. He stopped in front of the ladies' room. Screw it. He wasn't going to sit at the bar and argue with her until midnight. This was the end of it. He stepped inside the ladies' room and locked the deadbolt.

He looked under the stall door. String black panties were stretched between Mona's ankles. He watched her slide her feet back to the base of the toilet.

"Occupied," she said.

Conor leaned against the door. "Open up."

Her panties were still around her ankles as the door swung open.

"I knew you couldn't stay away from me," she said, wrapping her arms around his neck.

He grabbed her hands. "Mona."

She tightened her grip around the back of his neck. "We're good together," she said, pulling his head down, trying to kiss him.

He muscled her hands off his neck and pushed her away. "Stop it." He stepped back. "We're done. There's no more 'together.' No more talking about it. We're finished. And now, I'm leaving." He turned and stepped toward the door.

"You think you're too good for me?" Mona yelled.

The deadbolt pinched his finger as he jammed it to the side. He hissed, "Shit," opened the door, and walked out.

He stalked out into the dining area, her shouts following him.

"Screw you, Conor! Think you're better than everyone else! You have another girl, don't you? You big asshole! Conor! *Conor! Come back here!*"

He could feel the eyes of the room on him as he paid his tab, pocketed his wallet, and left. He thought about yelling, "Yeah, I do have another girl!" but held it in. Knowing Mona, she'd hunt Julia down and kill her.

He rode his motorcycle down Park Avenue toward

home. The thought to stop at the Red Fox to see if Sully and Fitz were there ran through him. They had to be wondering why he hadn't called. He even slowed as he passed the Fox but thought better of it. The fight with Mona had him rattled. The best move was to check on Julia and make sure she was okay. He'd call them tomorrow. If nothing else, he had a good reason for ghosting them.

Breaking up with Sully's sister had sucked the life out of him.

But he'd done what Sully asked. He'd talked to Mona. He'd broke it off. She wasn't his problem anymore, she was Sully's. He grinned, thinking, *Better him than me.*

After parking his bike, he trotted up the stairs toward his apartment. A door slammed somewhere on the first floor, vibrating through the soles of his shoes. He stopped in front of Julia's door and checked his watch. Nine-thirty-five. She was probably asleep, but what the hell. He knocked softly. The door flew open.

"Conor…I need your help," said Julia.

She wore a T-shirt. Her legs were bare. It was possible she was naked under the shirt. A smear of blood crusted under her left nostril, and she held a pair of scissors. A bruise shadowed her left cheek. He reached for her. She jumped back.

"Don't touch me," she said, raising the scissors defensively.

"What?" he said, keeping his voice low, watching her wipe at tears. "What's going on?"

Then he heard a grunt. He looked into the living room. A man was on the floor. His pants were pulled down, his junk was out, and his hands and feet were bound with electrical cord. A white bath towel gagged him. His eyes shifted from Julia to Conor, and then he started writhing and let out a muffled cry.

Conor took a step toward Julia. She backed into the wall.

"Take it easy," he said, raising his hands. "I'm here to help." He eased away and leaned against the kitchen counter. "Just tell me what happened."

She talked and he listened. It wasn't long before he felt his blood boil and his head pound. He looked at the man on the floor.

This guy was in for a long night.

CHAPTER SEVEN

"Give me the scissors," Conor said, reaching toward Julia.

She stared at James, gagged and tied up on the floor. She clutched the scissors against her chest. Conor lowered his voice. "He can't do anything. I promise. I just don't want you hurting yourself. Let me have them."

A trickle of blood leaked from her left nostril. She sniffed, and then said, "No," as she smeared the blood with the back of her wrist.

Conor squatted next to James and untied the white gag.

"Call the police," said James. "That girl is insane. She almost killed—"

Conor covered James' mouth. "Where's your wallet?" he said, then lifted his hand.

James blinked. "What?"

Conor rolled James on his stomach, patted him down, and pulled a wallet out of his back pocket.

"Untie me," said James, rocking back and forth.

Conor opened the wallet and took out the driver's license. He rolled James to his back and dropped the wallet on his chest. He held out the license. "You're James Stockton?"

"What are you doing?" sputtered James. "Untie—"

Conor stomped on James' shoulder. He watched James

wince, waited a moment, and then held the license in front of his face. "You're James Stockton?"

James nodded.

"You live on Turner Avenue in Massey, Ohio?"

James nodded again.

Conor slipped the license into his pocket. "What do you do in Massey?"

"I'm, uh… I'm a superintendent of a school district."

"Which school district?"

"Woodlands."

Conor made a 'Tsk, tsk' sound and shook his head. He turned, noticing Julia behind him, blank-faced, her eyes trained on James. A trickle of dried blood marked her upper lip. She tightened her grip on the scissors.

"Well, James Stockton, superintendent of Woodlands School District, you got a problem," said Conor. "Julia looks like she wants to cut your junk off. And me? I just want to beat your head in, maybe with a hammer. How's that sound?"

James squeaked. His bottom lip quivered. He had no problem slapping a girl around, but he turned to Jell-O when someone got in his face. It took all Conor had to keep from pummeling him.

He grabbed James. People who thought they were on top of the food chain—people who had money, a labradoodle, a mansion in the suburbs, and a job telling other people what to do—rarely had a backbone. Seeing a stream of piss run out of James onto the carpet proved the point. James thought he could do what he wanted to Julia because, in his mind, she was below him. She was a toy. James was in charge. He was untouchable.

Until now.

Conor rolled James to his belly and untied his ankles and wrists. Wrapping the electrical cord around his fist, he kicked James in the side.

"Zip your pants and stand up."

James pulled up his pants, stuck his wallet in his back

pocket, and struggled to his feet. Piss stained his chinos. He wiped at the stain with a trembling hand and looked at Conor. "What are you going to do?"

Conor swept his arm toward the front door. "Nothing. Get out."

James looked at Julia holding the scissors. "Can you tell her to move?"

Conor shrugged. "She's not doing anything. Start walking."

"But I can't—"

Conor lifted his fist. "Yes, you can."

James walked toward the front door. If Julia stabbed him, Conor wouldn't stop her. She'd earned the right to do whatever she wanted to him. He watched her pivot, leveling the scissors at James as he walked by. Then James was past her, opening the front door. Julia lowered the scissors. Conor flexed his hand, feeling the electrical cord tighten around his knuckles. He felt bad that Julia was letting this creep go home without a scratch.

"Hey, James," he said, pulling the driver's license from his pocket. He tapped a finger on the license. "Expect a visit from me." He stepped across the room, slipping the license into the pocket of his jeans. "We can hang out. Use your Jacuzzi and watch a game on your flat-screen. You know, pal around. That's okay, right?"

"I don't underst—"

Conor punched James in the throat. James dropped and crawled out the door, gasping and holding his throat. Conor followed him into the hall and kicked him in the stomach. Air whooshed out of James' lungs as he bowled over. Conor stood over him and stomped his crotch. James mouthed a silent scream, grabbed his junk, and balled up in the fetal position. Julia watched from the doorframe.

"If you want, I'll keep it up," Conor said, looking back at Julia. "When I'm done, he won't bother anyone ever again." He kneeled and grabbed James' ear. "I'm calling some buddies of mine in Massey. Maybe you know them.

They ride with The Locos. I fixed their bikes, and they owe me, so they'll be checking on you."

He twisted James' ear, listening to him wail.

"But watch out for Pedro," Conor whispered. "He's just out of the joint and, from what I hear, he really, really hated school. Got picked on. Bullied for years. And no one ever did a thing. He'd like nothing better than to get his hands on a school superintendent for payback. In fact, he'd love it."

Conor unwrapped the electrical cord from his hand and dropped it on James. He looked at Julia and spread his arms. "I got all night. You want me to cut him loose or keep it up?"

Julia wiped her bloody nose, dropped the scissors, and walked into her apartment.

"Guess we're calling it a night, James," said Conor. "But I'll see you soon. Count on it."

He picked up the scissors and stepped into Julia's apartment. Walking into the kitchen, he kneeled in front of the sink, opened the cabinet doors, and pulled out a bucket and some rags.

A good hard scrubbing cleaned most of the piss and blood out of the carpet.

Finished cleaning, he looked at Julia's beach painting above the couch. He touched the girl in the painting. It looked to him like Julia had painted a self-portrait. The girl was beautiful.

He dumped the dirty water, put the bucket and rags away, then walked to Julia's bedroom. The door was closed. He knocked lightly. "Julia?"

Silence.

He opened the door. Julia lay on the bed with her back to him, outlined in a touch of light leaking through the window across the room. He shut the door and eased onto the bed behind her.

"Hey," he said. "It's gonna be okay. He's gone."

She turned to face him. He reached for her. She pulled

away.

"Sorry," he said. "I forgot—no touching. I'll leave if you want."

"You can touch me," she whispered. Her eyes closed. Her breathing slowed. Then she slept.

He watched her breathe through barely parted lips, how her eyes moved behind closed lids, no doubt surveying a dreamworld. Her brow pinched and her neck muscles tightened. He touched her cheek, lightly brushing her scar. She exhaled and relaxed. He ran his fingertip down the bridge of her nose. Over her lips. His cell buzzed in his pocket.

It had to be Sully or Fitz.

He sat up, pulled his cell out, turned it off, and slipped it back into his pocket. They'd have to wait. Lying on his side next to Julia, he stared at her and ran his hand over her forehead and through her hair. It wasn't long before his breathing fell into rhythm with hers. The comfort of her bed, her body heat, the smell of her hair, all of it held him there like a spell until he, like her, slipped into a dream as relaxing as a hot bath.

CHAPTER EIGHT

"That's all I can tell you. Meet us at Fitz's trailer and we'll fill you in on the rest. But we gotta do this now. This thing has a fast turn-around, and you disappearing and ducking our calls hasn't helped."

Conor paced in front of his kitchen counter. "I wasn't ducking anything. I thought you guys got drunk and were talking shit."

"If I was talking shit, would I have left you three messages yesterday?" said Sully. In the background, Conor could hear Fitz yell, "And I texted you twice."

They were right. He should've got in touch earlier. He exhaled to calm himself. It was just his luck. And the day had started out so nice. Waking up next to Julia. Knowing that he'd finally ended it with Mona. Everything had been looking great—right up to the moment he walked in his door, turned on his cell, and his phone started buzzing with a call from Sully. When he answered, he got an earful. Somehow, someway, Sully and Fitz stumbled onto something. They'd been cagey about details, but swore up and down that it was real, the payout was huge, and that it was in their skillset. Beyond that, he'd have to wait to see them before they'd get into specifics. That was the good news. The bad news? They had to pull it off tonight, which gave them zero time to plan.

"So, when do you want to talk?" said Conor, walking across his apartment. He opened the sliding glass door at the far end of his living room and walked out on his balcony.

"Earth to Monroe," said Sully, rapping his knuckles on his cell before adding, "Now. We're at Fitz's trailer. Get over here."

"Give me thirty minutes—I gotta take a shower," said Conor. He could feel Sully's eyes roll as he said, "Sure. Take a shower. Eat breakfast. Paint your nails. Do what you have to do, but you're coming, right?"

"Soon as I can," said Conor. "See you in a bit."

After a quick shower, Conor grabbed a banana, ate it in three bites, and then headed out.

Two steps down the hall, he stopped. Julia had a rough night. It ended well, but she probably needed to see a friendly face. He knocked on her door and waited. Nothing. Odds were that she was still sleeping. He knocked again, quietly, but insistently. When that didn't work, he pressed his face against the edge of the doorframe.

"Julia, you in there?"

Still nothing.

"Julia. Open up. I want to make sure you're okay."

He paced in front of the door for a bit, and then tried the knob. Locked tight. For a brief moment he had a flash of dread. Was James dumb enough to come back? No way. That guy was either at a hospital or sitting at home with an ice bag on his balls. Taking a step back, Conor looked at Julia's door, and then his watch. Maybe she was still sleeping. After last night, she deserved it. He turned and walked away, his footsteps echoing down the concrete hallway.

Julia said she worked at Sacred Heart Cathedral, which was on the way back from Fitz's trailer park. If he had time, he'd stop in and see if she was there. If not, he'd come back and check her apartment again.

He picked up his pace, ran down the stairwell, and jogged over to his motorcycle. It roared to life and he pulled out. The wind blew his hair back as he opened the throttle.

It was time to hear what Sully and Fitz were all excited about.

* * *

Julia shuffled out of her bedroom and looked at her front door, wondering who could be knocking this early. Then she remembered.

Conor slept with her last night—after he got rid of James.

She ran a finger across her scar, remembering his touch.

How he smelled.

The way he breathed.

She touched the small cut on the back of her neck from James' belt buckle. Her whole body was sore. She rolled her head from one shoulder to the other.

The knocking started again—soft and insistent. She looked at the clock hanging over her kitchen sink. Almost eight in the morning. It had to be Conor. She took a step toward the door. The knocking stopped. Conor's low, breathy voice was unmistakable.

"Julia, you in there?"

She kneaded the back of her neck, imagining him leaning against her door in his jeans and black T-shirt, his long hair on his shoulders, his arms muscled and tan. She reached for the doorknob and stopped, seeing a drop of blood on the linoleum. Her back stiffened. She closed her eyes.

Just relax. James is gone, and Conor is one of the good guys.

She ran her tongue over a scab on her bottom lip. Her brow furrowed.

But James wasn't a bad guy at first. It took some time before he slapped me.

She turned away from the door.

Before he punched me.

She lowered her chin to her chest. Her hands turned clammy, and she started to shake.

Before he raped me.

Her breathing came quick and shallow. She walked to the kitchen to brace her shaking hands on the counter. It felt like her mind was breaking.

She looked at the door. She couldn't let him see her like this. He'd think she was mental.

Conor called softly, "Julia? Open up. I want to make sure you're okay."

She could hear Conor pace in front of the door. He turned the doorknob. Then she heard him walk away.

She walked back to her bedroom, crawled into bed, and buried her face in the comforter, feeling a sharp thorn of fear deep in her chest. She took a sip of water from a glass on her nightstand and looked at her watch lying there. Eight o'clock. She blinked, trying to make sense of what happened last night between her and James. A feeling of pride welled up at the memory of how she punched him in the nuts and tied him up. Then she thought of Conor, coming to help. How he'd taken James' driver's license. How he'd pummeled James. How he'd cleaned up her apartment and then came to her bed. She looked at her watch again. Almost twenty minutes had passed. Her chest tightened, and she pressed a hand over her heart. It thumped hard and fast.

Something's wrong with me, she thought.

She sat up, opened her nightstand, and pulled out a rosary. The black beads rattled as she untangled it.

She held it against her chest and prayed.

In an instant, a vision of her and Conor sitting on the riverbank came to her. She stopped praying, remembering how Conor asked if she had any dreams about her life. She placed the rosary on her nightstand, curled into a fetal position, and let her mind settle. Just thinking about Conor soothed her anxiety. Remembering his energy. His calming presence. He was someone she felt normal around, which was special. Her life had been a shitshow, giving her nothing in common with just about everyone she ever met. But around him she felt normal. And, oddly enough, electric.

Life felt exciting when she was with him. And yet, he gave her a sense of peace and security. How those two ends of the spectrum could share the same space within her, she couldn't say. The only word that seemed to fit was 'magic.'

"Well," she whispered. "I think I'm starting to figure out my dream, Conor." She rolled to her back and closed her eyes, crossing her arms over her chest where she felt the blend of excitement, peace, and security that Conor gave her. It was big and warm and alive in a part of her that had never been touched before. She smiled and said, "I don't have it all figured out yet, but I know one thing. It starts with this magic."

CHAPTER NINE

The door on Fitz's trailer would've been right at home in a dumpster. Most of the white aluminum frame was dented, and half the screen was flapping in the wind. The trailer wasn't much better. But it wasn't the worst place Conor had ever seen. Even if it was, Fitz had done pretty good for a kid who lost his dad because of Conor's colossal screw up of a father. Conor pushed the ripped screen out of the way and opened the door. Sully and Fitz stared at him from the couch. He stepped inside. Time to see what all the hubbub was about.

"Finally. The man, the myth, the asshole who never returns calls—give him a big hand, folks—it's dickwad of the year, Conor Monroe," said Fitz.

"Where you been, man?" added Sully.

Conor took a seat in a ratty armchair. Crushed empty beer cans covered the coffee table between him and the couch. He kicked a few out of the way as he put his feet up. "When's your maid getting here? This place could use a light dusting."

Fitz stood, walked to the kitchen, and opened the fridge. He strolled back with three cans of beer. Conor caught one thrown his way. "Little early, isn't it?" he said, holding the can of beer.

"Just drink," said Sully, cracking his open. "You're

gonna need it."

Conor opened his beer, and then leaned forward. "Alright, fill me in. What are we dealing with?"

The upshot was simple.

The bishop of the diocese was holding some kind of special mass to commemorate the hundred-year anniversary of Sacred Heart Cathedral. The safe in the Sacred Heart Cathedral sacristy was currently holding religious items the bishop brought to celebrate the mass, such as a chalice, a staff, a monstrance, and other Catholic voodoo. The items in question were made of gold. Melted down, that gold was worth about four-hundred thousand dollars.

Conor stayed quiet while the broad strokes were laid out. After hearing everything, he agreed with Sully and Fitz—it sounded great.

It wouldn't be hard to break into the church.

They could pick a time when it was empty, so security guards and other people wouldn't be a problem.

And best of all, Sully and Fitz reminded him of how he'd been an altar boy at Sacred Heart Cathedral before his mother left town. And as luck would have it, Father Kilgarren, God bless his departed soul, had given him the combination to the safe those many years ago. Back then there had never been anything worth stealing but communion wafers and sacramental wine, but he still remembered the combination, along with all his other altar boy duties. It was a terrible job. Getting up at the crack of dawn during the week. Spending Saturday nights serving mass rather than hanging out with his crazy friends. But there was always the thought that his sacrifice would bear fruit someday. Maybe even get a delinquent like himself into heaven. He'd never dreamed it could get him rich.

The hitch, however, was that as good as the job sounded, no robbery was easy. Every job had hidden razor blades. He started with the most logical question.

"I gotta say, it sounds good. But are you guys serious? Robbing a fucking church?"

Fitz rolled his eyes. "Like the Catholic Church is gonna miss four hundred thousand."

"They're supposed to help the poor, aren't they?" added Sully.

"Fair enough," said Conor. "I just hope we don't end up cursed or something, you know?"

"That ship already sailed," said Fitz.

Conor nodded and grinned. Fitz wasn't wrong. "So, how did you hear about it?" he asked.

Sully looked at Fitz, who sniffed and said, "I'll tell you, but you gotta promise not to interrupt until I'm finished."

"Why?"

"Cause I said so," said Fitz.

When Conor opened his mouth to argue, Fitz talked over him, raising a finger to emphasize each point he calmly presented.

"Because you already got our timeline all jacked up. Because we don't have time for your hand-wringing about the details. Because me and Sully already buttoned this whole thing up while you were out doing fuck all. And lastly, because you don't get to play devil's advocate after going AWOL while we sat here watching this job nearly slide through our fingers. That's why you're keeping your mouth shut, dumb ass."

Sully nodded. "Yeah. Dumb ass."

Conor drank his beer. He shrugged. "Points taken. Please continue."

"Alright then," said Fitz, leaning forward, his gaze pinned on Conor. "It was Duck and Artie."

"Duck and Artie!?" sputtered Conor. "The old Muppets that hang out at the Fox?"

Fitz pointed at Conor. "What did I say?"

Conor rolled his eyes. He also shut his mouth.

"That's right. Keep your fucking bullshit to yourself and listen," said Fitz. "I overheard them talking about it—right after I heard them say two guys had stolen all the money from the concession stands at the football game."

"And that was less than an hour after we dropped you off," added Sully. "There's no way they could've heard about those cash boxes that fast."

"Unless they're connected," said Fitz.

"Which means that whoever's talking to them knows his shit," said Sully.

Conor rubbed the stubble on his chin. "You know, breaking into a safe is a felony. Whoever's talking to them better know their shit, cause we're not risking prison for stealing communion wafers."

Fitz nodded. "Agreed. That's why we did some checking."

"I called the bishop's office," said Sully, tucking his long black hair behind his ears. "Told them I had a large donation, but I wanted a photo op with the bishop. They said he'd be out of town all weekend."

"At Sacred Heart Cathedral," added Fitz. "Then Sully called Sacred Heart to see if he could have his baby girl baptized this weekend."

Conor eyed Sully. "Let me guess—"

Sully nodded. "Yeah. No baptisms this weekend. And the secretary was nice enough to tell me it was because, 'We'll have a special guest in town.'"

"Okay. The bishop's coming," said Conor. "But how'd Duck and Artie find out about the gold?"

"Think about it," said Sully.

"The way we figure it, there's only one person that would know about us stealing those cash boxes and the gold being at the church," said Fitz. "It has to be that off-duty cop that sicced his rottweilers on you and Sully at the stadium. We checked him out. He also moonlights as a security guard at Sacred Heart. He's either running security for the bishop or knows who's doing it. And he probably told Duck and Artie all about it for a finder's fee."

Conor couldn't argue against any of it—it all made sense. All it took was one dirty cop. Telling Artie and Duck about the cash box heist was just gossip—keeping them informed.

But giving them information about the transportation and storage of items worth four-hundred thousand was what people in the breaking and entering business called, "actionable intelligence." And the best part was, although Duck and Artie now knew about the bishop's gold, it was what they didn't know that was going to hurt them—that a group of nobodies not only knew about it, but also knew the combination to the church's safe. Conor took a long drink of his beer, put the can down, and leaned in toward his friends. "I think we got something here," he said, smiling. "So, what's next?"

"We go in tonight at eleven o'clock," said Fitz. "We steal everything before Duck and Artie even know what happened."

"What do we need?"

"Not much," said Sully. "You got the combination. All we gotta do is get in, get out, and run."

"Is there a security system?"

"Oh, by gosh and Begorrah, who woot steal from ta house of ta Lort?" said Fitz in a terrible Irish accent. He held out his beer can.

All three started laughing. They tapped cans and chugged their beers. Conor crushed his empty beer can and tossed it across the room. It rattled into the kitchen sink.

"What about after?" he said. "If Duck and Artie are connected, I'm guessing they're gonna come for us."

Fitz stood, took Sully's empty can, and walked into his kitchen. "All we gotta do is hide the gold and stay outta sight until things die down. Nobody knows us. We're so small time we're not on anyone's radar. There's no way they're gonna know it's us unless we screw up."

Conor thought that over for a moment. It made sense. There was no way anyone could figure out it was them.

The hinges on the cabinet door under the kitchen sink squeaked as Fitz opened the door and dumped beer cans in the trash. He kneed the door closed. "We figured that, just to be safe, we should split up and leave town for a little bit afterward. Then, after a few days, we check in with Angel. He'll let us know if anyone's looking for us. And even if they are, we just stay gone."

"With four-hundred thousand in our pockets," added Sully.

Conor stood. Angel Silva was their boss who ran the auto repair shop. Good guy if he was your friend, but you didn't want to get on his bad side, which was where about ninety percent of humanity stood. "Yeah, if anyone would hear anything, it would be Angel," Conor said. "I can't believe I'm saying this, but I think this is perfect."

Fitz and Sully looked at each other and smiled.

Conor looked at his watch. "Alright then, eleven o'clock. Do we know how we're getting into the church?"

Sully shrugged. "I'll check it out on my way home. It won't be hard."

"Nah," Conor said. "You guys hooked all this up. I'll take care of it."

They all smiled at each other for a silent moment. Then Conor turned and followed Sully out the front door. The day had barely started and he was already busy as hell. He had to stop by the church to check on Julia, scope out a way to break in, go home, pack for a trip out of town, and get some sleep before meeting Fitz and Sully at eleven. Busy, busy, busy—but it was all good.

Outside, he sat on his bike, and then tied his hair back in a ponytail, watching as Sully got into his mom's dirty, white, murder van—which would carry the bishop's gold after they got it out of the safe. Sully started the van and rolled down his window. "Hey, thanks for talking to Mona last night," he said.

Conor smiled. "She wasn't happy, was she?"

"Pissed as hell," said Sully. "But she's not riding my ass about having you talk to her anymore."

"Good."

"Yeah, it is," said Sully. He started to roll his window up and then stopped and said, "Hey man, I gotta say, I'm excited about this job."

"Me too," said Conor.

Sully held eye contact with Conor, then looked down and shook his head. "Not the same as me. I mean, we've all been together a long time, and none of us have nothing, but we're different, you know? You were the big athlete in high school, and Fitz, well, he's always been the big man wherever he went. You guys find ways to fit in. Me? I've never been able to do that. And I'm thinking, if I have a little money—not a ton—just enough to live normal, then maybe I won't feel like trash, you know? Maybe if I get my own place, my own car, new clothes—maybe I'll fit in then, right?"

"You fit in fine, man," said Conor. He stood and reached through the van window, grabbing Sully's hand. "Fuck 'em, Sully. People don't like you the way you are, who cares? Me and Fitz got your back."

Sully squeezed his hand. "Got yours too, bro."

Conor waved as Sully backed out and drove away. The screen door on Fitz's trailer screeched open. Conor started his bike. He looked over. Fitz stood in front of his door—his arms folded over his bare chest. "We got this, brother," Fitz yelled over the sound of Conor's bike.

Conor revved the engine. He rolled over to Fitz and held up his fist. Fitz bumped him. "We do," yelled Conor over the rumble of his motorcycle. "But it ain't done yet."

"Words of wisdom from Mr. Sunshine," said Fitz, turning to go back inside.

Conor watched the door slam shut behind Fitz, the screen flapping. He put his bike in gear and drove away, shaking his head.

Somebody had to keep it real.

* * *

Heat rippled off the street as Conor rode through town. He needed to make one quick stop before going to Sacred

Heart.

The sun blazed off the library's stone courtyard as he stopped next to the curbside book drop. He pulled out his wallet, counted out a thick stack of bills, pulled a hair tie from his pocket, and then rolled and rubber-banded the cash.

Before he could turn off his motorcycle, a figure climbed out of the bushes next to the front doors of the library and stomped across the courtyard yelling, "Didn't I tell you to leave me alone?" The disheveled, dirty-faced man focused on Conor, his brow furrowed.

The sun was blazing, but the bum seemed unaffected. He was barefoot and wore jeans, a black sweater, and a dirty blue suit coat. Layers of clothes were standard for the homeless. You had to keep warm at night, but Conor figured his dad would've had more sense in this heat.

Conor recognized the sweater. It had hung on the hook inside the garage for years when he was a kid. His dad wore it when he went out to shovel snow or work on the car in the dead of winter. Conor wanted to yell at him to take the sweater off, clean himself up, and act normal. It was embarrassing. But he kept his mouth shut, even as his dad, smelling of days-old sweat, grabbed his shoulder.

"How many times do I have to say it? You live your life, and I'll live mine."

Conor couldn't believe this was a man he'd once looked up to. His father's hair was shoulder-length, gray, matted, and greasy. Dirt covered his face and beard. He smelled. He was a disgrace.

A security guard opened the front door of the library. Conor grabbed his dad's hand. "Security is watching. Keep it up, and he'll call the cops."

"Good. Nothing wrong with sleeping in a bed for the night."

The guard stepped into the courtyard. "Is there a problem?" he said, tapping the walkie-talkie on his hip.

"No problem," Conor said. "Just talking." Then he

handed the roll of money to his father and whispered, "I'm leaving town. Not sure if I'm coming back, but this should hold you over for a while." Not waiting for a response, Conor turned on his heel, walked over to his motorcycle, and pulled away from the curb. He glanced back.

His dad stood quietly on the curb, holding the roll of money in his dirty hand.

Conor felt like he should be mad at himself. It wasn't the smartest move to tell anyone, let alone his drunken bum of a father, that he was leaving town. If word got out, he'd be the prime suspect for robbing the church. But, oddly enough, he didn't care. His dad was still his dad. If he left without telling him, it would upset him, and his dad already had enough to be upset about.

He pulled away and motored up a hill toward the bell towers of Sacred Heart. The massive stone church rose into view.

Conor stopped at a red light, the steady thrum of his motorcycle vibrating through him. The church's stone steps fanned down to the street on his right, inviting parishioners in.

Lots of memories were packed in these two blocks. This is where he went to school when his dad's partner died and his mom left town. After that, the only job his dad could find was bartending at a dump outside of town. He'd kept it together only long enough for Conor to graduate high school. Then his dad turned into a guy that slept under bushes out in front of the library.

The light turned green. Conor rode by the high school, looking at the huge white banner strung across the chain link fence. The words 'Celebrating 100 Years—Sacred Heart Parish' were printed in bright blue. He scanned the parking lot behind the church, catching sight of a set of doors.

Those back doors would be the best way in tomorrow night.

He pulled in next to the rectory. If Julia was working,

there was no telling which building she was in. Best to check out the back doors of the church first to see if they were the best option for breaking in, then he'd look for her. Heat blanketed him as he climbed the church steps. Cool air whooshed over him as he stepped inside.

He dipped his fingers in holy water, crossed himself, and then walked toward the altar.

A door slammed near the altar.

Julia walked into view, carrying a bucket of cleaning supplies. She stepped around rows of potted purple and white lilies that covered the altar.

"Hey, Julia," he said, waving.

She startled and dropped the bucket. He thought about teasing her for being so jumpy, then decided against it. The dark circles under her eyes didn't look good.

"Thought I'd stop by to see how you're doing," he said, walking toward her as she gathered rags off the floor. "You okay?"

She straightened, holding the bucket against her chest. "I got a lot of work to do, Conor."

He grabbed the last few rags off the floor and dropped them in her bucket. "I stopped by your place this morning. Maybe you didn't hear me."

"Can we talk later? The Bishop's coming, and I have work to do."

As she turned away, he touched her hand.

"You sure you're okay?" he said.

"Just tired," she said.

Conor nodded. "I understand. It was a tough night. But tired or not, I'm coming over after you get home. I'm worried about you."

She bit her lip, trying to hold down a smile. "I really have a lot to do. But I should be home early if you want to hang out later."

"Like how early?"

"I don't know. Father Sal said I can go home after he talks to me. He already sent everyone else home."

Conor smiled. "Cool. I'll see you at home."

He walked toward the side of the altar toward a hallway that led to the back doors. Looking back to make sure Julia couldn't see him, he checked the lock. There was no deadbolt, so all he had to worry about was forcing the latch. A crowbar would do it. They'd be inside in less than a minute.

He dipped his fingers in holy water and crossed himself on the way out. Sunlight blinded him as he opened the door and walked around the church to his motorcycle. It started with a rumble. The black leather seat was hot as a grease fire. He looked at his watch. It was almost noon. He gunned his bike and rode out of the parking lot.

It was time to go home and pack because tomorrow, he, Fitz, and Sully were going to be rich.

CHAPTER TEN

Julia looked over her work. Everything gleamed. The gold accents on the altar. The brass candle holders. The wooden pews. The marble floor. Every surface that could be wiped, dusted, waxed, or polished had been cleaned. If she had to eat off this floor, it wouldn't be the worst thing she'd ever done. A door banged open and the scent of the lilies on the altar wafted over her. Father Sal's face lit up as he walked in, his head on a swivel as he moved past the votive candles flickering in front of a statue of Saint Joseph. He made his way along the communion rail toward the altar.

"Wow. Somebody's been working," he said, lifting his arms as he neared Julia.

Julia blew a lock of hair off her face. "Thanks, Father. It was hard."

"I'll bet," he said. He put his hands on his hips, nodding as he scanned the altar. "Fantastic job. Just great. So, did I catch you at a good time? I don't want to interrupt if you're in the middle of something."

"No, I'm done," she said, pulling her hair into a ponytail.

Father Sal sat on the marble communion rail. "Take a seat," he said.

The rail was cool. She glanced at Father Sal. Same outfit every day. Silver-framed glasses. Black pants. Black shoes. Black shirt. And, of course, his priest collar. Black brought out the pepper in his salt and pepper hair and beard. He usually looked amused, with a slight crinkle at the corners of his eyes. But today he looked different. His shoulders sloped down and he seemed pained, as if he was carrying a great weight.

"So, how long have you worked here?" he said. "Almost a month, right?"

"Yeah. It'll be a month tomorrow."

"You like it?"

"It pays the bills."

He laughed and readjusted himself on the rail. "I'm sure it does, but it's not a very good job. No health insurance. No pension. Not much of a future. You ever think of doing something else?"

Julia crossed her arms. "Did I do something wrong?"

He touched her shoulder. "No. You've been great. What I'm trying to—"

"Am I getting fired?"

He took his hand off her shoulder. "Julia, what happened to your face?"

She touched her bruised cheek. "It's nothing. So, when's my last day?"

Father Sal was quiet for a moment.

"If I'm being fired, you can at least tell me why," she said.

"You're not being fired," he said. Then he sighed. "But Sacred Heart is going through some changes. I just want to make sure you're prepared."

She watched him shift in his seat. "What do you mean, changes?" she asked.

Father Sal raised a hand. "All I'm saying is it would be in your best interests to look for something else."

"Why?"

He took off his glasses and cleaned them. "I'm going to tell you something, but I trust that you'll keep it confidential."

Julia nodded.

"Sacred Heart is being merged with two other parishes. The diocese is closing us down."

Julia looked away, focusing on the sun coming through the stained-glass window of the Virgin Mary. "Oh," she whispered.

"Yes, oh," he said.

"But what about the Bishop? Why would he come if they're closing the church?"

"This is a recent development," said Father Sal. "He's coming, but only to talk about the merger and attend the picnic."

"Great," said Julia, rubbing her eyes. She looked at her hands. The middle knuckle on her right hand was cracked and crusted with blood. Maybe this was good. Maybe she wouldn't be dousing her hands in bleach all day long at her next shitty job.

Father Salvatore stood. "I'm sorry, Julia. We'll be laying people off in two weeks. If I were you, I'd find a new job before everyone else starts looking." He patted her shoulder.

She sighed. "If we're closing, a lot more people than me are losing their jobs. Why are you telling me?"

"The other employees have family in town. They'll be fine," he said. "You, on the other hand, are alone. You could use the head start."

Julia watched Father Sal walk away, his voice trailing through the church. "If you can't find work, let me know. I know some organizations that can help with food and temporary lodging. And please, take care of whatever caused that bruise. I'm guessing whoever put it there isn't good for you."

Then he was gone.

Julia pulled out her ponytail and shook her head, running her fingers through her hair. A memory of Conor walking toward the altar, asking if she was okay, came to her. She stepped toward the altar to pick up the bucket of cleaning supplies, then changed course, walking toward the exit. "I'm on a real lucky streak," she said. "My ex tried to rape me yesterday, and I lost my job today. Can't wait to see what happens next."

Her black Ford Escort was so hot that the door handle burned her fingers. She got in and pulled her shirtsleeve over her hand to roll down the window. Long pants didn't seem smart in this kind of heat until you had to sit on a seat that had been sizzling in the sun for the past five hours. She started the car and cranked the air conditioning, sticking her face in front of the vent. It took a few minutes, but the air conditioning finally put a dent in the heat. She closed her window and backed out of her parking space, drumming her fingers on the blistering hot steering wheel.

A bead of sweat rolled down the back of her neck. She pulled out of the parking lot onto the street. The bell towers in her rearview mirror disappeared as she rounded a corner, driving through the heat of Brannigan toward home, unsure of—

Everything.

* * *

Conor carried an ice-cold six-pack into the shaded stairwell of his apartment complex. He opened a can, drinking while he walked up the steps to his apartment. Inside, he put the rest of the six-pack in the fridge next to a box of calcified baking soda. Pressing the cold can against his forehead, he went out on his balcony. It was so damn hot. He sat on an aluminum beach chair and wiped his face.

He still had to pack, but it could wait—at least until the sweat stopped pouring down his face.

Sipping his beer, he looked down at the parking lot. Julia's parking space was empty. He played with the pull tab on the beer can. For whatever reason, he couldn't get her out of his head. He'd only known her what, three days? He stood and gripped the balcony railing. What was it about her? Was it her looks? Her attitude? Her hard-luck background? He'd always been a sucker for long dark hair and dark eyes. Exhibit one was Sully's sister, Mona. Julia had the same dark hair and eyes. That definitely attracted him. But there was something else.

He wiped sweat off his brow and took a long pull on his beer. Underneath it all, Julia had something that made her a rockstar. A calm, almost playful, intelligence. Her smarts made her stand out. It was there in the little stuff, like hanging out at the river. Conor knew that if he'd taken Mona there, she would've thrown a hissy fit. It would've been too dirty. Too dark walking under the bridge. They never would've made it to the secluded pool where he and Julia sat and talked about their lives. And the way Julia handled her ex, James, was nothing short of mind blowing. The very thought of imagining that Julia—or any woman—would be able to overpower a man as big as James, tie him up, and gag him seemed impossible. Add that to the way she overcame her background, kept her head down, and just kept moving forward, and you had someone very special.

Conor downed the rest of his beer. Yeah, Julia was a class of woman he'd never run into before.

And he'd do whatever it took to get closer to her.

He barely finished his thought before Julia's car whipped into the parking lot. She pulled into her space under his balcony. He leaned over the railing as she opened her car door and stepped out.

"That was fast," he yelled, lifting his can. "You want a beer?"

She looked up and shaded her eyes. "I just had the worst afternoon. All I want is a shower and a nap."

"C'mon—just one?" said Conor, hanging over the rail.

She grinned, blinking into the sun. "And then can I take a shower?"

"Sure. Can I join you?"

Julia flipped him off, slung her purse over her shoulder, and walked toward the stairwell.

It didn't take more than a few minutes before Julia told Conor what was up.

Her ex-boyfriend's visit had freaked her out. She told Conor about her panic attack when he'd come to check on her. Although he was no psychiatrist, Conor could see she was still struggling. Her hands and voice trembled slightly when she talked about James. She was scared and he didn't blame her. Having someone physically bigger and stronger stalking you couldn't be fun.

"You know, he's not coming back," said Conor, glancing at Julia sitting in the beach chair next to his. "Not after the beating I gave him. Doesn't that help?"

Julia drank her beer. She squinted. "I know that in here," she said, tapping a finger on her head. "But something in here doesn't believe it," she added, tapping the same finger on her chest.

"I get it," said Conor. "He hurt you. That can stick with you for a while."

They sat in silence for a beat. Julia finished her beer. Conor handed her another.

"It's so stupid," she said. "I know he's gone, but I'm constantly looking over my shoulder."

Conor watched her tap the top of her beer can with a long fingernail painted black. She slid the nail under the tab, and popped the can open. He tilted his beer back, then wiped his mouth. "You're probably just freaked out because he knows where you live. Maybe you'd feel better if you went somewhere else."

"If he found me here, he'll find me anywhere."

"True. Plus, you'd have to get a new job."

Julia looked at him. "I have to do that anyway."

Conor's eyebrows raised. "Is that why Father Sal wanted to talk to you?"

She nodded.

"Damn," said Conor.

"I know," said Julia. "Nothing but bad news, right?"

Conor's brow furrowed. He sipped his beer. Then he

grinned. "Maybe it's good news."

"For who?"

"For you, if you want it to be," said Conor.

Julia looked confused.

Conor turned his chair to face her. He laid a hand on her knee. "You don't want to stay here because your ex knows where you live, right?"

"Yeah."

"And you got laid off from your job."

"I did."

"That means there's nothing keeping you here. You could go anywhere. Live anywhere."

Julia looked at him like he'd lost his mind. "Conor, you do know I'm broke, don't you?"

Conor leaned in. "But what if I wasn't?"

Julia cocked her head. "Huh?"

He stood and gripped the balcony railing, looking out over the parking lot. "I'm leaving tonight. If you want, you can come. We could go anywhere you want."

"What?"

"You heard me," said Conor, turning to look at her.

Julia opened her mouth, but no sound came out. She shut it, put her beer down, took a deep breath, and stood. "You're saying you're leaving and you want me to go with you?"

He nodded.

She stepped next to him. Her throat tightened. For some unexplainable reason, she felt like crying. She pushed the feeling down and gazed up at Conor. "Why?"

He kissed her. After the kiss, he laid his cheek against hers and whispered, "Why not?"

CHAPTER ELEVEN

Julia held her keys, smiling as she walked out of Conor's apartment. She felt like she was floating. Filled with joy. And to think that only a few minutes ago, everything had been unraveling.

James had found her and tried to assault her.

She was having panic attacks.

She'd lost her job.

But all that trouble was behind her now. Wiped away with Conor's kiss and the two words he'd whispered in her ear—*why not?*

She unlocked her door and went into her apartment. A few steps inside, she looked at the painting of herself sitting on a beach looking at the ocean. Her mind spooled back to when she was a child—to the place that provided the inspiration for the painting. To the place she told Conor she wanted to go.

She was maybe eight or nine when her mother first started taking her to a cottage in Maine for summer vacations. A distant uncle owned the cabin. She remembered the smell of saltwater and how the waves pushed and pulled at the shoreline, washing foam over the pebbled beach. That was before her mother hurt her hand working at a factory and started taking Oxy. Her memories of the days before Oxy were golden. She'd painted the beach scene a few years ago to remind her of that time. And now, for the first time in a long time, she felt like life could be good again.

She walked toward her painting, moved the coffee table out of the way, and shoved the couch until it was at a ninety-degree angle to the wall where the painting hung. Then she went into her bedroom and put on a pair of paint-splattered jeans and an old T-shirt. It took a few trips back and forth from her bedroom to set everything up. She dragged an old bedsheet out, spreading it on the floor underneath the painting, and then brought out her brushes and paints. She loved this painting, but it needed a little more added to it.

Her hand moved in sure, graceful strokes on the canvas. Barefoot, she moved around the canvas as she worked. She remembered her high school art teacher saying she was the best natural artist he'd ever seen. She smiled, wishing he could see her now.

Two hours later, she was done. She stepped back. The painting now included someone sitting next to her on the beach. He had long hair, wide shoulders, and his hands were braced in the sand behind him. Only the side of his face was visible, but it was easy to see that he was easygoing. Confident. And maybe a little dangerous.

She looked across her apartment, staring at the wall she shared with Conor.

A sense of calm settled over her.

She washed her brushes and put them away in the tackle box that held her painting supplies, thinking about all the things she needed to do before Conor picked her up tonight. Her eyes became unfocused as she worked a rag wet with paint thinner over the bristles of a brush.

He said he had to take care of some things later tonight, but that he'd pick her up around midnight. No worries about packing—an overnight bag would do. Once they got to a hotel or a bed and breakfast in Maine, they'd go shopping. Even with all that being said, Julia felt like she needed to clean her apartment, deposit her final paycheck, and call her landlord to tell him she was moving at the end of the month. This was the end of her time here. She was sure of it. Conor said he had more than enough money for both of them to leave forever—if that's what she wanted. It was what she wanted. She had no ties here. Not even a job. But Conor grew up and had friends here. He'd come back to visit at some point. But for her, this was goodbye. She had it all worked out.

Clean the apartment.

Get out of her lease.

Move everything she owned into her car.

And be ready to jump on the back of Conor's motorcycle when he showed up at midnight.

When Conor did come back to Brannigan, she'd come with him, get in her car, and drive away—with or without him. She hoped "with," but that didn't matter right now. Today, at this very minute, she was just excited to be leaving with him.

She put the paintbrush in its tray, closed her tackle box, and surveyed her apartment.

There wasn't a lot to do. The apartment came furnished so all the furniture stayed. Her belongings only amounted to some clothes, shoes, a few pieces of jewelry, makeup, towels, linens, and maybe a few lamps. It fit in her car when she came here, it would fit in her car now.

She glanced back at her painting, turned, and walked toward her bedroom. Her thoughts jumbled between what she needed to pack and her excitement over leaving with Conor. She smiled.

Midnight couldn't come fast enough.

CHAPTER TWELVE

Conor stopped packing clothes into the suitcase on his bed. He reached under his bed, grabbed an aluminum baseball bat, and turned, raising the bat. A man with a gray, matted beard, and long, gray hair pulled back into a ponytail stared at him. Somehow, he'd walked right into Conor's bedroom without making a sound. The man raised his hands.

"Take it easy. It's me."

Conor tilted his head back and exhaled hard. "You're lucky I didn't crack your head open."

His father, Mickey, tipped his head at the bat. "You want to put that away?"

Conor slid the bat back under the bed. He rubbed his face. "What are you doing?" he said, trying to calm his heart.

His father's gaze focused on the clothes and toiletries piled next to the suitcase on top of his bed.

"So, you are leaving," said his father.

"Yeah."

"On account of me?"

"No."

"Then why?"

Conor walked up to his father. "Let's go in the other room," he said. "You almost gave me a heart attack."

Conor led his father to the couch in the living room.

Then he grabbed a couple beers from the fridge and dragged a chair out of the kitchen. He gave his father a beer and sat.

"How the hell did you get in here?" he said, watching his father drain half the beer.

His dad answered with another tilt of the can. He burped and held up the empty. "Is that other one for me?"

Conor gave him the other beer.

His father opened the can and settled back. "Where you going?"

"Can't say."

"Why?"

"Because you're a drunk," said Conor. "You might tell people that don't need to know."

His dad took a deep breath and exhaled. "Can't argue with that." He took a long pull on his beer and looked out the sliding glass door that led to the balcony. The day was sunny and clear. "If you can't tell me where you're going, can you at least tell me why?" he said.

"Sorry," said Conor. "Same answer."

"Makes sense," his father replied, still staring at the perfect summer day visible through the sliding glass door. "You know, ever since you said you were leaving, I've been sober. I wanted to talk to you with a clear head."

Conor watched him tilt his beer to take another long swallow.

"I need to say a couple things," his dad continued, clearing his throat. "One is, I love you. Might not seem like it, but I do. The other is, I know why you're leaving. Can't be easy living here." He tapped his beer can. "Must be hard hearing people say what a lousy bum your father is."

"They don't say that to me," Conor said. "Not if they're smart."

His dad smiled. "You always did have a chip on your shoulder. I used to be like that. Fighting a battle every day." He took a long pull of his beer. When he lowered the can, his eyes were unfocused. It looked like he was staring at nothing as he said, "You know what I do now?"

Conor shook his head.

"Think about when you were little and me and your mom were together," his father said. "I had the whole world in my hands and didn't even know it. I loved life back then."

Conor watched his father's chest expand. He filled out before Conor's eyes, becoming the man who used to come into the house singing and flashing money, giving Mom a playful swat on the ass as he danced with her through the kitchen. If he took a shower, dyed the gray out of his hair, and smoothed out a wrinkle or two, he would look exactly like that man, except for one thing. This version of his father had a noticeable tremor in his hands. Today's sobriety had obviously been hard on him after all his years of hard drinking.

"Anyway, I'll finish what I came to say and leave you to it," his dad said. "Everybody wants things. Money. Security. Respect. Power." He put his beer down, stood, and leaned over Conor, putting his hands on Conor's shoulders. He whispered, "And here's the secret. None of it matters. All you need is somebody to build a life with. The rest is crap."

He straightened and stepped back toward the sliding glass door. Turning his back on Conor, he opened the door and walked out on the balcony. He pointed at Conor. "Just remember. Don't be a screw up like me."

Conor looked down, feeling embarrassed that his father thought so poorly of himself. When he looked up, his dad was gone. Then he heard him singing somewhere down in the parking lot, his voice fading as he walked away.

Conor walked out onto the balcony. He looked over the edge and slowly walked around its perimeter. No ropes or anything hung off the railing. So how did his dad get onto a balcony that was two stories up? Then he saw the row of garbage cans. The metal lid of one of the cans was smashed in, like it had bent under the weight of someone standing on it.

He shook his head, laughing softly. Because his father had fallen so low, Conor sometimes forgot that his father was once a man of infinite skills. Conor grew up thinking his dad was the strongest, smartest man alive. Finding a way to climb up onto a two-story balcony was the least of his powers. As a kid there wasn't a week that went by without his dad teaching him something. When Conor wanted to learn how to fight, his dad took him out in the garage and taught him things that got him out of situations that should've put him in the hospital. When Conor wanted to know how to meet girls, his dad took him to a local bar and soon had a bevy of women hanging around, listening to his stories, enjoying his flattery, and laughing at his quick wit. Although he'd tried to copy his father's gift for gab, that skill never stuck. He figured it was one of those things you either had or you didn't. It wasn't something a person could just copy—at least not for him.

His father's lesson tonight, however, was different. Showing Conor how to be faithful to his girl and his friends was impossible—Mickey Monroe was known all over town as the exact opposite. He'd lost both his best friend and wife because of his drinking. But in spite of that—or maybe because of it—he'd dried up long enough to be a father for one more day. Although he couldn't show Conor how to be faithful, he'd made an effort to tell him how to do it. Forget about money, power, and all the rest of it. Just find someone to spend a life with. It was the best of his father's hard-gained wisdom, and the most Conor could ask for.

With his father's voice still echoing in his head, Conor conjured an image of Julia back at the river with her dark hair dripping water down her beautiful face.

He held the image of Julia as long as he could. A warm spot grew in his chest, then receded as Julia's image faded. He turned, walked back into his apartment, and locked the sliding glass door.

Today's lesson from his dad was one he'd remember. All he—or anyone else—needed was somebody to build a life with.

Conor picked up the empty beer cans in the living room

and put them in the trash can under his kitchen sink.

All the rest was crap.

He walked back toward his bedroom to continue packing.

It was time to leave the crap behind.

CHAPTER THIRTEEN

Sully stopped the van in front of the hospital, jumped out, and ran around to open the passenger door.

"Sullivan, what are you doing?" his mom said, clutching her purse as she stepped out. She pulled her hospital badge from her purse and rubbed it clean on her pink nursing scrubs. "You don't have to open my door."

Sully shut the door. "I'm just being nice, Ma."

"I already said you can have the van tonight," she said, clipping on her badge. "Just make sure Mona picks me up at five tomorrow morning, or there's going to be trouble. You hear me?"

Sully watched his mom walk toward the staff entrance. He stuck a piece of gum in his mouth and waved as she went into the hospital. Basic intelligence told him he shouldn't tell anyone he was leaving, that it would raise a red flag that he and Conor and Fitz were up to something. But he hated the idea of leaving without letting his mom know. He blew a bubble and got back in the van. After they got settled out of town and sold the gold, he'd have to give her a quick call to make sure she knew he was okay—that he was just taking some time off with his friends. He'd fallen off the radar before, so his mom wouldn't be completely surprised by his disappearing act. It just bothered him to think that she might worry. His mom was the nicest person. She worked so hard. And after dad died, she got little to no help from Mona or him.

He drove by Brannigan Senior High. He shook his head, looking at the school. Without Dad around to keep them straight, he and Mona were hellions. Always in trouble with teachers and the principal, costing Mom money and time with their shenanigans. And now that they were out of school, they were still a drag on her. Living at home. Eating her food. Even asking for spending money now and again. His mom deserved better.

His gum snapped as he chewed. Yeah, she did deserve better, but after tonight, he'd be able to give her better. After they sold the gold, he'd come back and take care of her for a change. Maybe he'd pay off her mortgage. How nice would that be? It might even make up for all the shit he'd put her through. Probably not, but it would be a start. He rolled down his window and spat out his gum, driving down the street toward home.

Parking the van in the driveway, he walked upstairs to the kitchen and filled a glass of water at the sink. Mona lay on the couch in the living room with her phone pressed against her ear, smiling while she talked.

"Whatta you doing?" he said, walking into the family room.

Mona glanced up. Her face shifted from sweet to sour.

Sully checked his watch. He sat on the couch next to her and drank his water. She turned her back on him and mumbled into her phone. "It's nothing. My stupid brother just got home."

Sully tapped her shoulder. She ignored him. He tapped again and said, "Did you feed Bruno and take him for a walk?"

Mona looked up. Bruno, their big, fawn boxer, lifted his head from the ratty pillow he slept on next to the heating vent in the kitchen. Mona gave Sully a death stare. "I'm on the phone."

"Well, he still needs to eat and go for a walk," said Sully.

He finished his glass of water and walked into the kitchen, placing the empty glass in the sink. Bruno's tail thumped on the floor. Sully sat on the floor next to Bruno and put the dog's massive head in his lap, rubbing his ears. Ma bought Bruno ten years ago. He was supposed to be her guard dog after Dad died. Sully stroked Bruno's head. Although his mother brought him home when he was a pup and treated him like her baby, the dog gravitated toward Sully, following him everywhere. Even when he'd run the streets with Conor and Fitz as a teenager, Sully always made time to walk him, take him out in the yard, and throw him the ball. Bruno was a good dog. Sully hugged him. Bruno licked his hand. Sully turned toward Mona.

"Listen," he said, lowering his voice to a growl. "I'll feed him and take him out, but I might not be home for a while. You need to take care of him while I'm gone. Don't leave it all on Mom."

That caught Mona's attention. She straightened. "Where you going?"

Sully gave Bruno a final pat and stood. "None of your business." He walked to the refrigerator, grabbed a can of dog food, got a spoon, and shoveled the meaty, gristly mess into a metal bowl next to Bruno's makeshift bed. The dog got off his bed and sat perfectly still, looking up at Sully.

"Did you tell Mom you're leaving?" Mona asked.

Sully held a raised hand at Bruno. He waited for a count of five, then said, "Get it." Bruno wagged his tail and started eating. Sully put the empty dog food can in the trash and talked while he washed his hands at the sink. "Don't worry about me. And by the way, Mom said you have to pick her up at five tomorrow morning."

"I'm not picking her up. You pick her up."

Drying his hands, Sully rolled his eyes. He walked into the living room and tossed the hand towel at Mona. "I already told you. I'm gonna be gone. I got something to do tonight with Fitz and Conor. I'm not even gonna be here at five."

Mona threw the towel back at him. She stared at Sully as she talked into her phone. "Don't worry. It doesn't matter what my stupid brother says—I'm still going out tonight. Let me call you back in a minute. I gotta talk to him." She ended the call and shook her head. "You don't tell me what to do. I'm going out with Derek Ryder tonight. If Mom needs a ride, you pick her up, and then you can leave. And you can tell Conor that you had to hold off on whatever you're doing because I had a date with Derek."

"Fine," said Sully. "Don't pick Mom up. But she's gonna be walking home cause I'm gonna be gone. So, too bad, so sad for you. Have fun dealing with her when she kicks your ass for not picking her up."

With that, Sully turned and walked back into the kitchen.

"There he goes," said Mona "Walking away from me, just like his friend, mister 'I'm better than you,' Conor Monroe."

The dog leash clinked and jangled as Sully pulled it off the coatrack next to the front door. He held it up. "I'm taking Bruno for a walk." He clicked the leash on to Bruno's collar, opened the front door, and looked back. "And I'm gonna remember how much of a bitch you were when I'm rich, so watch your mouth, Mona."

Sully walked out and closed the door behind him, relishing Mona's confused look. It was rare that he got the last word. No one got under his skin more than her. She was, without a doubt, the one person on Earth who could make a man—any man—lose his shit. Why she was such a fucking pain in the ass was a mystery he couldn't figure. According to his friends, Mona won the lottery on looks and a body that wouldn't quit. If she wanted to, she could walk into any bar in town and get drinks and food all night long without spending a cent. Guys were that crazy about her. You'd think that having so much handed to her would make her halfway nice. But no—she had to always fuck with him. And that attitude of hers always made him say shit he never meant to say, like he just did, goddammit.

He mumbled under his breath as he walked Bruno down the driveway, wishing he could take back that thing he said about being rich. Stupid, stupid, stupid.

He watched Bruno squat and crap.

But Mona would have to be more than a pain in the ass to figure out that his leaving with Fitz and Conor and his comment about being rich added up to more than big talk. She'd have to be a fucking genius to figure out they were planning a robbery tonight. He didn't think she was, but she'd surprised him in the past. If she figured it out and started blabbing around town, who knew whose attention she might attract?

He picked up Bruno's poop with a doggie bag and continued down the block.

Thank God there wasn't much time for her to think about it. He, Fitz, and Conor needed to get in, get out, and get gone before anyone caught wind of what they were up to. That shouldn't be hard to do. When was the last time they had a job where they knew the combination to the safe and there were no guards to worry about? Still, he'd seen a lot in his short life, and from everything he'd experienced, he knew he could count on one thing.

He looked back toward his house. Mona was on the deck, watching him. Bruno tugged on his leash. He continued down the street, feeling anxiety tighten his chest.

Nothing was ever easy.

CHAPTER FOURTEEN

Julia shut her car door and locked it. It had taken half the day to get everything packed. Clothes, bed sheets, pots, pans, toiletries, and shoes—lots and lots of shoes—filled her car. She tossed her keys, catching them as she walked toward her apartment building.

It was late—around a quarter to eleven. All she had to do now was wait for Conor.

She ran up the stairs to her apartment. Once inside, she looked around. Her gaze stopped on the painting in the living room. The beach. Sunlight filtering over the ocean horizon in a blaze of color. Clouds filling with light. Waves rolling in. The sea grass bending in the breeze. And Conor sitting shoulder to shoulder with her in the sand as daybreak fell over them.

A flush of excitement filled her. Her stuff was packed. She'd called the property manager and ended her lease. Her apartment was cleaned. But she still needed to move that painting into Conor's apartment before they left. It needed a few days to dry before she could stick it in her car. She smiled, staring at the painting. It wouldn't be long before that scene became reality. All she had to do was—

Crap. She'd forgotten something.

She walked into her bedroom and pulled a pen and a pad of paper from her nightstand. She sat on the floor and started writing.

Dear Father Salvatore,

A good friend is going on a trip and he asked me to come with him. We're leaving tonight, so please have someone else cover my remaining shifts. I wish I could've given you more notice, but it was unexpected.

I also wanted to say thank you. With all your employees and the other people needing help in your parish, I know that someone like me can't be high on your list of priorities, but you let me know I needed to find another job before you told the rest of the staff. I appreciate you trying to help me.

With Sacred Heart closing, I imagine you'll be moving on to another parish. The people in your new church will be lucky to have you. Please remember me in your prayers. I'll certainly remember you in mine. Thank you for everything.

Julia Terranova

She signed the letter and sealed it in an envelope, printing 'Father Salvatore' on the front. If she was going to drop this off at Sacred Heart, deposit her check at the ATM, and make it back before Conor got here, she had to get moving. She grabbed her purse and hurried out the door to her car.

Pulling to a stop at a red light, she looked into the rearview mirror and tucked her hair behind her ears. A drop of sweat rolled down her back. The night hadn't taken much edge off the heat. The light turned green. Before she could accelerate, a motorcycle drove by in the left lane, followed by a van and an old SUV. One street ahead, they cut left onto a side street.

The van's headlights had lit up the motorcycle. There was no mistaking it. The man on the bike was Conor. She followed them but got hung up by oncoming traffic before she could turn. By the time she was moving again, Conor's caravan was blocks away, motoring up the hill toward Sacred Heart. She watched them disappear down a side street.

A bad feeling settled in her chest. There was no reason for it, at least not a logical one, but still, there it was, filling her head with questions. Where was Conor going? Who was in that van and the SUV? What were they doing?

She pulled into the church parking lot. The engine ticked as she got out. She walked across the parking lot, holding the letter to Father Salvatore.

She fingered the envelope as she walked, thinking the best place to put it was inside the screen door of the rectory. It was stifling hot, but the night was quiet. She glanced up at a washed-out moon that slipped behind dark clouds threatening rain. She quickened her steps, walking along the side of the church toward the rectory.

A figure darted across the far end of the walkway, disappearing around the back of the church. Two more figures followed. She stopped, listening, then started walking again, entering the dim circle of light in front of the rectory's front door. She could knock and tell Father Salvatore she'd seen people sneaking around the church, but it was probably just kids. She stuck the envelope in her pocket and kept walking. Even if it was just kids, she wanted to take a look.

No one was in sight around back. She exhaled. It had to be kids. She turned to leave. A crack of splintering wood broke the silence.

As quietly as she could, she crept around the back of the church. Peeking around the corner, she watched three figures slip into the side door of the church.

She looked back toward the rectory. If she told Father Sal, he'd call the police. The image of Conor on his motorcycle filled her head. She walked to the door, running her hand over the splintered trim next to the door handle. She stepped inside, hearing low whispers.

A hazy light filtered over the altar, but it was enough to

see Conor and two other men walk across the altar into the sacristy.

She followed them. Stopping outside the sacristy door, she peeked in. Conor kneeled on the floor next to the safe. Another man with dark wavy hair and a big man with short hair and a moustache stood over him, watching. They were so focused that they didn't notice her. It only took a few seconds before she'd seen enough. As she left, she let the church door bang shut behind her, not caring if Conor heard. It didn't matter.

She pulled the envelope from her pocket as she walked toward the rectory. Conor was a thief. She looked at the envelope. She wasn't going anywhere with Conor, but there was no need to write a different letter. This letter would tell Father Salvatore all he needed to know.

She was leaving town tonight.

She stuck the envelope inside the rectory's screen door and walked to her car. All the signs were there but she had somehow missed them. Conor came from a broken family. Except for mentioning that he did some work as an auto mechanic, he never did tell her how he made a living. He had time to take her for a ride around town in the middle of the week. And all those weeks before she met him, he'd kept the weirdest hours. Leaving at dark. Coming home late at night or in the morning. As nice as he was, it was clear to her now. He was a thief. A criminal. He was trouble—the last thing she was looking for. Nothing but a good-looking, smooth-talking thief.

Wind rocked her car as she drove. Rain began to spit. According to the radio, a cold front was bringing a bad storm.

A flash of rain covered her windshield. She turned on her wipers and clicked off the radio, focusing on the road as she headed out of town, unsure of where she was going. It didn't really matter. It just needed to be as far away from here as possible.

She wiped away tears of frustration and sadness,

thinking it was funny how things changed so fast in life. Fifteen minutes ago, she looked forward to her future. And now all she could do was dread it. All because of Conor.

She drove by a sign that read, 'You are now leaving Brannigan. Come back soon!'

"Fat chance," she mumbled, hoping with all her heart that Conor's night would go just as badly as hers.

It was the least he deserved.

CHAPTER FIFTEEN

Conor held his phone out, lighting up the face of the safe. He spun the dial one way, then another, then another. He glanced back over his shoulder at Fitz and Sully. "The moment of truth," he said, grabbing the latch. He pushed down. It didn't move. He tugged on it. Nothing. He sat back and stared at the dial.

"More like the moment of goof," said Fitz.

"Stop messing around, Conor," hissed Sully.

A bang from somewhere in the church made them jump. Fitz put a finger to his lips, then slipped out. He stepped back inside the room in less than a minute. "The wind must've banged the outside door shut. I made sure it's closed," he whispered.

Conor turned his attention back to the safe. He shook his head. "Maybe they changed the combination," he said.

"If they did, we're fucked," said Sully.

Fitz eyes narrowed. "We are not fucked. Try it again, Conor. Get that shit open."

Conor stared at the dial. The scowl on his face turned into a smile. He directed the light from his phone on the dial again, then leaned in and spun it. Three twists later, he stood, looked at Sully, and held out his hand toward the safe. "Be my guest," he said.

Sully kneeled.

Conor looked at Fitz. "My dyslexia kicked in. The last number was twenty-one, not twelve."

"And I thought Sully was the dumb one," whispered Fitz.

Sully pushed down on the latch. It clicked. He looked back at Conor, grinning. Then his gaze shifted. He stood, staring past Conor.

Conor felt hair raise on the back of his neck. He turned.

Two figures stood in the sacristy doorway. Darkness obscured their features. They stepped into the room. The moonlight coming through the windows illuminated their faces. Conor recognized them immediately. It was the men who were talking to Mona at Ricky's Pub, Derek Ryder and Johnny Tong. After he chased them away from Mona, they had dinner with the convict, Barry Cline.

"What are you boys doing?" said Derek.

Conor took stock of the two men. Neither had a gun. That was the good news. The bad news was that they didn't need a gun to do serious damage. They stepped forward and Derek pointed at Sully. "Your sister told me you guys were up to something. I told her, 'They can't be dumb enough to do what I think they're doing.' She said you were. I guess she was right."

Fitz stepped toward them. "We got here first, and there's three of us, so who you calling dumb?"

"Do you know who we work for?" said Johnny.

"I saw you having dinner with Barry," said Conor. "We're not scared of that convict. Save yourself the trouble. Tell him we were gone before you got here."

Johnny stepped toe-to-toe with Fitz. He was half-a-head shorter than Fitz, but a foot wider. He looked down at the ground and shook his head, laughing. "You have no idea of the shit you stepped in, do you? Just walk away. You'll thank us later, believe me."

Fitz glanced back at Conor and Sully. He winked. Then, turning back to face Johnny, he threw a left hook, twisting his hips and shoulders, putting every ounce of his strength and weight behind the punch. The crack of Fitz's knuckles on Johnny's face sounded like someone snapped a two-by-four.

Johnny reeled backward. He bounced off a wall and covered his mouth. He touched his mouth, looked at the blood, then raised his fists.

Conor mumbled, "Well, that didn't work."

Fitz said, "Shit," and backed away from Johnny.

Conor pushed Sully toward Fitz. They could handle Johnny Tong. He'd take Derek.

Derek eyed him and said, "Really?"

Conor raised half-clenched fists and backed into the center of the room. Derek rushed in. Conor blocked a jab. A hook axed him in the liver, sucking the strength from his legs. He backed up, trying to catch his breath. A kick knifed into his thigh, making the muscle hum as if it had been hit with a bat.

Derek's eyes shined bright as he moved in for the kill. Conor threw a straight right. Derek slipped it. Conor slid to the side and banged a hook into Derek's ribs. Derek grunted and dropped his arms. Moving inside Derek's guard, Conor threw two gut punches, then put his weight into an uppercut. It connected with Derek's jaw.

Derek fell, rolled, and scrambled to get back to his feet.

Conor waited. He timed it. Derek was almost standing when Conor dipped his hips and stepped in. He drove his shoulder into Derek's waist and lifted him. He ran a few steps, bent at the knees, and jumped.

Time crawled as he arced through the air. He glimpsed Johnny Tong on the floor, covering up from an onslaught of punches and kicks from Fitz and Sully. Then he felt the impact of the hardwood floor add to the force of his shoulder into Derek's midsection. Derek's ribs cracked. Conor rolled away, leaving Derek balled up in the fetal position.

"Let's go, Conor!" yelled Fitz. "Get the gold, Sully!"

Conor stood. The room rolled under his feet, and he

dropped to a knee. He looked around. Johnny was on his hands and knees with Fitz standing over him. Sully was across the room, sticking his head inside the safe. They'd be out of here in a minute. They'd ride away into the night with the gold. He'd drive home to pick up Julia. It was all going to work out.

Then Johnny Tong jumped to his feet, shoved Fitz out of the way, and ran toward the open safe.

All Conor could do was watch. Sully was on all fours with his head inside the safe. He yelled, "Sully!" as Johnny kicked the safe door. The door slammed shut on Sully's head. When it swung back open, Sully fell backward onto the floor. He landed flat on his back, motionless.

Johnny shoved Sully's body aside. He looked in the safe. "There ain't nothing in here," was all he managed before Fitz kicked him in the face. The door to the safe swung wide. Conor stared into it. It was empty.

Fitz picked up Sully from the floor. He walked stiff-legged across the room, struggling with Sully's dead weight. "C'mon, Conor. We gotta get him to the hospital."

Conor led the way, opening doors for Fitz on their way out of the church. He helped Fitz lay Sully in the back seat of Fitz's Bronco. Sully's eyes were open, but sightless. He stepped away as Fitz started the Bronco. A gust of wind rattled leaves and shook trees up and down the street.

Fitz stuck his head out the window, squinting into the wind, one eye nearly swollen shut. "C'mon!" He slapped the side of his door. "Get in! Let's go!"

Conor shook his head. "You take him to the hospital. I'm getting the guys who did this to him."

"We already got the guys who did this," said Fitz, pointing at the church. "We beat the shit out of them."

Conor backed away. "Not Derek and Johnny. The guys who sent them."

Fitz squinted, confused. He put the Bronco in gear, then said, "Get to the hospital as soon as you can," and squealed away. Conor turned and ran toward his motorcycle.

There was no gold.

Sully was hurt bad.

And Julia was waiting for him.

But he had to set things right with the guys who were responsible for this shitstorm. Those old codgers spinning their webs at The Red Fox, Duck and Artie.

The wind squalled and rain spat as he kickstarted his bike and pulled into the street. Fitz heard about the gold from Duck and Artie. Those old crooks had to be the ones who sent Johnny and Derek. And now they were going to be joining Sully in the hospital.

The ride to The Red Fox went by in a blur. Needles of rain pricked his face as he opened the throttle.

He parked on the sidewalk in front of The Red Fox just as the skies opened up, dropping buckets of rain. Shoving the front door open, he looked around. The bar was packed. His gaze settled on Duck, smoking alone at his table by the front window. Conor shook the rain out of his hair and walked over.

"I know you," said Duck, sliding a chair out. "Keep an old man company."

Conor watched him pull a twenty from his wallet.

"I'll get you a beer," Duck said, waving the bill at the bartender. Conor kept his expression flat as Duck winked and said, "I love beer, but it gives me gas something awful."

The bartender walked over and put a bottle of beer on the table in front of Conor.

Duck grinned and tapped his cigarette in an ashtray. Conor grabbed Duck by the arm, pulled him up to his feet, and said, "We gotta talk."

Duck prattled on as he pulled him through the crowd toward the back of the bar.

"Aren't you Mickey Monroe's son? How is he? Always wished I could help him."

"You know, the bartender is following us. You better be careful. Mike's a big boy, and he can get riled up."

"Slow down, son. I'm an old man."

There was no line in front of the men's room—a miracle for a Friday night. Conor kicked the door open, pulled Duck in with him, and slid the deadbolt. He faced Duck, looking him up and down.

"I'm no queer, if that's what this is about," said Duck.

Conor noticed the closed door on the toilet stall. He banged on it.

"I'm taking a dump here. How 'bout a little courtesy?"

"Artie! It's that Conor Monroe kid. He pulled me in—"

Conor kicked the stall door open. Artie sat on the toilet with his pants around his ankles. His eyes opened wide as Conor grabbed the sides of the stall and kicked him in the face. Artie's head cracked against the wall behind the toilet. He slumped forward, head hanging between his knees, his pants pooled down around his ankles. Conor shut the door.

"You have my attention," said Duck, his eyes flat.

Conor poked him in the chest. "Did you send Derek Ryder and Johnny Tong over to the church tonight?"

Someone banged on the locked door and yelled, "You okay, Duck?"

Duck looked at Conor. "I don't know how you heard about what's in that safe, but it's mine. You and your friends have no right to it."

The pounding on the door started up again. Conor stared at Duck. "Tell him you'll be right out."

Duck licked his lips, his gaze shifting between the door and Conor. "I'm fine, Mike. Check back if I'm not out in a minute." He waited a beat before eyeing Conor and whispering, "If I was you, I'd leave before that minute is up."

"One of my friends is in the hospital because of you," said Conor.

A small rivulet of blood ran from under the toilet stall toward the drain by Duck's feet. Duck stepped away from the blood. "If one of your friends got hurt, it's because he was somewhere he shouldn't have been, doing something he shouldn't have been doing," he said. " He drew himself up to his full height. "You know, this isn't going to go well for you or your friends. In all the years I've known your father, he never acted like this. I'm not sure what I'm going to do about it, but I'll do something. Your conduct bothers me."

Conor turned his back on Duck. He touched his temple, feeling his pulse pound. "My conduct?"

"This isn't something I'll forget. I'm afraid I'm going to have to—"

Conor punched him in the mouth. Blood spurted from Duck's lip as his head snapped back, cracking the mirror behind the sink. His knees buckled and his face bounced off the edge of the sink. He fell on the floor and rolled through Artie's blood. Conor grabbed the back of his neck.

"Couple things to remember about my conduct," Conor said. "If people hurt my friends, I hurt people back."

He smeared Duck's face in the blood. Duck lifted his face, gasping, blood staining a shock of white hair above his forehead. Conor stepped on the back of his neck.

"And another thing," he said, listening to Duck wheeze. "My dad doesn't know you." He took his foot off Duck's neck. "So, stop talking about him and start thinking about my friend that's in the hospital. Better yet, start praying for him, because if he doesn't pull through, you're gonna see me again."

He opened the men's room door and looked back. "And by the way, I don't know who told you about that safe, but either they're stupid, or you're senile, because it was empty. This whole disaster of a night is because you don't know what you're doing anymore. Time to retire, Duck."

Conor stepped out of the men's room and saw the bartender pushing through the crowd, holding a bat. Conor met him halfway and jabbed his thumb toward the men's room. "They're gonna need more toilet paper." He patted the bartender's shoulder and walked out. He glanced back once and saw the bartender talking on his cell phone.

A driving rain soaked him as he rode toward his

apartment complex. Before he went to the hospital to meet up with Fitz, he had to stop and talk to Julia. He had to tell her what happened. How he'd planned to steal the bishop's gold, and how it all went to hell. She might not like hearing that he was a thief, but he felt like he needed to come clean. After tonight's epic failure, it was time to make a new plan. One where they both decided what to do. Whether that meant staying here, or going somewhere else, he was ready. It was time to see what life could be like with someone at his side. But he needed to step on it. It was already a quarter past midnight. Fifteen minutes was a long time to keep a girl as perfect as Julia waiting.

He squinted through the rain, motoring up a hill toward the apartment complex. A car turned on its high beams behind him, racing toward him. That fucking bartender must've called someone. He glanced in his sideview mirrors. He couldn't make out who it was—the lights were blinding. But the car was bearing down on him. He sped by the entrance to his apartment complex. One thing was sure—whoever was following him was trouble. The last thing he wanted was to bring trouble to Julia's door. He downshifted and took a quick left. It shouldn't be hard to lose whoever it was in this rain. He heard the screech of tires and glanced back. The car skidded into the turn, barely missing a line of parked cars. He could hear the car's engine roar as the driver floored the accelerator. Up ahead, Conor could see the bridge that went over the Mohican River. There were no street lights on the other side of that bridge. Nothing but dark roads winding through parkland. Even some dirt roads. And he knew them all. Whoever was tailing him would never be able to keep up with him once he got past the bridge. And after he lost them, he'd head back to get Julia.

He flew up an incline toward the bridge. The car closed in from behind. His motorcycle went airborne as he crested the hill.

The bike settled with a heavy thud on the bridge. The front wheel landed solidly. The back wheel hydroplaned on the wet asphalt. The tail of the bike swept right, then left, fishtailing. He muscled it, trying to keep it on the road. For a moment, he got control. Then the car tapped his back end. If he hadn't lost speed from hydroplaning, he would've already been over the bridge. But he did lose speed. Just enough for the car to tag him.

A motorcycle moving at high speed is a dangerous machine. The combination of weight and speed can kill a man as easily as a man can squash an ant. The nudge from the car unleashed that danger in an eyeblink.

The motorcycle's back end swept out to the right. Conor put both feet on the ground, straining to keep it upright. The back wheel caught asphalt, then lost traction again. He felt the bike sliding out from under him. There was no option.

He jumped.

He expected to hit the asphalt. But his bike had slid more than he thought. It crumpled into the guardrail. He flew over the guardrail, plummeting toward the river below. The river, swollen with rainwater, roared. He plunged into its cold, raging current.

He spun head over heel. A whine filled his head. He needed air. His back slammed against a boulder. He broke the surface and gasped. The current drove him back underwater.

He rolled over and over in darkness. His head smacked a rock, filling it with an explosion of light. He tumbled and tossed like a leaf in a hurricane. This couldn't go on much longer. Any moment now, he'd pop to the surface, climb out of this river, get back on his motorcycle, pick up Julia, and ride out of town. He just needed air.

His head slammed into another rock. He breathed in involuntarily, cold water filling his lungs. His whole body went slack. The current gathered him up and carried him along. He relaxed and went along for the ride, listening to the roar of the river transform into the rumble of his motorcycle.

He was driving to the apartments. Everything glowed. The trees. The street. The grass. Everything. Jewels of rain fell as he pulled into the parking lot. A downed tree limb was under Julia's balcony. He pulled next to it, watching its leaves tremble in the soft rain. Julia leaned over her balcony's railing. He cut the engine on his motorcycle.

"You made it!" she yelled. Then somehow she was behind him, sitting on his motorcycle with her arms wrapped around his chest. He started his motorcycle and pulled out of the parking lot. Julia's grip tightened around his chest.

"This is the best day of my life," she said, kissing the back of his neck.

"I can't breathe," he said.

The glow from the street, the trees, the grass, and everything else brightened. He drove into the glare as Julia's embrace became a relentless pressure, crushing him. It felt like his heart would explode, but it didn't matter.

Julia was with him.

He opened the throttle full bore.

They were leaving.

It was time to start a new life.

He inhaled, drawing cold water into his lungs.

Everything was perfect.

CHAPTER SIXTEEN

Conor Monroe opened his eyes. Couldn't see a thing. It was dark. And cold. His head ached. He shivered, breathing through chattering teeth. A hand covered his mouth. Someone whispered, "Quiet."

He recognized the voice. It was his father, Mickey Monroe. His broken, homeless bum of a father. Which begged the question.

Where the hell was he, and what was his dad doing here?

He took stock of his situation. His clothes were wet. The air smelled of oil and gas. He was lying on a roughed-up leather couch. His head hurt. None of it made sense. Then muffled voices filtered through the quiet. A light clicked on outside the room, illuminating a crack under a door. Conor's eyes adjusted to the feeble light. He scanned his surroundings. He could see a desk. Catalogs filled the shelves above the desk. Mickey stood over him, holding an index finger against his lips. The men's voices outside the door grew louder.

"I said I'll let you know if I see him."

"If you hide him, you're dead. If you help him, you're dead. If you—"

"I know, I'm dead. Just get the fuck out—he's not here. If I see him, you'll be the first to know."

Conor sat up. He knew the first voice. Wasn't sure about the second. The men outside the room walked away, their voices receding. A door banged shut in the recesses of the building. Footsteps approached. The door swung open. A tall figure entered, switching on a light.

Conor shaded his eyes. A man in blue coveralls stared back at him, standing a couple inches over six feet. Clean shaven with long, straight black hair tied back in a ponytail. Broad cheekbones. Eyes with a slight Asiatic tilt. It was Angel. So that explained where he was—the back office of Angel's garage, where he'd worked off and on as a mechanic for the past few years. But the big question still hung out there.

Why was he here?

Angel eyed him, then glanced at Mickey. "How's he doing?"

"Seems okay," said Mickey, turning toward Conor.

Conor opened his mouth to talk. He belched. Nausea rose up through his gut. He hugged his arms around his chest as his teeth chattered. His dad hung a coat over his shoulders.

"I was in a little camp of mine on the Mohican River, just down from the bridge at Fox Glenn Park," said his dad. "I went to piss and saw you on the riverbank. Thought you were dead. What happened?"

Conor huddled in his dad's coat. It was damp and it was rank, which was to be expected, but it was warm. The sickness in his stomach settled. He hung his head between his legs. It started to come back to him. He and Sully and Fitz tried to rob Sacred Heart cathedral. The bishop had supposedly locked a gold staff, chalice, and other Catholic voodoo worth around four-hundred thousand in the church safe. It was supposed to be a sure thing. And after he got his cut, Conor and his girlfriend, Julia, were going to leave town and start a new life. One last big heist—the kind of cliché you read about in a crime novel. But, just like a crime novel, it all came crashing down.

There was no gold. All he, Fitz, and Sully had found in that church was a fight that put Sully in the hospital.

Angel pointed at Conor. "Why do Artie and Duck have people looking for you?"

Conor leaned back, closing his eyes. Artie and Duck. That sparked his memory. Artie and Duck were the old guys that occupied a front table at The Red Fox. They looked and acted like pensioners who were running out the clock on their last days. But, if Conor had to guess, they ran everything, and they had the muscle to make sure that anyone who stepped out of line was quickly reminded of who was in charge. And that was the problem. He, Sully, and Fitz had stepped out of line. The job of breaking into the cathedral's safe had been set up by Artie and Duck. It was supposed to be for one of their crews, not three knockabouts from the neighborhood.

Another bolt of nausea wrenched Conor's guts. He clapped a hand over his mouth, gagged, and then threw up. Cold water and bile splashed on the floor. He spat, waiting for his stomach to calm.

Angel tapped his shoulder. "Conor. What happened?"

"A lot," Conor said between shallow breaths.

Mickey smiled. "Did you have something to do with Artie and Duck getting the shit beat out of them last night?"

Conor looked up. An image flashed of him kicking Artie in the face, followed by an image of Duck crawling across a piss-soaked bathroom floor, blood dripping from his nose. Conor wiped his mouth and mumbled, "Maybe."

Angel stared. "You gotta be kidding me."

Conor exhaled, shaking his head. "Me, Sully, and Fitz heard about a job that Artie and Duck set up, but it was bullshit. There was nothing in the safe. Then Duck and Artie's guys showed up. We had to fight our way out and Sully got hurt." A wave of anxiety rolled through Conor as he remembered dumping Sully's motionless body into the back of Fitz's Bronco. "Fitz took Sully to the hospital. I went to the Red Fox to see Artie and Duck. They got what they deserved for what their guys did to Sully."

Angel shook his head. "So, you tried to steal from Artie

and Duck, got caught, Sully got hurt, and you went to the Red Fox to beat them up as payback."

"Yeah."

"You're a fucking idiot."

Conor shrugged. "I know."

"So, how'd you end up at the river?" said Angel.

Conor took off his dad's dirty coat. He stood and pulled off his boots and socks as he talked.

"I guess one of Artie and Duck's guys followed me after I left the Fox. I was riding over the bridge at Fox Glen Park when he clipped me. My bike went into a slide and I jumped off. I don't remember anything after that." He grabbed the front of his shirt and twisted it. Water trickled on the floor. "Guess I ended up in the river."

Barefoot, he started to strip out of his wet clothes.

Angel glanced at Mickey in disbelief. Mickey shrugged.

Naked, Conor walked by Angel. He grabbed a pair of coveralls off a hook on the back of the office door. His bare feet slapped the concrete as he walked back to the couch. He sat, pulled on the coveralls, and said, "That job was supposed to give me enough to leave town with this girl I've been hanging with. I was supposed to pick her up hours ago."

"She's going to have to wait a little bit longer," said Mickey. "You're in no condition to be doing anything."

Conor spit on the floor. He stood. "I gotta go. She probably thinks I ditched her."

Angel stepped over and pushed Conor back down on the couch.

"Duck's guys are looking for you," said Angel. "They see you walk out of here, I'm next. You're staying here."

"They won't see me," said Conor, trying to stand again.

"Not tonight," said Angel, shoving him.

Conor recognized the look on Angel's face. There was no way he was leaving without getting into it with Angel. And that wasn't something to be taken lightly. "How long do I have to stay?" he asked.

Angel stared at Conor. "We'll talk about it later." He switched his gaze to Conor's dad. "Mickey, take the easy chair. Conor, stay on the couch. I'll sleep in one of the cars in the garage." He pointed at Conor. "You try to sneak out and I will ring your fucking bell, so stay put." He walked out of the room and came back with an armful of canvas tarps. He tossed one to Conor and one to his dad. "Go to sleep. We'll figure this out tomorrow."

Conor watched Angel leave. He waited for his dad to settle into the easy chair and click off the overhead light before he pulled the tarp over himself and turned onto his side.

As soon as things calmed down, he'd explain everything to Julia. He didn't get the big payday, but they could still leave town. If she let him, he'd make it right.

* * *

Conor stretched. His dad was gone, but a pizza box was on the floor. He ate the last two cold slices of pepperoni and looked at the clock. Unbelievable. It was after five. Half the day was gone. He rubbed an aching lump on the back of his head. His whole body hurt. He walked out of Angel's office, feeling bruised all over. Apparently, spending last night stealing, fighting, and drowning had worn him out. Angel turned and looked at him from under a car perched on a hydraulic lift. He dropped a wrench, stepped over to the open garage door, and pulled it down.

"What are you doing?" said Angel. "Somebody could've seen you."

"I'm thirsty," said Conor.

Angel closed the other bay door. He waved for Conor to follow as he walked into the customer waiting area. He locked the front door and closed the blinds. "Come here," he said, stepping behind the front counter.

Conor sat on a stool at the front counter.

Angel filled a paper cup from the water tank behind the

counter. A bubble billowed to the top of the tank. He handed Conor the cup.

Conor drank the water in one gulp. He handed the cup back.

Angel filled it again.

"So, I checked things out," said Angel, handing the water to Conor. "You beat the hell out of Artie and Duck." He opened the cash register, pulled money out, and counted it. "Artie's in the hospital with head trauma. Duck is in bad shape too, but he's walking around. Word is he's willing to pay a lot to get his hands on you."

Conor finished drinking. He threw his cup in the trash can behind Angel. "You hear if Sully is okay?"

Angel rubber-banded the cash. "No. Your dad left this morning to check on him."

Conor watched Angel count and band his money for a while before he said, "So, you and my dad are…What are you?"

Angel shut the register with a clang. "We're friends. Is that a problem?"

"No. It's just, well…He's a bum."

Angel zipped the deposit bag and shoved it under the counter. Rummaging around, he pulled out a bottle of vodka and a couple shot glasses. "He's a lot more than a bum."

"Yeah. He's also a drunk."

Angel grabbed a deck of cards out from under the counter. "You up for a game of blackjack?" he said. "Loser takes a shot."

"Sure."

Angel shuffled the cards. Someone knocked on the front door. Angel put the cards down and shouted, "We're closed."

Conor heard his dad say, "It's me."

Angel opened the door. Conor's dad stepped inside and pointed at the bottle of vodka. "Having a party?"

"Blackjack. Loser takes a shot," said Angel.

"Deal me in."

Angel eyed him. "Is that a good idea?"

"Don't start."

Angel counted three stacks of chips and dealt the cards. Conor won the first hand then went on a losing streak until his chips were gone. He drank a shot, feeling the burn as he took Angel's place behind the counter to deal.

"By the way," said Conor, dealing the cards. "Thanks for not turning me over to Artie and Duck's crew last night."

"No problem," said Angel, watching Mickey drain a glass of vodka, smack his lips, and then turn to Angel.

"I checked around," said Mickey. "Fitz dropped Sully off at the hospital and then disappeared. He never made it back to his trailer last night—I checked. Nobody knows where he is. And I visited Sully at the hospital." He took a deep breath and sighed. "He's on a respirator."

Conor turned his cards. Sixteen was showing. He took a hit. Five. "Twenty-one," he said, raking in everyone's chips.

His dad poured another glass of vodka, then glanced at Angel. "Fitz might have done more than disappear. Somebody might have found him. You should let Conor stay until we figure out what's going on."

Conor stopped shuffling the cards. "Fitz is fine. He's probably holed up somewhere."

Angel played with his stack of chips. He glanced at Conor. "Like where?"

Conor's chest tightened. The last time he saw him, Fitz was driving Sully to the hospital. After that, no one knew where he went. And according to his dad, he wasn't in his trailer. So where did he go? He shook his head. "I don't know. But he can take care of himself."

"Does he know you put a beating on Artie and Duck?" said Angel.

"No."

"Then he doesn't know people are looking for you and probably him. They might already have him."

The room went quiet.

Conor broke the silence. "But Fitz didn't do anything to them. I did."

"You and Fitz and Sully all tried to steal from them last night. The beating you gave Artie and Duck didn't help, but they have more than enough reason to do very bad things to all of you," said Angel. He walked over to the blinds, lifted them enough to peek out and added, "You're staying here for a couple days."

"I'm not your problem," said Conor. "My bike's probably in the impound lot. If you get it, I'll ride out of town tonight."

Angel poured himself a vodka. "No. You're chilling out for a few days. Anyone sees you leave from here, I'm fucked. We're letting this thing with Duck settle."

"That'll take longer than a couple days," said Conor.

"All the more reason to stay," said Angel, holding out his hand. "Give me your cell. No calls in or out as long as you're here, not even to that girl you're leaving town with."

"What?" said Conor.

"Give it to me," said Angel.

Conor didn't move.

"You want me to take it?"

Conor looked at his dad, who shrugged. Cursing under his breath, Conor handed over his cell.

"It's called, 'keeping you safe,'" said Angel.

"So, am I going to ever meet this girl, Conor?" said Mickey.

"I don't know."

"She pretty?" said Mickey.

"Very," mumbled Conor, watching Angel pocket his cell phone.

Angel met Conor's gaze. "You have a problem?" he said.

Conor folded his arms over his chest and rolled his eyes.

"I didn't think so," said Angel. "Deal. Let's play some cards."

CHAPTER SEVENTEEN

Julia drove by the 'Welcome to the City of Massey' sign. She felt sick. Her old boyfriend, James Stockton, lived here, but it was the only place she knew. Where else could she go?

Her mind circled around thoughts of Maine—how great it would've been to go there with Conor. But last she saw of him, he was breaking into a safe at Sacred Heart. If he hadn't done that, they'd probably be halfway to the East Coast by now. She turned off the classic rock coming from her radio, needing silence. Why did he have to do that?

She knew Conor was rough around the edges. But if he would steal from a church, what else would he do? After seeing that, it made sense to leave and drive back to this horrible town. The town she grew up in. The town she got raped in. Massey.

Pulling into a convenience store, she turned off the ignition. She tilted down the rearview mirror and gave herself a once-over. Not a pretty sight. Digging eyeliner, mascara, and lipstick out of her purse, she went to work. The makeup didn't help much, but it was something. Really, how good could a girl look after driving most of the night before sleeping in her car at a truck stop?

She went into the convenience store. The guy behind the counter smiled way too wide when he rang up her cigarettes. Passing her change back, he gripped her hand for a moment and ran his thumb over the back of her hand. She pulled her hand away and threw the change at him. It felt good listening to him curse as she walked out.

Back inside her car, she looked up an old friend on her cell. Angela Duncan. Starting the car, she searched for Angela's address, put it into Google maps, and then pulled out of the parking lot.

Angela would let her crash at her place until she figured things out. They'd been tight when they'd worked the cleaning crew at Woodlands High School. Julia smiled, remembering how Angela would sing classic rock, like Zeppelin, Foreigner, and Bad Company, shaking her ass and whipping her long blonde hair around while they mopped floors, trying to one-up each other with their dance moves. And when they weren't dancing, Angela was sneaking up on her, kissing her neck from behind and talking in a low voice, play acting that she was a boyfriend who'd come to take her away. All fun all the time—that was Angela. The only thing Angela ever bitched about was Karla, their boss. Karla only had her job because her dad was on the school board. It was part of life. People used connections all the time, but it sure chapped Angela's ass. And it probably explained why she'd been distant before Julia left. Julia shook her head.

She probably thought I was sleeping with James to get ahead. That's why she stopped talking to me. Thought I was another Karla.

A sign that read "Windsor Farms" came into view on the right side of the road. She pulled into the development. The temperature cooled in the shade of the huge oak trees towering over the road that wound its way into the development. It was a nice place, built to look like some kind of old southern plantation. A white, split-rail fence lined the edge of the road. Lots of old trees, a clubhouse, a pool, and tennis courts completed the picture as you drove further in. Julia remembered that she and Angela had gone to a couple parties here thrown by pampered college kids back when they were janitors. She turned onto Angela's street, White Birch Lane. Each rowhouse had a parking space and a nice, leafy-green tree out front. Julia pulled into a spot in front of her old friend's house. She glanced in the rearview mirror. The jagged scar across her cheek blazed—an ugly reminder of when she'd moved down in the world. She averted her gaze, scanning the splendor of Windsor Farms. Somehow, someway, at the same time she was being beaten and raped into submission by James, Angela had moved up. It would be fun to hear how she'd done it.

Good for you, Angela, she thought, opening her car door and stepping out to gaze at Angela's rowhouse. *At least one of us is going in the right direction.*

* * *

Julia sniffed her armpits before she knocked on Angela's door. A shower was way past due. She knocked and crossed her arms, checking her watch. A little past noon on a Sunday. Hopefully, Angela was here. She didn't know what she'd do if Angela wasn't home. She had no job, and her last paycheck wouldn't last long.

She knocked again.

Nothing.

She put her ear against the door.

It was quiet inside.

She turned to leave, feeling a cold stone of despair settle in her stomach. Now what? She couldn't go back to Brannigan—she'd already quit her job. And she didn't have much gas in her car anyway. The best move would probably be to sit in her car and wait. Maybe Angela was working. Maybe she'd come home later.

She took a step away from the door when she heard it. Someone thumping their way down a flight of stairs inside the rowhouse.

Julia turned.

The door opened.

It was Angela. Her hair was super long and a blinding shade of blonde. She'd lost weight in the waist and hips—but somehow kept her big chest—and had a tan that nearly matched the orange of her gym shorts, but it was definitely her. No one's face lit up quite like Angela's when she smiled.

"Julia?" said Angela.

Julia smiled back at her. All she could manage was a quick "Hi" before Angela squealed and jumped on her, squeezing her in a hug.

It was early, but Julia took one of the beers Angela brought from the kitchen. She sat on a couch, watching Angela sprawl across a rattan chair with overstuffed floral cushions. Angela lit a cigarette and blew a cloud of smoke. She picked a piece of tobacco off her tongue and folded her bare legs under her.

"Been a long time," said Angela. "What are you doing back here?"

Julia scanned the town house. "Looks like you're doing okay for yourself."

"Can't complain," said Angela. She took a drag on her cigarette, swigged her beer, and cocked her head. "Last I heard, you were seeing that superintendent, Mr. Big Shot James Stockton. Then you disappeared. Not even a goodbye. What happened?"

Julia nodded. "I got a job out of town," she said, touching the scar on her cheek. "Sorry about ghosting you, but it came up all of a sudden."

Angela pointed at the scar. "What happened there?"

Julia lowered her hand. She stood and walked to the big picture window with a view of the parking lot. She picked up a photo of her and Angela smiling and holding up beer bottles. "This was a fun party," she said, tapping the photo.

Angela stubbed out her cigarette. She walked over, took the photo from Julia, and placed it on the window ledge. "You okay?" she asked, gripping Julia's shoulder.

Tears welled in Julia's eyes.

Angela hugged her. "It's okay. I got you."

Julia let Angela lead her back to the couch. Having someone hold her and tell her everything was going to be fine felt good. She didn't know how much she'd needed it until now. "I need someplace to stay, but just for a little bit," she said, sitting on the couch.

"Long as you need," said Angela, sitting next to her.

"I don't have much money."

"Don't worry about it. Just tell me what's wrong."

Julia laid her head on Angela's shoulder. "There's this guy. We were going to go away together," she said, feeling Angela play with her hair.

"Can't trust guys," said Angela.

"I saw him breaking into a church with a couple other guys. They were trying to break into a safe. Can you believe that?"

"You deserve better."

Julia sighed. "He seemed like such a good guy."

Angela circled a finger around Julia's ear. "Men can fool you. It's happened to all of us."

"He was really cute."

"That's how they suck you in," said Angela. She rubbed the back of Julia's neck. "You need help bringing your stuff in?"

Julia grabbed Angela's pack of cigarettes. She lit one and took a drag, handing it to Angela. "You sure it's not going to be a problem for me to stay?"

Angela nodded, took a drag, and then handed the cigarette back to Julia. "You can sleep with me. I got a king size bed. It's big enough for both of us."

Julia smiled. "You mind if I take a shower before we get my stuff?"

Angela raised her eyebrows. "I wasn't going to say anything, but yeah, take that shower. You are ripe, girl."

* * *

The shower relaxed Julia. When she was done, she realized how tired she was. She wrapped a towel around her and walked into Angela's bedroom. Angela was on the bed in a white muscle shirt and panties, reading a magazine. Julia put on a black T-shirt and jumped on the bed next to Angela. "You're looking tight. You been working out?"

Angela looked over the top of the magazine. "I've been dancing." She hid behind the magazine again.

Julia pulled down the magazine. "What kind of dancing?"

"The fun kind," said Angela.

"Oh my god," said Julia, smacking Angela's thigh. "You're a stripper!"

Angela lifted her shirt, flashing Julia. "If you got 'em, use 'em."

"I can't believe it," said Julia. "Really?"

"It's not bad," said Angela, tossing her magazine on the floor. "Listen. If you need work, we're looking for another girl. You'd rake it in with that body of yours."

"My tits are too small," said Julia, laughing. She lay down on her side. "But I can't even think about it now. I'm exhausted."

Angela spooned her and talked into the back of her neck. "You sleep. I'm gonna clean up downstairs and then I'll join you. I gotta work tonight."

Julia listened to Angela pad out of the room. She watched the bedroom door shut, closed her eyes, and fell asleep.

* * *

Angela lit a cigarette and stood at the bottom of the stairs with an ashtray in one hand and a cigarette in the other. She blew out a cloud of smoke. She'd always been a good friend to Julia. Danced with her. Partied with her. She'd had feelings for that girl, which was why it had been so disappointing when she'd heard that Julia was catting around with James Stockton. Angela knew how it worked. Julia gave herself to James and got something in return. Like everyone else, she was making a deal. That had been bad enough. The worst, however, had been how Julia left without saying a word. Never even called or texted. But she sure didn't have any trouble coming over when she had nowhere else to go.

Typical. She only thought about herself, just like everyone else.

"So, you won't be surprised if I do the same," Angela whispered.

She smoked her cigarette to the filter and gazed up the steps, listening, but Julia never made a sound. A last cloud of smoke eased out of her as she put the ashtray on the coffee table, and then walked into the kitchen. She dialed a number. When James Stockton answered, she took a deep breath and smiled.

"Hey, honey," she whispered. "Your old girlfriend Julia is here." She shook her head. "No, I'm not kidding. She's sleeping in my bed right now." She laughed softly. "Yeah, that's me. Very thoughtful." She walked into the living room, lit another cigarette then stepped quietly back into the kitchen. "No, there's no guy. She's alone." She tapped ash into the sink. "I'm gonna take her to Sweeties tonight. See if Billy can get her on the stage. You help make that happen, like you did for me, and she'll be there waiting for you." She narrowed her eyes. "But you're gonna owe me." She listened for a moment, then shook her head. "I'll let you know what I want. Let me think on it a bit. See you soon."

She walked upstairs on tiptoe. Slipping under the covers, she tucked in behind Julia and nuzzled her. Julia smelled good. All soapy and clean. Julia let out a small, satisfied groan and Angela kissed her neck.

"It's okay, baby," she whispered. "I got you. Everything's gonna be just fine."

CHAPTER EIGHTEEN

Duck zipped up and flushed the toilet. He turned on the water in the sink, looked in the mirror, and grimaced while he washed his hands. The black around both eyes had faded to a sickly purplish yellow. He dabbed his split lip with a washcloth, winced, and threw the cloth in the sink. He stared at his reflection. Conor Monroe was going to be shitting broken bones for this. He opened the medicine cabinet, pocketed a straight razor, and then limped downstairs to his dining room. Taking a seat at the head of the table, he scanned the assembled group.

Johnny Tong, the big Samoan prizefighter, had a knot on his forehead and his face was puffy and bruised.

Derek Ryder, the cauliflower-eared cage fighter, winced with every breath. His ribs were fractured.

Across the table, Barry Cline looked great, but that was to be expected. Barry was supposed to lead the Sacred Heart robbery. He drove Johnny and Derek to the church on Duck's instructions. It hadn't been hard to figure out that those boys, Conor, Fitz, and Sully, were up to something. Sully Bomba's sister, Mona, told Derek all about it. How Sully was shooting his mouth off about something big that was going to make them all rich. It didn't take a rocket scientist to figure out that Sully and his friends had heard about the bishop's gold. And it shouldn't have been hard to stop them—they were three, half-assed thieves with no rep and no serious friends. But somehow, someway, those three lost causes cleaned out the safe and put a hurt on Duck's best muscle, Johnny and Derek. Sure, Sully was in a coma, but Johnny and Derek were in terrible shape, Artie was in the hospital, and Duck felt like he'd been shoved in a sack and thrown out the back of a truck barreling down the highway. But Barry? Not a scratch on him. That pissed Duck off as much as those boys cleaning out Sacred Heart's safe. Barry, the ex-con with his perfect haircut that sported just a touch of gray at the temple. Designer, frameless glasses. Clean-shaven. Crisp, white button-down shirt with a blue tie. All that and a fresh manicure with clear-coat gloss on his fingernails. Barry came out of this looking relaxed and satisfied, like he'd just enjoyed a day at the spa.

Duck bit his bottom lip, tasting the dried blood.

Good old Barry. Didn't even get his hands dirty while Artie got a free trip to the hospital and I got my face beat in by that punk Conor Monroe.

Duck nearly choked on his spite. He took a deep breath and turned his gaze on Derek.

"So," he said. "Where is this Conor Monroe fella?"

Derek waved at Johnny Tong. "Me and Johnny have been all over town. The kid is nowhere. Tell him, Johnny."

Johnny straightened. "We got eyes on his apartment, the hospital where Sully's laid up, and most of the bars in town." Johnny looked around the table, nodding. "He shows up, we'll be the first to know."

"And what about you?" said Duck, focusing his gaze on Barry.

"What?" said Barry, putting his elbows on the table and steepling his hands.

Duck walked over to Barry and stuck his face in front of him. "Are you having trouble seeing?" He circled a finger around his beaten and bruised face. "I blame this on you. And Artie's in the hospital. You need to make this right."

"I did everything I could to make it right," said Barry. "I chased him as soon as Mikey called me. Ran him off the road into that river. He must've drowned. What else could've happened?"

Duck pounded the table with his fist. "We've been up and down that river! There's no body! No body means he's still alive! Understand?"

"You need to calm down," said Barry.

Duck took a breath. "You know what'll calm me down? Ten thousand of your dollars on the street for anyone that brings me Conor Monroe's head."

Barry's brow wrinkled. "That's a lot of money."

"And," said Duck, raising his voice, "twenty-five for anyone that brings him in alive so I can kill him myself."

Barry shook his head. "I can't—"

"Do I need to call a detective about Mickey Monroe's partner?" said Duck.

Barry set his jaw.

"Who's Mickey Monroe's partner?" said Derek.

Duck smiled at Barry.

Barry slid his gaze over to Derek and said, "Mind your own fucking business," before pursing his lips and nodding at Duck. "I'll put the money on the street."

Duck felt a wave of satisfaction. He didn't like using old jobs as leverage against his men, but in this case, it was warranted. Barry's murder of Mickey Monroe's partner happened over a decade ago, when Barry was just getting into the game. Duck had ordered it to ruin Mickey's life. And ruin is just what Mickey got. The man had built up a reputation as someone who could get things done—someone people had started to respect. That meant he was competition, or in other words, a man who needed to be put in his place. And now his son Conor was following the family tradition of being a pain in the royal ass. Duck exhaled with a low growl. Somehow, that kid had cleaned out a safe with four-hundred-thousand dollars of gold, beat up Derek and Johnny, and then put a cherry on top by coming into The Red Fox and painting the bathroom red with his and Artie's blood. Gossip moved fast, and this story would move faster than most. That meant Conor needed to be put down before anyone got the bright idea that Brannigan was open for business for any hard ass with an attitude.

Duck nodded at Barry. "Get your money on the street, put the word out that I want Conor Monroe, and let's wrap this up. I have to go check on Artie at the hospital."

"What do you want us to do with him?" said Johnny, turning to look at a man sitting on the floor in the foyer. Bound with duct tape, the man sat motionless with his back against the wall and his chin on his chest.

Duck walked over to the man and squatted.

"You don't look so good," he said, pulling duct tape off the man's mouth. He turned Fitz's bloody face one way, then the other.

Fitz spat blood on the floor, stared at Duck, and smiled. "Neither do you."

Duck looked at Barry. "You sure he doesn't know where the gold is or where Conor is hiding?"

Barry shook his head. "He would've told us by now."

Duck turned to Fitz. He leaned in close. "Before I let you go, there's something you should know."

"That you need a breath mint?" said Fitz.

Duck patted Fitz's cheek. "That's funny. Your dad used to be funny, back when he was Mickey Monroe's partner."

"Fuck you," said Fitz.

"Here's the thing," said Duck. "You know how everyone thinks Mickey accidentally shot your dad during a blackout drunk?"

Fitz struggled against the duct tape.

Duck whispered, "Mickey didn't kill your father. I had Barry kill him. I told Barry to meet up with Mickey at the Fox. They had a couple drinks—Mickey's with a little something extra, of course, because his head got too big. He thought he could work around me and Artie. So, I taught him a lesson. My boys dragged him to some club that he and your daddy were going to knock over that night. Things didn't go well for your dad. And Mickey? Well, let's just say he woke up with the gun that killed your daddy, wondering why the hell he'd shot his partner."

Fitz's eyes hardened. He clenched his jaw.

Duck pulled the straight razor from his pocket. "You feel better now that you know the truth, right? Good. Now let's get that tape off so you can go home to your trailer, with the rest of the hillbilly trash."

Fitz's nostrils flared. His eyes were black pinpoints, holding Duck's gaze. Setting his jaw, he leaned forward to give Duck a better angle for cutting his hands free. Duck slipped the straight razor under Fitz's neck and cut his throat. He stood, turning to the men at the table. "You're cleaning this up," he said, wiping the razor on his pants.

Derek, Johnny, and Barry watched Fitz's mouth work for air like a fish out of water, blood spilling over his chest.

Duck closed the straight razor and turned toward them. "I want one thing. Conor Monroe. And if you can't find him, I'll find someone who will. Now get busy." He stepped over Fitz and walked toward the front door.

Derek straightened. "Can we get a contractor?"

Duck stopped, his hand on the doorknob. He turned. "Like who?"

"I know a guy that finds people, among other things. I can give him a call. I guarantee he'll find Conor. He'll kill him, bring him back here—whatever you want."

"Who is he?" asked Duck. "Some knucklehead friend of yours?"

Derek laughed, then grabbed his side. He took a slow breath and shook his head. "He doesn't have friends. His name is Joe Cracker Jones. He hurts people and likes doing it."

"He sounds like a problem," said Duck.

"More like he gets rid of problems. Nothing stops him. He's a pit bull."

Duck touched his split lip. He walked over to the table, took out his cell phone, and laid it on the table in front of

Derek.

"Call him," he said. Then he looked back at Fitz slumped over in a pool of blood. "And when you're done, get rid of Fitz."

* * *

Joe Cracker Jones swiveled on his bar stool. "I understand. I'll see you tomorrow." He pocketed his cell and drained his beer. "One more," he said to the bartender, who stared at him from the far end of the bar with the rest of the patrons. The bartender filled a mug, and then walked over, putting the beer on a coaster.

"Shouldn't you leave before he wakes up?" said the bartender.

Cracker glanced at the long-haired biker lying face-down on the floor. The man was a giant. "Have I caused you a lick of trouble since I been here?" said Cracker.

The bartender looked back at the patrons who were watching, turned back to Cracker, and then shook his head.

"That's right," said Cracker. He drained half his mug, belched, and then nodded at the biker. "He was rude, standing in front of the tv. I asked him to move. He didn't. So that's what he gets." He pointed at a plate with a hamburger and fries sitting on the bar. "Slide his food on down here."

The bartender handed him the plate.

Cracker watched the ball game, drank his beer, and ate the biker's fries.

CHAPTER NINETEEN

Conor watched Angel stretch next to the racks of free weights that filled the far corner of his garage's basement, but the bulk of the space—about nine hundred square feet—was open wrestling mat. Angel liked to spar. Well, really, he liked to fight. Conor knew that. He'd heard the stories about Angel being some kind of special forces bad ass years ago. But it couldn't have been that many years ago—Angel could still throw down with the best of them. No doubt it was because he trained every day. He lifted, ran, and threw fists and kicks at whoever was dumb enough to spar with him. Conor wasn't a fan—too many aches and pains afterward. But Angel insisted. And Conor knew he couldn't decline the invitation. Angel was taking a big risk hiding him here. If Duck found out, Angel would be fighting for more than staying in shape—he'd be fighting for his life.

Conor sighed. Stripped down to his shorts, he checked himself in the mirrored wall. The fight with Duck's crew at the church had painted his thighs, arms, and shoulders with bruises. Sparring with Angel would only add to his collection. Time to get this over with.

He tied his hair into a ponytail, put on gloves, and padded over to Angel.

"Ready when you are," he said.

Angel cracked his neck. "Were you really gonna leave

town with a girl?" he asked, rolling his head from side to side.

Conor nodded. "Yeah. We were gonna go up to Maine and hang out. That safe being empty at Sacred Heart kinda killed the plan, though. Can't live if you don't have money—know what I mean?"

Angel pulled on padded gloves. "You always have a job here."

"Part time at eighteen bucks an hour? That's why I was leaving."

Angel laughed. "Lots of people would kill to make anything." He waved Conor toward him. "Enough jawing. Let's go."

Conor watched Angel bounce on his feet. Angel threw a lazy left hook. Conor ducked it. Two jabs popped him in the mouth. *Bam, bam.*

Conor pulled out his mouth guard and wiped his mouth. He looked at a smear of blood. He stuck his mouth guard back in, put his hands up, and then walked toward Angel, bobbing his head.

Angel confused Conor with feints, sneaking a jab in here, an uppercut there. An occasional kick knifed into Conor's thigh to keep things interesting. But it didn't take long for Conor to catch up to Angel's timing and land a few counters. Feeling good, he went on the offensive, backing Angel up with a jab followed by a hard right to Angel's ribs. Then Angel got busy. None of his punches were full speed, but he wouldn't stop. Left to the face. Right to the body. Right to the chin.

Conor covered up and retreated. Two body shots in Conor's ribs took his breath away. "Thought we were sparring," he huffed, grabbing Angel and tying him up.

"I am," said Angel.

Conor shoved Angel away. He circled him, then lunged, catching Angel with an overhand right to the temple. Angel staggered. His eyes rolled back.

Conor's left hook whistled toward Angel's chin, on

course to snap his head around and drop him. He pulled it in. No reason to take Angel's head off. The man was out on his feet. He dropped his hands and said, "You okay?"

An elbow came from nowhere, smashing Conor's face.

Conor grabbed his nose and dropped to his knees. It felt like the floor tilted as he tried to stand. Angel grabbed his shoulder and eased him back down.

"Give it a minute," said Angel.

It took a while for his balance to settle. Conor sat and scooted backward until his back was against the wall. Angel handed him a towel.

Conor looked at the floor between his legs, waiting for his head to settle. He wiped his face. Blood smeared the terry cloth. He pressed the towel to his nose. "What the fuck was that?"

"An elbow," said Angel.

"I know it was a fucking elbow. Why'd you do that? You saw me drop my hands."

"A fight doesn't have rules," said Angel. "Better you learn that here than when it matters."

A door squeaked open. The sound of footsteps came down the basement stairs. Conor stood next to Angel, still feeling a little woozy. His dad stepped into view halfway down the stairs.

"What's up, Mickey?" said Angel.

Mickey nodded at Conor as he descended into the basement. "I checked around about this girl of yours. Looks like she disappeared too, just like Fitz."

Conor slung the towel over his shoulder. He picked up his jeans from the floor. "How would you know?" he said, slipping into his jeans.

"I know more than you think," said Mickey. "I know she lived next door to you. I know she worked at Sacred Heart." He cocked his head. "And I know her name is Julia Terranova."

"Not bad," said Conor.

Mickey threw his shoulders back and smoothed his hair,

looking smug. "Father Sal told me she moved into town and started working for him a few months back. Said she lived in your apartment complex—and that she left him a note saying she quit her job the other night. Hasn't shown up for work since."

Conor looked at Angel. "I should probably check her apartment to make sure she's not hurt or anything."

"No," said Angel. "That's not happening."

Conor slipped into his T-shirt. He lowered his voice to a whisper. "Before the job at Sacred Heart, Julia's old boyfriend stopped by her place," said Conor, his gaze flicking over to his father standing at the base of the stairs before settling back on Angel. "The guy was a real piece of shit. He tried to rape her. I need to check on her."

Angel moved toward the stairs. "Let's have some lunch. I don't think well on an empty stomach."

* * *

Conor waited in Angel's office with his dad, sipping a beer while Angel paid the pizza delivery guy. Angel brought in the pizza, paper plates, and some napkins. Conor grabbed a slice and took a seat on the couch next to his dad. Angel sat at his desk and opened a beer.

"I know you want to make sure your girl is okay," said Angel, taking a bite of pizza. "But going to her apartment isn't going to help."

"Why?" said Conor.

"Because if someone sees you, we're both in trouble. And even if she is there, what are you gonna do? You got no money. That Sacred Heart job was a bust."

Conor's dad nodded. "Girls don't like broke-ass criminals. Take it from someone with experience."

Conor finished his pizza. He threw his empty beer in a trash can across the room. "This girl's different," he said. "Money don't matter to her."

"I been around a long time," said Angel. "Never met a

girl like that."

The time he'd spent with Julia told Conor different. They had fun going out to eat hot dogs. Riding through the countryside on his motorcycle. Simple things. But even those things required a little money, and he had none. He looked at his father, and then at Angel.

"So, what do you suggest?" he said.

Angel tossed another beer to Conor. "If she's in town, there's no need to rush over there. She'll still be there next week. And in the meantime, I might have something that fixes your money problem." He nodded at Mickey. "It's something your dad's been working on."

Mickey grinned. "It'll fix *all* our money problems."

Conor's stomach tightened. He'd spent years maintaining an arms-length relationship with his father. The man had gotten his partner killed (or accidentally killed him—opinions varied), sent Conor's mom running for greener pastures, and eventually turned into a homeless bum. Conor's high school years had been pretty desperate times. A glass of tap water and a box of macaroni and cheese had been dinner more times than he could remember. His father tended bar and worked minimum wage labor jobs—when he was lucky enough to get them—and drank himself into a stupor every night. A white-picket-fence, blue-sky existence it was not.

"If my dad's involved, I'm out," said Conor, eyeing Mickey. "Even if it's a sure thing, he'll screw it up," he said, folding his arms over his chest.

Angel lowered his voice. "Your dad carried you here on his back," he said, sipping his beer. "Without him, Duck's guys would've found you. You'd be dead."

"So? He'll still fuck it up ," said Conor.

The room fell into an uneasy silence. Conor sipped his beer. His dad mumbled, "Can't fuck it up any worse than your last job."

Conor turned toward him. "What did you say?"

Mickey cleared his throat, then said, "You heard me."

Every muscle tightened in Conor. He talked through clenched teeth in a whisper. "Why do you think I even did that job?"

"What?" said Mickey.

"You heard me. Why did I try to rob Sacred Heart?"

Mickey looked at Angel and shrugged, searching for the answer.

Angel took a step toward Conor. "Take it easy, Conor. There's no need to—"

"Shut up, Angel," said Conor. He stood from the couch, turned, and pointed at his father. "It was because of you."

"Huh?" said Mickey.

"You're the reason I tried to rob Sacred Heart," said Conor.

"What did I do?" said Mickey.

"You shot your partner in a black out drunk," said Conor. "You chased mom away. Then you became a homeless drunk. What kind of chance do you think that gives me?"

Mickey bowed his head. "I pay for my mistakes. Every day."'

"That isn't enough!" said Conor. "It doesn't fix anything. It sure doesn't fix all those years I was wearing clothes from Goodwill. It doesn't give Fitz his dad back. It doesn't make it any easier hearing people talk about what a fuck up you are, and how I'm just the same, does it?"

Mickey stared at Conor. He opened his mouth, then shut it. He lowered his gaze to the ground.

"That's enough, Conor," said Angel. "Sit down."

Conor glanced at Angel. He bit his lip. He sat, and then nodded at Angel. "I don't care what kind of job it is. There's no fucking way I'm doing it with him. You can't believe anything he says."

Angel shook his head. "You don't have to believe him." Angel tapped his chest. "Believe me. I checked it out."

"What is it? Sawing the tops off parking meters?" asked Conor.

"You ever hear of Grandma Moses?" said Angel.

"Grandma who?"

"She was a painter," said Angel. "Your dad found out about her. She gave two of her paintings to Louis Bromfield, the guy who owned Malabar Farm before it got turned into a state park."

Conor shrugged. "So?"

"So, those two paintings are worth three hundred grand. And they're hanging in an old farmhouse," said Angel.

Conor watched his dad drain his beer, put the bottle down, and mumble, "It's the easiest money we'll ever make."

CHAPTER TWENTY

"No, no, no. You can't wear that," said Angela.

Julia watched Angela take a step back, tilting her head one way, then the other. It felt like Angela was undressing her, which wouldn't be hard—she was wearing jeans so tight she couldn't feel her thighs and the cut-off T-shirt she wore barely covered her chest. "What's wrong with this?" said Julia, adjusting the shirt to cover her boobs.

Angela's gum cracked as she chomped away. "You're a leg and ass girl," she said, walking over to Julia and stepping behind her.

Julia felt Angela's hands slide under her shirt and cup her boobs.

"These are too small for you to be wearing this kind of shirt," said Angela, squeezing them.

"That's enough," said Julia, pushing Angela's hands away. "What should I wear?"

Angela smiled wide and smacked her gum. "Girl, you're gonna look good enough to eat when I'm done with you."

* * *

Julia looked out the window while Angela drove. Suburban ranch houses gave way to farms and an occasional trailer until they stopped at a four-way light with a diner and a gas station on opposite corners. Julia tugged the tight black leather skirt riding up her thighs. "This skirt is too short," she said.

"It's not too short. You have a big ass," said Angela. "But Billy likes big butts, so don't worry about it."

"I don't have a big butt," said Julia, seeing Angela bite her bottom lip to keep from laughing. "I don't," she repeated.

Angela patted Julia's thigh as she turned left.

A half mile down the road Angela pulled into a gravel parking lot, throwing up a cloud of dust as she skidded to a stop in front of a squat, windowless, one-story, cement-block building painted jet black. A sign near the road read 'Sweeties' above a cartoon drawing of a curvy girl in a bikini sitting in a champagne glass.

Julia got out of Angela's bumblebee-yellow Mustang. Walking on gravel wasn't easy in high heels. Halfway across the parking lot, she stopped to dig a piece of gravel out of a shoe. By the time she managed it, the front door to the club was open. A long-haired man stepped out of the shadowed club interior, the sun glinting off a gold front tooth.

"Well, well, Angela. Bring your lady friend on in," he said, eyes roaming over Julia.

Julia followed Angela into the club, pulling her skirt down as she walked by the man. She followed Angela to a circular bar that filled the middle of the room. Three gold poles were on a stage behind the bar. "Who's the gold-toothed creep?" Julia whispered, pulling her skirt down.

"Billy Kelley," Angela whispered. "His family owns this place, but he runs it."

"Little runt, isn't he?" said Julia, expecting her comment to pull a laugh or at least a smile from Angela. It did neither. Angela watched Billy lock the front door.

"He has a mom, three brothers, and two sisters," Angela whispered. "Any one of them would punch you in the mouth as easy as they'd look at you."

Billy walked over with a bow-legged cowboy stroll. Julia smiled as he looked her up and down. He twirled a finger over her head. She looked at Angela, confused.

"Show him what you got," said Angela.

Julia turned in a slow circle.

"Not bad," said Billy, putting a toothpick in his mouth. He looked at Angela. "Can she dance?"

Angela rolled her eyes. "Ask her."

"You brought her. I'm asking you," said Billy, pointing his toothpick at Angela.

Angela huffed and grabbed Julia's hand, pulling her up on the stage.

"I don't know how to dance," Julia whispered.

Angela unzipped Julia's skirt and tugged it down, letting Julia step out of it. "That's why I'm here," she said. "Just follow my lead and shake that big ass."

"It's not big," hissed Julia.

Angela snapped her fingers at Billy. "Play some music."

Billy's eyes widened. "Don't bark at me."

Angela turned and slapped Julia's ass.

"You want to see this move, you better put some music on. Just saying," said Angela.

Billy grinned. He moved behind the bar and turned the music on. The tune was simple old-school rap. Strobe lights came on, blinding Julia. Angela put her arms around her and grabbed her butt, moving it one way then the other.

"Move your ass," Angela whispered in her ear. "Now put your hands over your head and move 'em with the beat. Nice and slow. That's it."

"Take your hands off," said Julia, trying to pull away.

Angela gripped her hips.

"Be cool," Angela whispered, running her hands up between Julia's legs to her crotch. "I'm just trying to—"

Julia whirled around, shoved Angela, and stared at her. The music played and the strobe lights blinked. The girls stood frozen, facing off. Billy's voice broke the standoff.

"What the hell is this?" he yelled. "Ain't no dance I ever seen."

Julia glanced at Billy. She thought over her options.

There was nowhere to go if Angela threw her out. She didn't have a job. She'd be living in her car if this didn't work. She grabbed Angela's hand, smiled, and started dancing. Angela pulled her close.

"You need to chill. Let me show you how this is done," said Angela. She stepped back, slipped out of her shirt, and then held out her hands.

Julia reached out. Angela grabbed her hands, then she grabbed her hips, then her thighs, all the while moving and rubbing up and down against her. Julia glanced back at Billy. His eyes were black pinpoints and his mouth hung open a tiny bit as he watched. She threw her hair back and shook her ass. He grinned. Maybe she could do this. Angela circled behind her and slipped her hands around her stomach, one finger playing under her G-string, the other moving up under her tank top. Julia closed her eyes. Strobe lights popped behind her eyelids while Angela rubbed her nipples.

"Slow down," Angela whispered. "Keep it sexy."

Julia tried to relax and move with the music. Angela kissed her neck, her shoulder, and moved down her arm. Then Angela's mouth was on the back of her thigh. Then her inner thigh.

The song finished.

Julia didn't move. She heard Billy hit a switch. The strobe lights stopped. Angela walked across the stage, bare chested, boobs bouncing. She picked up Julia's skirt, came back, handed it to Julia and winked. "You got it," she whispered.

"That was nice," said Billy, his gold tooth twinkling. "Real nice. You dance before?"

"She's danced," said Angela, pulling her shirt over her head.

"I could tell," said Billy, climbing the steps onto the stage. "Here, let me help you with that," he said, stepping behind Julia to zip up her skirt.

Julia smiled. "Thanks."

"Glad to help," he said, then turned toward Angela. "You hear from Tina?"

Angela nodded. "She's still sick."

Julia watched Billy Kelley turn toward her. Everything about him screamed hard redneck. But he seemed sweet, almost like a little boy, as he said, "Would you like to dance tonight? It would really help me out. Whatta you say?"

"I'll bring her with me tonight," said Angela, taking Julia by the hand and walking her off the stage.

"That's great. See you at nine tonight, Julia," said Billy.

Once they were outside, Angela started talking.

"All that girl-on-girl stuff was for Billy's benefit," she said. "Didn't want him judging you on your dancing, if you know what I mean."

Julia nodded. She got in the car and grabbed Angela's hand. "Thanks," she said.

Angela smiled. "Told you I'd take care of you."

The engine started with a roar.

"So did you tell him about me before we came?" Julia asked.

Angela shook her head. "Just said I was bringing a girlfriend. That was a cold audition. You hit it out of the park."

"You didn't tell him my name?" said Julia.

"Nope."

Julia settled in her seat, pulling her skirt down. She tried to remember if she'd told Billy Kelley her name, or if he asked what it was. Maybe in all the excitement she'd forgotten, but she didn't think so.

And yet, he'd said, "See you at nine tonight, Julia," as she walked out the door.

CHAPTER TWENTY-ONE

Cracker pulled a wrinkled piece of paper from his pocket. He looked at it, looked at the address above the front door of the two-story white bungalow, and then knocked. All the houses on this street looked the same. Old. He crumbled the paper and dropped it on the stoop. The front door opened. A man with a smashed face and impossibly wide shoulders filled the doorframe.

"You Joe Cracker Jones?" said the man.

Cracker eyed the man. He looked like one of them island people—Tongan or Samoan or something like that. A lot of them was in the cage-fighting game. Big and strong, but they always came out too fast, got winded, and then fell apart. Cracker pushed past the man and stepped into the foyer. An old white-haired man with a bruised face and a split lip sat at a table in the dining room on his right. A hand gripped Cracker's shoulder.

"Hey, I asked you a question."

Cracker turned, looking at the face of the Samoan or Tongan or whatever the man was, who was now holding his arm. One thing was sure, the man had been a fighter. Had scar tissue over both eyes that would bleed really nice with an elbow.

"Johnny, let him go."

Cracker turned toward the voice. The old, white-haired man was on his feet.

"You must be Joe Cracker Jones. Thank you for coming," said the old man. "I'm Duck. Would you like to sit down?"

Duck gestured at the table where two men were already seated. Cracker pulled his arm out of Johnny's grip and walked over. He eyed a man at the end of the table with an anvil-shaped head and cauliflower ears. Duck sat next to the other guy, who looked to be some kind of businessman in a suit and tie. Cracker ignored the businessman and nodded at the man with cauliflower ears.

"You're the one who called me. Derek Ryder, right? We was on a couple fight cards together. So, what's this all about?"

"Mr. Jones, I'm hoping you might help us solve a problem," said Duck, leaning forward in his seat.

"Who should I talk to here, Ryder?" said Cracker, shifting his gaze from Duck to the businessman. "Which of these boys is in charge?"

Derek glanced at Duck.

Cracker turned toward Duck. "So, tell me, Mr. Duck, what is it you need?"

"It's Duck, not Mr. Duck," said Duck, exasperated. He looked at Derek. "I thought you said he could take care of our situation. He acts like he doesn't have a brain in his head."

"He'll take care of it," said Derek. "Just tell him, and he'll—"

Cracker let out a sharp whistle, stopping the conversation. He stared at Duck. "Mr. Duck, if your situation involves shaking hands, introducing ourselves, sitting at a table, and making a big production out of this, then I'm not your man. But if you want to pay me to hurt or beat a man to death, then we can talk. Now which of these situations are we dealing with?"

Duck sputtered, then pointed at Barry. "You tell him."

Cracker turned to the businessman.

"Can you find and kill a man for us, Mr. Jones?" said

Barry.

"Don't know," said Cracker. "Depends on what man and how much you're paying." Cracker felt the big island boy Mr. Duck called 'Johnny' grab his shoulder. He knew it wasn't out of the norm to have muscle like Johnny hanging around for protection, but Johnny here had put hands on him twice. He was getting way too familiar.

"Why don't you sit down?" said Johnny. "Your bullshit is wearing thin."

Cracker turned. "I had a daddy that used to put hands on me. Didn't like it then, and I don't like it now."

"You don't listen, do you? Sit down," said Johnny, shoving him.

Cracker stumbled. He faced Johnny, looked him up and down, and then head kicked him to the floor. Johnny fell like he'd been axed.

"Told you I don't like hands on me," Cracker said. He turned to the businessman. "Now, who's this man you want dead?"

Barry looked at Johnny, out cold. He shifted his gaze to Cracker and said, "His name's Conor Monroe."

"You sure you want him dead? How 'bout I just rough him up?"

Barry looked at Duck.

"Dead," said Duck, touching his split lip.

Cracker nodded at Duck. "He open your lip?"

"That's none of your business," said Duck, his voice rising. "I just want him in the ground."

Cracker shrugged. "Don't matter none to me. You want him dead, he's dead. Just seems childish to kill a man for punching you in the mouth and giving you two black eyes. Maybe you deserved it."

Duck's face reddened. "If you're not interested, you know where the door is. We can always find someone else looking for an easy payday."

"Can't be too easy if you had Derek call me," said Cracker. He turned toward the businessman. "What's it pay?"

"Ten thousand," said Barry.

"Ten if you deliver him dead," added Duck. "Twenty-five if you let me watch. Only payable after he's dead."

"I can live with twenty-five," said Cracker. "Anything special I need to know about this Monroe boy?"

"He's tough," said Derek, putting a hand over his ribs.

"He do that to you?" said Cracker, pointing at Derek's ribs.

Derek nodded. "I was beating him bloody. Next thing I know, I'm on my back. Busted ribs."

"Everybody gets lucky," said Cracker.

"He sure did," said Derek.

"I meant you," said Cracker. "If I'd cracked your ribs, I'd have gone to work and cracked a few other things. Monroe must be sweet on you."

Derek's eyes narrowed.

"So," said Cracker. "I need to know where this Monroe boy lives, drinks, eats, who his friends are, where his family lives—things like that."

"Derek can put that together for you," said Barry.

Cracker turned to leave. "All right then. Get my twenty-five thousand ready. I'll call when I have him. You can watch me kill him." He looked at Derek. "Shouldn't take long, so pay attention to your phone."

Cracker bent down and rubbed Johnny's chest until Johnny stirred. He helped Johnny to his feet. "You awake?" he said, holding Johnny's shoulders and looking into his eyes.

"Yeah," slurred Johnny.

"Good," said Cracker. He moved his gaze over Duck, Barry, and Derek. "I'll see the rest of you boys later." Then he punched Johnny in the back of the head. Johnny dropped in a heap. Cracker gave the men a moment to stare at Johnny before adding, "By the way, I imagine you have people looking for this Monroe fella. Tell them to quit. I don't need nobody flushing him out and setting him running before I find him. That would be what they call, 'a breach of contract.'" He focused his gaze on Duck. "And I will not abide that. If you make that mistake, believe me, I will get paid, but you will be the worse for wear." He turned and stepped on Johnny's hand as he walked out, snapping one of his fingers.

Outside, looking up into the afternoon sun, Cracker could hear the boys inside talking to that Johnny fella, trying to wake him up. They sounded upset. Cracker raised his arms toward the sky.

It felt good to be alive.

* * *

Cracker sat in his truck outside the old, abandoned General Motors plant on the outskirts of town. Surveillance cameras were set up around the property, so he couldn't just cut through the fence and walk in, but there was a sign with a realty company's phone number. After calling their office, Cracker parked next to the main gate under one of the cameras. The sign above the gate read 'Warning. Twenty-four-hour surveillance. Trespassers will be prosecuted.'

The half-hour it took for the real estate agent to show up gave Cracker time to call Derek and get Conor Monroe's address and the names of his friends. Then he ate a protein bar and thought things over. Twenty-five grand to kill this Monroe fella in front of Mr. Duck was a good payday, but they'd need a place to fight where Mr. Duck and that businessman could enjoy the show. This abandoned GM plant would be perfect. He just hoped Conor was a respectable fighter. It was no fun fighting someone without skills. But by the looks of Derek Ryder, Conor Monroe might make things interesting. Not like them Orientals in their death matches. Broken knee, broken elbow—it didn't matter, they kept coming. Took a broke-ass neck to get their attention. But even though Monroe wasn't from the Far East, he might put up a respectable fight.

A man could always hope.

Cracker finished eating his protein bar. He wiped his hands, watching his rear-view mirror as a car pulled in behind his truck. A woman got out and waved at him.

He got out of his truck, nodded, and smiled.

She talked a mile a minute as they walked toward the empty factory, rattling on about leasing and build-out options on the vacant space. They stepped inside, and he waited while she found the lights. It smelled like metal shavings and oil. Overhead lights clicked on, revealing a long, wide expanse of concrete floor. It reminded Cracker of an aircraft hangar he'd once fought in down in Mississippi—wide open space with a ceiling that was three stories high. The building was huge, but he immediately saw what he was looking for. He walked toward a black chain-link, two-story cage in the middle of the empty factory, walking around it until he found the door. He stepped into the cage as the realty agent clicked after him in her high heels, talking breathlessly, because she had twenty or so pounds to lose and was trying her very best to keep up.

"This is the tool crib," she said, following Cracker into the cage. "It's a secure space for storing tools or equipment. The footprint is four hundred square feet, all of which is caged top to bottom with reinforced, black-vinyl-coated, steel chain link." She grabbed the door and rattled it. "Once you put a lock on this door, your valuables will be very safe."

Cracker looked over the cage. It was as good a spot as any to fight to the death. He looked at the woman. "Are there surveillance cameras inside here?"

"Yes, but they aren't functioning. If you'd like, I can set you up with a local security company. It shouldn't take long to have them back online."

"I'll let you know on that," Cracker said. He pursed his lips, deep in thought. "My main problem is how do I get back in here to show my boss this space? He needs a hundred thousand square feet, fast."

The agent smiled. "You can call me any time to set up

an appointment."

Cracker shook his head. "My boss is a son-of-a-bitch. He won't wait for you. Not one minute. Best bet is to give me a key."

The woman sighed. "I can't do that. It's against policy."

Cracker walked out of the tool crib, leaving the agent behind.

"Mr. Jones?" she said, her voice rising as she ran after him.

Cracker stopped to let her catch up.

"I can't give you a key," she huffed. "But I can leave one at the office for you to pick up whenever you want. Will that work?"

"I don't think so," said Cracker. "But there's other spaces in town, so don't worry yourself. I appreciate your time."

The agent hissed through clenched teeth. "God, I can get in trouble for this," she said, taking a key off her key ring and pulling a business card out of her purse. "Here's my spare, but please get it back to me as soon as your boss has seen the property. Can you promise you'll do that, Mr. Jones?"

"I can," said Cracker, taking the key and her business card. "Right after he sees it, I'll drop the key off with your receptionist. Thank you for your understanding."

The woman smiled. "I hope he likes it," she said.

"He will," said Cracker, pulling out the piece of paper with Conor's last known address. "He's gonna love it."

CHAPTER TWENTY-TWO

Conor parked Angel's '68 Camaro convertible a few parking lots over from his apartment building. The car looked like hell—filthy and covered in gray primer—so it wouldn't attract much attention. But if anyone did try to tail him, there wasn't a thing wrong with the engine. It would outrun most anything, which was one of the reasons Angel had agreed to let Conor use it.

Conor cut the engine. Angel thought going to Julia's apartment was just plain stupid, but he'd handed over the Camaro's keys after Conor had agreed to help steal the Grandma Moses paintings, and after Conor had also agreed to Angel's instructions.

"If someone follows you," Angel had said, "Do *not* come back here. If someone catches you, tell them you stole the car from me. Do not—I repeat, do *not*—involve me in your problems. If you do, I'll help Duck find you and string you up. I'm not going down because you have to check in on some girl. Got it?"

Conor had done his best to calm Angel's fears, thanking him and telling him he'd be right back after checking Julia's apartment.

It was a lie, but the less Angel knew, the less he'd worry.

Conor scanned the parking lot, looking for any suspicious cars or people. Everything looked normal for a Monday afternoon. There were a few cars in the parking lot—probably belonged to stay-at-home moms and retirees—but that was it. He got out of the Camaro and strolled across the blacktop, making his way toward the dark stairwell that led to Julia's apartment. The walk was out in the open, which made him nervous. He looked up at Julia's balcony. It was empty. None of the other balconies had people on them either. Everything looked clear, but—

He jumped as a long-haired, shirtless, teenage boy flew out of the stairwell on a skateboard, wheels clacking over the cracks in the parking lot asphalt. Conor took a moment to gather himself. Stupid kid. He started up the stairs toward Julia's apartment.

When he got to Julia's door he froze. He swiveled his head one way and then the other, looking for movement. There was nothing. The hall was silent and empty. He looked at Julia's door again. The frame next to the doorknob was splintered. Maybe Duck and Artie had figured out they were connected. Maybe some of their guys were inside right now, working Julia over to get info on where they could find her boyfriend, Conor Monroe.

Conor took a deep breath and slowly exhaled to calm himself. He pushed her door open a crack and listened. Nothing. He slipped inside, closing the door behind him.

There were no signs of life. No bowls or plates in the sink. No magazines or books on the living room coffee table. No shoes on the floor next to the front door. But there was a big painting on an easel in the living room. Conor walked over to it.

He smiled at the memory of the first time he'd seen this painting. It was when he met Julia. When she thought someone was in her apartment and he walked through it to make sure no one was inside. This painting, however, was different than the one he saw. She'd added him to the painting, putting him next to her on the beach, watching the sun rise over the ocean. Seeing them sitting together, sharing that moment, made something in his chest grow warm. He traced a finger over Julia's face, remembering her dark hair. Her brown eyes. The way her body felt when he held her.

He sighed, scanning the apartment. One thing was certain—she'd moved out. She'd waited for him to pick her up and take her away, and when he didn't show, she left. Who could blame her?

"Sorry, Julia," he said, touching the painting once more before walking out.

He closed her door, turned to leave, and then stopped. He hadn't planned on checking his apartment. There was nothing in it he needed, and there was a real danger that someone from Duck's crew was inside, waiting for him. He crept over. He touched the splintered door frame. It looked like the same person who'd broken into Julia's apartment had broken into his. That pissed him off. He took a step back from his door, seething at the idea that one of Duck's guys had busted into Julia's apartment because of him. He kicked his door open.

The place was ransacked. Every piece of clothing, every dish, and every spoon and utensil had been tossed on the floor. Conor cursed, looking at the mess. He kicked a pile of books out of the way and walked into the living room toward the balcony. There was a note taped on his television screen. He pulled it off and sat on his couch, reading it.

Conor Monroe,

An old fella by the name of Mr. Duck has asked me to kill you. I'm guessing it has something to do with you giving him a couple black eyes and a fat lip. He thinks an awful lot of himself, which is good enough reason for him to take a whipping from you, but business is business, and my business is taking you out. In addition to being honest, you'll be pleased to know that I'm a man of honor and will provide you with a fair fight. I will not shoot you, cut you, or try to kill you in any other manner than a hand to hand fight. If you walk out alive, good for you. If you don't, I get paid, which is good for me. Seeing as how we both have skin in the game, we shouldn't beat around the bush. In order to speed the process, I'm asking you to visit any local bar at your earliest convenience and tell the bartender you would like them to call me, Joe Cracker Jones. I will pick you up and take you to a suitable location where we can fight until one of us slips away to our everlasting reward. I urge you to be clear of mind when I pick you up, as you will need to have all your faculties when you face me. There is nothing I hate worse than a sloppy fighter, and I will make you pay dearly should you indulge yourself with alcohol or drugs before we are formally introduced. Of course, I know it's normal for a man to determine that a fight of this kind is less than ideal. A man may even believe he can somehow avoid the issue. I urge you to not travel this path, as I have begun checking around to locate your friends, family, and associates. I will also be putting your photo into the hands of quite a few people in town. Mark my words, I will find you. I will also be back in this apartment from time to time, checking to see if you have read this note. I will know if you have been here, and every minute you are not coming to me is another minute that I will be coming to you. That will make me unhappy. If you make me find you, people you know and love will be killed. Don't make me do that. Be a man, meet me face-to-face, and let's take care of our business as quickly as possible.

Have a blessed day,
Joe Cracker Jones

Conor read the note twice. He looked around the apartment at the mess, and then looked out the balcony's sliding glass door into the summer afternoon. Sunshine. Green grass. Trees rustling in a breeze. He walked over to the television and taped the note back on the screen but wasn't sure it was exactly where it had been. He took it off, tried sticking it in a couple different spots, then crumpled it and threw it on the floor.

When he walked to Angel's Camaro, he had to fight the urge to run. He got in the car and started it, scanning the parking lot. There was nothing to see but the same few cars baking in the sun. He cranked the air conditioner, feeling off balance.

He'd dealt with bad guys his whole life. This Cracker

guy, however, was crazy. A fight to the death? Who did that? And writing a note saying he'd kill people Conor knew unless they fought? The cops could probably put him in jail for writing that.

"But he knows I won't call the cops," Conor said, pulling out of the apartment complex. "He knows the cops are the last place I'll go."

The smart move would be to head straight back to Angel's and tell him about this Cracker guy. The problem was Sully. He hadn't seen his friend since he was lying unconscious in the back of Fitz's Bronco. He had to check on him. If he'd been knocked into a coma, Sully and Fitz wouldn't leave his side. Sully deserved the same. It had been two days since they'd broken into the church and gotten ambushed by Duck's guys. Two days of hiding without knowing how either of his friends were doing. There was no telling where Fitz was. He probably ran out of town after dropping Sully at the hospital. After things settled down Conor would track him down. But Sully was lying in a hospital bed. He deserved a visit, no matter what the cost. After all, Conor was in the room when it happened. He'd watched Johnny run over and kick the safe's door closed on Sully's head, leaving him lying motionless on the floor. He'd replayed the scene in his mind a hundred times, wondering if he could've stopped Johnny. There was no way to know for sure, but he was positive of one thing. He didn't try. And now, Sully was in a coma.

It took a few extra minutes driving through back alleys to get to the hospital, but he made it there without incident. He kept his head down as he walked to the information desk to ask where he could find Sully. Then he bypassed the elevator, went to the stairwell, and ran up to the third floor.

Visiting hours were over in ten minutes.

He hurried down the hall and stepped into Sully's room.

There lay Sully, under the covers with his eyes closed and a tube running down his throat, his chest rising and falling in rhythm with a machine that breathed for him.

Conor pulled a chair next to the bed. He grabbed Sully's hand. Sully didn't move. Conor patted Sully's hand.

"Hey man, sorry this happened to you." He squeezed Sully's limp hand. "But I gave Artie and Duck a beating right after their guys did this to you. Got 'em good too—they're gonna feel it for a long time. Haven't seen Fitz since, but no one's heard anything, so I don't think they got him. He's probably laying low after he heard what I did." He shook his head. "But Duck hired some guy to kill me. Can you believe that?"

The machine breathing for Sully stopped for a moment, letting out a high-pitched tone. Conor froze. Sully stiffened, and then relaxed as the tone stopped and the machine fell back into rhythm. Conor relaxed. He patted Sully's hand.

"Hey, don't do that," he said. "If you're gonna die, have some manners and do it after I leave." Raking a hand through his hair, he sat back. He eyed the clock hanging next to a small flatscreen television on the wall. Visiting time was almost up. He leaned in close to Sully and whispered, "So, listen to this. The guy Duck hired to kill me left a note in my apartment. He said I either fight him to the death, or he'll kill my friends and family." He leaned back and laughed. "Can you believe that? What friends and family? Fitz is hiding. You're lying here in a coma. My dad's a homeless bum. The only person I have is this girl, Julia. And I gotta tell you, Sully, she's something. Came from a bad situation. Her mom overdosed and then she got put in the foster system. But she moved past all that. And she understands me. You know what I mean? If anything ever happened to her—"

His grip on Sully's hand loosened as he remembered the splintered door frame at Julia's apartment. He set his jaw. The guy who wrote the note—Cracker whatever-his-name-was—he broke her door. Which meant he saw the painting of them sitting together on the beach, holding hands.

"Shit. He knows that Julia and me are together," he whispered.

Conor stood. He had to find Julia before the guy chasing him did. But how?

His eyes narrowed. His dad. He said he'd talked to Father Sal at Sacred Heart. Father Sal said Julia left a note, saying she was leaving town. He stepped next to Sully's bed and put his hand on Sully's chest. "I gotta go," he said. "You keep fighting. I got faith in you, brother. I'll check on you again soon." He patted Sully's chest and then walked out.

* * *

Out in the garage, Angel banged away at something. Conor looked at the clock above Angel's office door, looked at his dad sitting on the beat-up leather couch, and shook his head. It wasn't even five o'clock, and his dad was drunk. Getting any information out of him about Julia was gonna be a chore. He waited for Angel to finish, hearing an especially loud bang of metal on metal, followed by Angel's muffled yell of "Gotcha." He looked at his dad, barely able to stay upright on the couch.

"So, tell me again," Conor said. "Julia left a letter with Father Sal, right?"

"Yeah. A letter," said Mickey.

"And she said she was leaving town?" said Conor.

"Yeah."

"Did she say where?" asked Conor.

Mickey shook his head. He burped and covered his mouth with a dirty hand.

"Did Father Sal say anything about where she was going?"

Mickey shook his head again, then said, "Is there anything to drink? Angel's contact in Europe is gonna wire us three hundred thousand if we get the paintings. Three hundred, can you believe it?"

Conor watched his dad rise unsteadily to his feet. He pushed him back down on the couch. "You don't need another drink," said Conor. "Just sit down and sober up."

He walked over to Angel's desk and poured a cup of coffee from a pot on the desk. "Drink this," he said, putting the mug in his father's hand. The office door opened.

"Lower your voices," said Angel, closing the door. He pulled a rag from his dirty overalls and wiped his hands, looking at Conor. "I can hear you in the shop."

Conor thought about telling Angel about the guy that was hired to kill him, then decided against it. Angel was spooked enough knowing Duck was on the warpath. "Sorry," he said, staring at his dad. "He's drunk and it's pissing me off."

"I am not," bellowed Mickey.

"Keep your voice down," said Angel.

"I am not," whispered Mickey.

Angel looked at Conor and rolled his eyes.

Mickey sipped his coffee. He made a face and then spat coffee on the floor. "That's terrible," he said, sticking out his tongue.

"It should be," said Angel. "It's from last night." He picked up the pot of coffee and dumped it in a utility sink. He glanced back at Conor as he rinsed the pot. "Was your girlfriend in her apartment?"

"No," said Conor. "She wasn't at work either. But I'll find her."

"People go to places they're familiar with," said Angel, walking back to his desk with the coffee pot. He put in a filter and started brewing a new pot. "Where's she from?"

"Massey," said Conor.

"She got family or friends there?"

Conor shook his head. "An old boyfriend who beat the hell out of her. That's about it."

"Well, I'll tell you what," said Angel. "A couple bikers from The Locos owe us for fixing their rides when they cracked up on 311. You remember?"

"Yeah. Ronnie and Pedro," said Conor. "I was going to call them and see if they could rough up the guy that tried to rape my girl."

Angel pulled his cell from his pocket. "It's up to you, but they live in Massey. I'm sure they could find her. You want to talk to Ronnie?"

Conor nodded.

Angel dialed a number, and then handed his cell to Conor. "Here. If she's in Massey, they'll find her."

Conor gave Ronnie the lowdown on his situation. He described Julia while he watched Angel walk over to his dad, talking to his father in low tones as he took his coffee mug. Angel washed out the mug, poured in fresh coffee, mixed in a creamer and half a sugar, and then handed the mug back to his father, smiling as his dad took a sip. Hearing Ronnie say, "If your old lady's here, I'll let you know," Conor mumbled a thanks and hung up the phone. He stared at Angel, feeling embarrassed. Angel treated his father better than he did.

"I'm gonna sit out front for a while," said his father, getting off the couch with Angel's help. Conor watched his dad sip his coffee and wobble out of the office, closing the door behind him.

"So, " said Angel. "Everything cool? They gonna find your girl?"

"Yeah," said Conor.

Angel nodded and walked toward the door. "Good," he said, grabbing the doorknob. "Let me know how it goes."

"Wait a second," Conor said.

Halfway through the door, Angel turned to face Conor. Conor looked at him but couldn't find the words. Angel lifted an eyebrow. Conor cleared his throat. He looked down and mumbled.

"What?" asked Angel.

Conor raised his head, forcing himself to look at Angel. "Why are you so nice to my dad?"

Angel stared at him for a bit. It felt like judgment to Conor. Judgment for all the years he steered clear of his father. For all the times he avoided any contact with him because he was embarrassed to be his son. It felt like he could shrivel up under Angel's gaze. Feeling ashamed of how he treated his father was a new twist in their relationship, and it wasn't one he felt good about.

"You know, your dad's a good guy," said Angel. "He's just got a disease. Yelling at him doesn't help."

Conor felt his face flush. He looked down. "But he's a drunk. I can't count on him for nothing."

Angel walked over and put a hand on Conor's shoulder. "He wasn't a drunk until his friend died. He blames himself. And everyone else blames him too. Regret can do bad things to a man."

"Well, maybe he should blame himself," said Conor.

"And maybe he shouldn't," said Angel. "You don't know. I don't know. Nobody knows, cause we weren't there." He pointed at Conor. "You need to ease up on him. He's done a lot for you."

Conor shrugged. "What, like showing me how to pick a lock?"

"He did more than that," said Angel.

"He showed me how to peel a safe," said Conor.

Angel laughed and then said, "You know what? Never mind. Stay away from your dad—he's trouble."

"Too late," said Conor. "The damage is done."

Angel smirked. He opened the door to leave and stopped, looking back over his shoulder. "Listen. I'll tell your dad he needs to dry up before we pull this job. If he doesn't, he's out. You okay with that?"

Conor nodded.

"Good," said Angel.

Conor listened as Angel went back to work in the garage, the air vibrating with the ring of metal pounding metal. He sat down at Angel's desk and let the ringing fill him. His body thrummed with the vibration. He turned on the desktop computer, opened the browser and searched 'Joe Cracker Jones.'

The search brought back over a million results. He pulled his chair closer, clicked the first link and watched a video clip of the man hired to kill him.

An hour passed before Conor logged off. He stared at the blank screen. Cracker was a wrecking crew. No one in any of the fights made it out of the cage conscious. And the end was always the same. Cracker bending over, his mouth opened impossibly wide as he stuck out a tongue tattooed with a Confederate flag and screamed into his opponent's face. According to comments under the videos, that was what Cracker called his 'rebel yell.' The rednecks loved it because it always signaled the bloody end was coming.

Conor mumbled, "I'm in trouble," and stood.

It was time to stop messing around, steal the paintings, and get out of town.

CHAPTER TWENTY-THREE

"I know it's your first night, but don't freak out. The main thing is to just look good," said Angela, picking through outfits hanging in the strippers' dressing room. "If you look good, it don't matter how you dance. The guys pay to watch booty like yours."

Julia felt out of place in the bustle of all the strippers. The dressing room was laid out like a cut-rate hair salon with mirrored stations lining the walls. Girls in various stages of undress jiggled around her, walking, primping, and rubbing lotion over their bodies, their boobs glowing in the harsh light. The hardest part was knowing where to look. Julia couldn't help but stare at the tits and thighs and hips and lips and eyes and hairstyles of all kinds. She felt out of her league. People had always told her she was pretty, but these girls were unreal. How was she supposed to compete with all these girls who looked like they'd just walked out of a Playboy centerfold? And the nervous flutter in her stomach wasn't helping matters. She felt like she had to go pee again, and she'd already gone three times. She turned her attention to Angela, who was picking through the rack of outfits along the back wall.

"This'll look good on you," said Angela, holding two hangers. Julia followed her over to an empty mirror.

Angela hooked the hangers on the back of a chair. Julia looked at the clothes as she stripped. A black fur bikini top and a metallic gold G-string. "What's with this?" Julia said, picking up the furry bikini top.

"Just put it on," said Angela. "And the G-string too. We're going on in a minute."

"You sure?" asked Julia, making a face.

Angela took the hanger with the G-string off the back of the chair and held it up. "Either put 'em on or go out there naked. Me? I'm wearing whatever I can. They pay to have us take it off, you know."

Julia slipped into the G-string. Angela helped tie the bikini top. A girl whistled from across the room.

"Damn, Angela," the girl said, teetering in spiked heels. "Tell your girlfriend to stay off my stage unless she wants trouble. I ain't sharing my booty tips."

"Ain't your stage, Shalonda," snapped Angela, looking the girl up and down. "And if you want trouble, you know where to find me. I'm here every night." Angela tapped a foot, hand on hip, and held Shalonda's stare until she walked away muttering under her breath. Then Angela turned to Julia. "Don't worry. She runs her mouth but never backs it up. Just relax. This is gonna be fun."

Julia nodded. She looked in the mirror. Angela had done her makeup and hair before they'd gotten here. Her dark, shoulder-length hair fell in big shiny curls over her shoulders. Her mascara and eye shadow were thick enough to ink a newspaper, but somehow Angela made it work. The only thing Angela hadn't been able to do was cover her scar. No matter how much foundation Angela put on, the scar wouldn't disappear. But other than that, Julia thought she looked crazy sexy. She slipped her feet into a pair of black high heels and pursed her lips in the mirror. The bassline of a heavy, funky beat vibrated up from the floor, through her feet, and up her legs.

"Let's go, girl," said Angela, grabbing Julia by the arm. "That's our music."

Julia followed Angela through a curtain. The bar's strobe lights blinded her for a moment. She could barely hear the announcer's voice over the music.

"Welcome, Cookies and Cream!"

Wonder which one I am, Julia thought, as she followed Angela sashaying across the stage. Angela said they'd dance together tonight. Julia wasn't sure what that meant, but she was out of her body at this point, moving on autopilot. Whatever Angela told her to do, she'd do. She just wanted to get this over with. She stepped across the stage, felt Angela's hands wrap around her—her hips grinding against her—then Angela whispered in her ear.

"Remember, it's all an act. Just follow my lead."

Julia nodded. The music filled her head. A hand reached up, stuffing something in the back of her G-string, followed by more hands grabbing her legs, shoving money in her G-string, Angela's mouth was on hers. The music swirled around her in a kaleidoscope, mixed with yells, cigarette smoke, and groping hands. Angela licked her neck, then slipped her tongue into her mouth.

She kissed Angela back, letting herself sink into it, her body swaying, every nerve ending firing. She came up for air. Men held money toward her, their pupils hard black pinpoints anchored in swirls of cigarette smoke, focused on everything but her face. She watched Angela kneel in front of her, throw her head back, and flick her tongue in the air. She backed up against the pole in the middle of the stage and closed her eyes, leaning on the pole while she danced. Angela stood and stepped behind her, massaging her breasts. The crowd yelled. None of it mattered. It was all part of the game. She relaxed, letting Angela grind into her. It was okay.

As long as it paid, the world could suck her dry tonight.

* * *

"You did a good job out there."

Julia looked up at Billy Kelley. He smiled, flashing his gold tooth. She turned back to the mirror and continued touching up her makeup.

"I mean it, really," said Billy, putting a hand on her shoulder.

"Thanks," she said.

"Bet you made a couple hundred," he said, rubbing her shoulder.

She stared at her reflection, saying, "Mm-hmm," as she lined her eyelid with a mascara pencil. Billy's hand slid down to her chest. She froze.

"We killed it out there."

Billy lifted his hand. He turned toward Angela, fanning herself with a stack of bills as she walked the length of the dressing room.

"What are you doing here, Billy?" Angela said, stopping next to Julia. "You ain't supposed to be in our dressing room. I could turn you in for sexual harassment."

"Just stopped in to tell Julia she did a good job," said Billy, as he walked out of the room. He stopped at the curtain that led into the club and pointed at Angela. "By the way, you got that customer coming in for a lap dance in five minutes. Don't forget."

Julia watched Billy disappear through the curtain into the club. She looked up at Angela. She'd come blowing in here like a diva, fanning herself with that handful of bills, and now it looked like the air had been taken out of her. Julia touched her hand.

"You okay?" she asked.

Angela stared at the curtain that led into the club. "I'm fine." She smiled and held up the money. "Why wouldn't I be? We got something going with this girl-on-girl act."

"I guess," said Julia. "When do we go on again?"

Angela rolled her money, rubber banded it, and put it on the table in front of Julia's mirror. "We're dancing solo the rest of the night. You know, jiggle around, bend over—that kind of thing. Our act is a once-a-night thing. Don't want them getting bored with us." She held her hand out. "Give me your money. Billy will hold it for us. These girls will steal anything that ain't attached to you."

Julia handed her cash to Angela.

Angela rolled Julia's money, banded it, and put it on the table next to hers. "I gotta do this lap dance. Wait here until I get back."

"One of the other girls said I should mix with the crowd," said Julia. "She said lap dances are where I'll make the real money."

Angela nodded. "Yeah, but you do the wrong thing with an undercover cop, and he'll toss you in jail. Just take it easy. I'll be right back. I'll show you how to do lap dances tomorrow."

"Good," said Julia. "I'm wiped out anyhow. Feel like I ran ten miles."

Angela laughed as she walked toward the curtain. "It takes some getting used to," she said. "I'll see you in a bit. Just relax."

The curtain closed and Angela was gone. Julia turned and cursed under her breath. Angela said she was going to give their money to Billy for safekeeping, but their rolls of cash were still on the table. Julia picked up the money and hurried after Angela.

The club seemed different from when she was on stage. Everything moved slower. The music wasn't as loud. The lights weren't as bright. Even the men seemed less…less…hungry looking. Now they just seemed like regular guys. She weaved through the tables, noticing that some of the men were polite, even cordial, as she walked through the club. Two guys in biker cuts nodded at her.

"Nice job up there," said one as she walked by their table. Julia glanced back and saw that their cuts were from The Locos biker gang. She flashed a peace sign and said, "Live hard." Both men lifted their bottles of beer and yelled, "Die young." She smiled and moved on. Everyone in Massey knew The Locos' creed, but she'd never said it to any of them before. That was reserved for members and their old ladies. She grinned. *And now, hot-ass strippers like me.*

She kept walking, feeling more relaxed with every step. She was a stripper, and damn if it didn't feel good. Angela's lesbian act on stage freaked her out, but based on the money these men were throwing at them, Angela knew what she was doing. Billy Kelley was a little too handsy, but all in all, this job wasn't bad. She walked toward the white curtain that ringed the private lap-dance section of the club, gripping the thick rolls of cash.

Slipping through the curtain, she scanned the area. It was the size of a two-car garage. Four separate lap dance areas, each with a white leather couch and a mini bar, were set up in the corners of the room. A common-area bar filled the middle of the back wall. It was so dimly lit in here that the guys needed eyes like hawks to know what they were looking at, which helped out some of the older strippers. Julia let her eyes adjust and saw Angela in a corner. Her back was turned. She was mixing a drink, and from what Julia could see, she was alone. Whoever she was supposed to give a lap dance to hadn't arrived yet. Julia took a step toward Angela to give her the money and stumbled as a large man pushed through the curtain behind her, shoving her out of the way.

Julia opened her mouth to give the man hell and then froze. She'd only gotten a quick glance, but there was no doubt. It was her ex-boyfriend, James Stockton.

She backed out of the room, expecting him to turn and recognize her at any moment. A cold sweat broke over her as she slipped through the curtain. She hurried through the club, keeping her gaze fixed straight ahead until she was back in the dressing room. She sat in front of her mirror, stared at herself, taking deep breaths to calm herself while her mind relived the time she spent here in Massey with James Stockton.

The whole six months of her time with James spooled out. She could hear the clink of silverware and bell-toned clink of fluted glasses during dinners at fancy restaurants. See the bellhops pulling their bags during weekend trips to high-end hotels. Taste the crafted cocktails mixed by bartenders in black-tie outfits at swanky nightclubs. Worse, she could feel the heady thrill of it all. It had been a dream—far removed from her janitorial job in the high school that was part of the school district he oversaw as superintendent. The overwhelming, dizzying shine of being with a powerful man had intoxicated her. Then there was the creeping realization of realizing that everything they did was secret. The restaurants and nightclubs were always out of town, as were the weekend trips. It didn't take long to see that James didn't want anyone to see them together. Out of town, he had no trouble attracting attention with his big, booming voice. Talking over people. Ordering them around. But back in Massey, he didn't even glance in her direction or whisper a "hi" when he saw her mopping a floor or pushing a trashcan at the high school. She'd tried to break it off nicely. Said the age difference was too much for her. That he'd probably be happier going out with someone closer to his age. His response? The beating followed by the rape. Leaving town, getting a new job, and meeting Conor had given her a flicker of hope for the future. But even that didn't last. James stomped it to dead ash after he'd tracked her down and broke into her apartment. And he would've raped her again if Conor hadn't come by. The beating Conor gave James was something that prick would never forget.

Or forgive.

She lifted her hand to her face, running a finger along the scar on her cheek.

I just have to take it one day at a time. I have to be careful. And smart.

She turned her head in the direction of the curtain that opened to the club where James was being entertained by Angela.

And no matter what happens, I have to be ready…

She took her finger off the scar and stared at her face in the mirror and whispered, "To fight."

* * *

Angela handed James Stockton his dirty Martini with a blue-cheese-stuffed olive. The sight of it made her gag. It looked like an oily puddle of water with flecks of half-digested cheese.

"Are you sure her boyfriend isn't around?" James said, looking around the room.

Angela held her arms out. "You see him? Maybe he's hiding under a couch."

"Don't get smart," said James. "I mean, is he going to come busting in here looking for her?"

Angela shook her head. "Julia don't want anything to do with him. Plus, he don't even know she's here." She tilted her head. "You scared of him or something?"

"Of course not," said James. He leaned back on the couch, sipped his drink, and smacked his lips. "I just don't need to get in an altercation in a strip club. It wouldn't look good." He patted the couch. "Sit down."

Angela sat next to him. She forced herself to smile as he rubbed her thigh and loosened his tie. Angela unbuttoned the top button on his dress shirt. He licked his lips.

"Is she out in the club?" he asked.

"She's in the dressing room," Angela said, wincing as James kneaded her thigh.

"Well, I didn't come out here for nothing. Get her in the private room and lock the door. I need to talk to her."

Angela pushed James' hand off her thigh. She stood, shaking her head. "Nuh-uh," she said. "It don't work like that." She swallowed hard and screwed up her courage. "Here's the deal. I want out of this titty bar, and I want that executive secretary job in the board office you promised me. Give me that, and I'll put her in that back room with a bow around her ass. And if you don't think that's fair, I'll tell her you've been sniffing around. You'll never see her again."

"Calm down," James said, reaching for her. "You know you can trust me."

She slapped his hand away. She needed to be careful. He'd spun a rosy line of bullshit when Julia had first left, telling Angela he only wanted a girl he could take care of and hire as his executive secretary. Next thing she knew, he'd talked her into his bed. But surprise, surprise, none of his promises had come true. What had come true were cuts in the budget that eliminated her maintenance job, followed by James getting her a job here at Sweetie's and coming in for a weekly lap dance that sometimes went too far. So much for him taking care of a girl.

She thought of Julia sitting in the dressing room, oblivious to the trouble coming her way. She liked Julia. She could see them being friends forever—and maybe more. There was only one problem. Life wasn't a TV commercial with a smiling husband, a nice house, and neighbors coming over to eat hamburgers off the grill while the kids played in the backyard and a dog bounded in the sun after a Frisbee. Life was big shots like James taking everything from you, making you dance, show your ass, and worse. As much as she liked Julia, in this life, it was every girl for herself.

She stepped closer to James, ran her fingers through his short, thinning hair and looked him in the eye.

"Can you get me that job or not?" she asked. He nodded. Knowing what this meant for Julia made her feel a little sick, but she smiled.

"It won't be official until the board authorizes it," said James. "But they'll do it. If I tell them to jump, they jump."

"I want a signed contract," she said.

James dipped his fingers into his Martini, grabbed the olive, and ate it. She could see blue cheese between his teeth as he talked.

"You bring me Julia tomorrow night, and I'll give you the contract. I'll take care of everything."

She kissed him on one cheek, and then the other.

***

"You want me to sleep on the couch downstairs?" said Julia, walking into Angela's bedroom wearing white cotton underwear. She toweled her hair dry as Angela pulled on a pink satin top.

Angela turned toward Julia. "You need a shirt?"

"I have one," said Julia, walking over to the bed. She grabbed a black T-shirt off the floor. It was the shirt she'd worn to bed last night—one of Conor's shirts. She pulled it on, the smell reminding her of him. Clean and soapy mixed with a musk of his sweat.

Angela got in the bed, fluffed her pillow, and lifted the cover. "You're not sleeping on any couch," she said. "Get in here, girl."

Julia slipped under the cool covers next to Angela. Angela turned off the lamp on her nightstand, fluffed her pillow, and rustled around a bit to get comfortable. The scent of her cinnamon body wash filling the darkness. Finally settled, Angela pushed back into Julia, letting Julia spoon against her back.

"You did good tonight," Angela whispered.

"Thanks," Julia said. A long stretch of quiet filled the room, but Julia could tell Angela wasn't sleeping. "Hey, Angela," she said.

"Yeah."

"What was James doing in the club tonight?" She felt Angela stiffen.

"The same as every other guy," said Angela. "Why?"

Julia laid a hand on Angela's hip. "Just keep an eye on him," she said, rubbing Angela's hip. "He's not what you think."

Angela turned over, facing Julia. The whites of her eyes glowed in the dark. Julia could smell a hint of beer on Angela's breath from the drafts Billy poured them after Sweeties closed. Angela touched her scar.

"He gave you this, didn't he?" she said.

Julia pulled Angela's hand off her face, and then nodded.

Angela kissed the scar. "I'm sorry," she said.

"It's okay," said Julia.

"I hope you got something out of it."

Julia touched the scar. She took a deep breath and exhaled. "You know I can't work at the club if he's around. If he sees me, he'll try to hurt me."

"He only comes for me," said Angela. "You'll never have to see him."

"You shouldn't either."

Angela rubbed Julia's thigh. "Men are terrible," she said, moving her hand to Julia's lower back. Her hand lingered there, then Julia felt Angela's other hand slide between her thighs and begin to gently rub.

"We could leave," said Angela. "Just you and me. We could make each other happy."

Angela's hand felt good. And what she said sounded familiar—about leaving together and making each other happy. An image of Conor appeared in Julia's mind. His long hair. His green eyes. His muscled arms and shoulders. His smile and the way he could be so gentle and so strong at the same time. If he hadn't stolen from that church, they could be together now. She would've gone anywhere with him.

Angela rubbed faster. Soft, insistent pressure, circling around and around. Julia pushed against Angela's fingers, finding a rhythm. She moaned, a memory of Conor's lips on hers, his breath mixing with hers, his strong hands holding her. Angela's voice broke her concentration, breathless and husky.

"That's it, Julia. I'll take care of you. We're good together."

"Stop," said Julia.

Angela kissed her neck, still talking.

"We'll leave tomorrow. Neither of us will have to see James again. We'll just leave and do our act at another club. We can go any—"

Julia grabbed Angela's face. "Angela, stop," she said.

Angela pulled her hand from between Julia's thighs.

"I can't do this with you," said Julia.

Angela rolled to her back and stared at the ceiling. "You still thinking about that guy?"

Julia grabbed Angela's hand. "His name is Conor."

"Must be something special."

"He was."

"Was?"

"Maybe still is," said Julia. "I don't know."

"You gotta be kidding me," murmured Angela. "Guy treats you like dirt, and you run right back to him. Typical."

"He never treated me like dirt."

"You said—"

"I said I saw him stealing from a church," said Julia. "That's all. He was nothing but nice."

Angela faced Julia. "Don't bullshit me. He did something. Had to. You wouldn't have come knocking on my door unless he did."

Julia rolled to her back and looked at the ceiling. "He lied to me. That's all. I've had too many people lie to me. I'm not putting up with it anymore."

"Please, girl," Angela snorted. "Everybody lies."

Julia stared at the ceiling as Angela rolled over in a huff. Julia touched her back. "Are you mad?" she asked.

"Yeah."

"Why?"

"Because you think some guy not telling you he's gonna rob a church is lying. What guy's gonna tell you that? He'd have to be the stupidest man in the world."

"It's not just that he didn't tell me," said Julia. "It's just that…I trusted him. He was the first person I trusted in a long time."

Angela rolled over and looked into Julia's eyes. "What about me?"

Julia stroked her arm, holding her gaze. "What?"

"Do you trust me?"

Julia nodded.

"Then why can't we—"

Julia cupped Angela's face. "It wouldn't be right. I'm still thinking about him. And I can't be with you until he's out of my head. It wouldn't be fair to you."

Angela pulled Julia's hands off her face and turned away.

"I'm not trying to hurt you," said Julia, tucking in tight against Angela's back, hugging her.

"I know."

"Are you okay?"

"I'm perfect," Angela said.

Julia could barely hear her as Angela added, "You better get some rest. You're gonna have a big day tomorrow."

CHAPTER TWENTY-FOUR

Cracker got in his truck. He could feel the girl up on the deck watching his every move, along with her growling dog. That black-haired hellion in a yellow bikini—Mona Bomba, sister of Conor Monroe's comatose friend, Sully—had once been Monroe's girlfriend, but she'd be no help in finding him.

Cracker started his truck and backed down the drive.

The way she'd talked, she'd just as soon cut Monroe's throat as look at him. She'd spit all kinds of venom about Conor being responsible for her brother Sully being brain dead. She'd acted like it was revenge for Sully that made her mad, but Cracker could tell it was something else. He knew jilted when he saw it. The way he figured it, Monroe had gotten himself some new tail, and Mona wasn't gonna let that stand.

Cracker scratched the back of his neck. Good for her. Mona was a fighter.

The brakes on his truck squealed as he stopped in the street. He heard barking. Mona's big old boxer had gotten away from her and was barreling down the driveway. Cracker rolled down his window and whistled, holding his hand out the window. Mona wasn't far behind the dog, running in her bare feet. Lord, she was put together. How Monroe had given her up was beyond Cracker, which could only mean that Monroe's new girl had to have some kind of magical hold on him. If he could get his hands on that girl, it would surely bring Monroe out of hiding. The truth was Monroe's new girlfriend was most likely his only shot at getting his hands on Monroe because the man appeared to have no friends or family.

Derek Ryder filled him in. Said his running buddy, Fitz, had mysteriously disappeared. Conor's father was a homeless bum he hadn't talked to in years. His mother had left Monroe and his daddy about fifteen years ago. Conor Monroe had no brothers or sisters. The only other person of note was his friend, Sully Bomba, and he was taking a long nap in the hospital. Monroe was a ghost. His apartment had been clean as a tomb. The whole idea of using someone to find him seemed like a complete bust, and Cracker had even entertained the thought of telling Duck that this Monroe boy was ungettable. But then, on a hunch, Cracker had broken into the apartment next to Monroe's. Neighbors were often friends, and sometimes more than that. Monroe's neighbor, bless her, turned out to be of the 'more' variety. The painting in her apartment showed someone that looked just like Monroe, according to the photo Derek had given him, and he was holding hands with a girl on a beach. And there was a name on the bottom of the painting. Julia Terranova. That made things pretty damn easy. All it took was Cracker going to the apartment manager's office and saying he had a package for Julia Terranova. The landlord pointed him to the same apartment where the painting was located, but he told him she hadn't been there for a few days, that she'd put in notice on her lease, and that he'd best check with her employer, Sacred Heart Church. Which was where he'd been headed when Derek had called and filled him in about this Mona girl, how she'd been Monroe's squeeze not too long ago. So, he'd driven here and checked Mona out, which brought him to his current situation of watching Mona's boxer coming for him like he was wearing a pork chop necklace.

Cracker snapped his fingers at the big boxer, who was a

stride away now, running full bore. The dog leaped, all fangs and slobber. Cracker moved in a blur, catching the dog by the throat in mid-air. He twisted his hand around its collar and lifted. The dog's legs kicked and clawed the side of his truck. Eyes bugged out, its tongue turned blue as it twirled in his grasp. It made a gagging sound. Cracker held it up in the air until its eyes dulled. He would've held it a bit longer, but Mona was almost on top of him, spitting and screaming. He didn't have time for this nonsense. He dropped the dog. Its head hit the asphalt with a clunk. He put the truck in gear and drove away, glancing in his rear view.

The dog struggled to its feet. Mona stood in the road, one hand on her big ole beautiful hip, the other pointing at him as she yelled. Cracker turned his attention back to the road. Monroe had himself a hard-ass hottie in Mona. If Julia Terranova was half as hard, it was gonna be a real pleasure trying to hold on to her long enough for Monroe to come in and fight. He stuck his hand out his open window, riding it up and down in the wind.

It was bound to be fun finding Julia and messing with her. Nothing was any good unless it took effort.

***

Walking in the afternoon heat was getting on Cracker's nerves. He'd knocked on doors at two of the three Sacred Heart school buildings, but they were locked, and nobody was home. He needed to talk to somebody who could tell him where he could find Julia Terranova. He walked across an asphalt playground toward the church. Somebody had to be in the church. A priest appeared around a corner, making his way up a grand set of stairs that led to the church's front entrance. Cracker ran toward him.

"Hey," he shouted. "Excuse me. You have a minute?"

The priest put his hand on one of the big entrance doors, stopped, and turned, waiting as Cracker ascended the stairs.

"Can I help you?" he said.

"I hope so," said Cracker, holding out his hand.

The priest shook Cracker's hand. "I'm Father Sal. What can I do for you?"

"I'm looking for a Julia Terranova. Heard she worked here."

"And you are?"

"A friend," said Cracker. "A very dear, old friend."

The priest tried to pull his hand away. Cracker tightened his grip.

"I have important news from her daddy," Cracker drawled. "If you could just point me in her direction, I'll be out of your hair."

"It was my understanding that she didn't know her father," said the priest, looking down at his hand. "And, even if she did, it wouldn't matter. She doesn't work here any longer."

"Oh, that's right," said Cracker, squeezing the priest's hand. "I get things mixed up. Not her daddy—a relative from a long-lost branch of her family. Someone she isn't properly acquainted with."

The priest paled. Cracker could see a slight sheen of sweat on the man's forehead.

"Can you please let go of my hand?" said the priest.

Cracker bore down. The priest's knees buckled and he let out a gasp.

Shouldering the door on the church open, Cracker hustled Father Sal inside, keeping a tight grip on his hand.

"Looks like you need to sit down," he said, dragging the priest inside.

* * *

Cracker started his truck. He let the air conditioning run while he looked over Julia's employment application. The priest had said he didn't know where Julia had gone, and Cracker believed him. Hard not to believe a man who'd pissed himself. But the holy man had gone the extra mile to be helpful, giving Cracker a copy of Julia's employment application. All kinds of good information was on this piece of paper—places she'd worked and lived before coming to Brannigan. And references. People you used as references were people you stayed in touch with. Like, for example, this here Angela Duncan girl, who Julia listed as a co-worker and personal friend.

Cracker punched in the phone number for Angela on his cell, and then pulled out of the church parking lot. The phone rang as he reached into a plastic grocery bag to grab a protein bar. He took a bite as a woman answered.

She sounded sleepy. Damn near one in the afternoon and the girl sounded like she'd just woke up. Cracker stopped chewing long enough to ask if he was talking to Angela Duncan. When she asked who was calling, he asked if she knew Julia Terranova. That got her talking, asking him where he'd gotten her number. How he knew her name. She didn't sound sleepy no more. She sounded mad and a little flustered. But he had to hand it to her, she never said a word about Julia.

He hung up, shoved the rest of the protein bar in his mouth and chewed. Angela knew something about Julia, otherwise she wouldn't have gotten all jumpy. And according to Julia's application, he just had to go to a little town called Massey to visit Angela and get to the bottom of her jumpiness.

A little face-to-face talk with Angela would move things right along. He was gonna find this Julia to get Monroe to come out of hiding. Then he was going to beat him to death. Then Mr. Duck would pay him. It was gonna be a good time for all involved.

Cracker turned onto the off-ramp for the interstate, heading toward Massey. He searched for some country music on the radio, stopping when he heard an old Johnny Cash tune. Johnny was good. He played simple, straightforward music and sang the same way. Cracker turned up the volume and got himself another protein bar, taking a big bite. He chewed and hummed along.

* * *

Conor finished his last set of squats. He stepped forward stiff-legged to the rack and eased the three-hundred pounds off his shoulders. He toweled the sweat from his face and thought back to the video footage of Cracker sticking out his tongue and screaming his rebel yell before finishing his opponents. If that maniac found him, he had to be ready to run or fight. He threw the towel down and caught a glimpse of himself in the mirror. Bruises still shadowed his torso from his fight with Duck's guys at the church. He stretched his arms over his head and twisted, watching his abs flex, then dropped his arms to his sides. Veins laced his arms, chest, and shoulders. He'd felt better, but if it came to it, he could fight. The better option was to steal the paintings, get the money, and run. He turned toward the sound of a door opening. Angel stuck his head around the side of the door at the top of the basement's stairs.

"Come on up," said Angel. "Your dad's here. We're going over the job."

Conor pulled on jeans and a white T-shirt. He wiped his face with the towel, took a sip from a bottle of water, and then looked in the mirror.

"Get the paintings, get the money, get Julia, and then get out," he whispered. "I can do this."

Conor walked into Angel's office. His dad sat in a chair in front of Angel's desk. Angel came in behind Conor and pointed at a stack of metal folding chairs propped against the wall. "Get a chair," he said, then walked behind his desk.

Conor pulled a chair over and sat next to his dad. Angel spread an architectural drawing over the top of his desk.

"This is it. Louis Bromfield's house," said Angel. "The park system runs tours through it three times a day. They'll walk us right in, no problem."

Angel went on to explain the layout, circled all the alarm

systems in blue, then drew a red X on the locations of the two Grandma Moses paintings. Conor asked a couple questions, but mostly listened. He looked at his dad, thinking how he'd nailed this job. It was almost too easy.

"So that's it," said Angel, rolling up the drawing. "Mickey will drop you off. You walk in, you hide, and then you steal the paintings after they close up for the night. Mickey will pick you up at the Mount Commons parking lot across the street. I got a buyer in Europe. He'll set up the provenance, the certificate of authenticity, and move both paintings through private auction."

"What's provenance?" asked Conor.

"Don't worry about it," said Angel.

"How much we getting?" asked Conor.

"Three hundred," said Angel. "But we gotta pay for transport. When it's all done, we'll clear ninety-five each."

Conor smiled. Angel slapped him on the back.

"I told you it was good, didn't I?" his dad said.

Conor gave his father a quick glance, then stared at Angel.

"Instead of my dad, how 'bout you take me over and pick me up?" he said.

Angel sighed. "No. I have eyes all over me every time I step out of the garage. Your dad's perfect. Nobody cares where he goes. Plus, he's been sober since I talked to him yesterday, haven't you, Mickey?"

"Haven't had a drop."

Conor eyed his dad. "You got the DTs?"

Mickey gripped his hands together. "I feel great."

"I don't like this," said Conor.

His dad grabbed his shoulder.

Conor turned. For the first time in a very long time, Conor noticed his dad's eyes were clear and bright.

"I won't let you down," Mickey said, tightening his grip on Conor's shoulder. "You can count on me."

Conor fixed a hard stare on him. "This is like—you know—your last chance. Screw this up and we're done."

His father nodded. “I know.”

Angel put a backpack on the desk. “Okay, then. Now that we’re all a happy family, here’s what you’ll need to get the job done.” Two cardboard tubes stuck out of the top of the backpack. He pulled one out. “Just remember, if any of us gets caught, we shut up and serve our time. The money will be here for you when you get out.”

Angel handed Conor the cardboard tube. Conor pulled a plastic end cap from the tube and slid out a thick, rolled-up, piece of paper. “I printed off reproductions for each painting,” said Angel. “After you get the original out of the frame, tape the fake into the frame, and put the original in the tube.“ Conor nodded, slid the reproduction back into the tube, and laid the tube on the table. Unzipping the top of the backpack, Angel rummaged around a bit, and then pulled out something that looked like a flashlight.

“This is your saw,” said Angel. “Extremely low vibration. Six point seven inches long. Ten thousand strokes per minute. It’ll cut right through the walls behind the paintings.”

Conor examined it. “What about vibration sensors?”

“They’re using contact sensors,” said Angel. “If the frames are moved—or if the glass is broken or removed—the sensors will trip. But you’re coming in from behind the paintings. The sensors won’t even know you’re there.”

“How do I know where to cut into the walls?” said Conor.

Angel took a magnetic stud finder out of the backpack. “The frames are anchored with four big bolts. Find the anchors, draw a square, and start cutting.”

“How do I get out of the house without tripping an alarm?” said Conor.

Angel put the saw back in the backpack and then looked at Conor. “All the doors and windows are alarmed, so you’re going into the attic and cutting your way out through the bottom of the cupola on the roof. It’s marked on the drawing.”

Conor turned to his dad. "You sure you're up for this?"

Mickey took a deep breath and exhaled. "Yeah," he said. "One hundred percent."

The room was quiet. Angel's cell buzzed in his pocket. Angel answered it, then handed it to Conor.

"It's Ronnie from The Locos," said Angel. "Says he's got something for you."

Conor took the phone. He stood and paced around the room, talking low. He smiled, clicked his fingers at Angel and whispered, "Pen and paper." Angel handed him a legal pad and a pencil. He wrote something and said, "You're the man, Ronnie. Thanks, brother." Then he hung up the phone and whooped, extending his hand toward Angel.

"Give me the keys to your Camaro. Ronnie and Pedro saw Julia stripping at a club in Massey last night."

Angel shook his head. "It's the middle of the day. Barry's crew will see you."

Conor clenched his jaw. "No they won't. Just give them to me."

Angel crossed his arms over his chest. "No." He waited, staring. Not moving a muscle.

Everything in Conor told him to back down. Instead, he returned Angel's stare, counting silently to ten in his head. When he got to ten, he wasn't sure exactly what he'd do, but it wouldn't be fun for him or Angel. He got to eight when Angel cocked his head.

"Well," said Angel. "Looks like you're ready to throw down over this girl, so I'll make this simple. You tell me why she's worth putting you, me, and your dad in harm's way, and—if it's good enough—I'll give you the keys. And if this is about nothing but you having a hard-on for her, you're out of luck."

Conor relaxed his hard stare on Angel. The answer was simple. He'd been in her apartment. He'd seen that Joe Cracker Jones had broken into her place, which had probably sent her running back to Massey where the only work she could get was stripping. Or her ex had paid her a second visit, dragged her back to Massey, and put her to work in a strip club. Not a pleasant thought, but not out of the realm of possibility. Either way, it was on him to make it right. Her life had been nothing but shit raining down, and somehow, someway, she'd been unlucky enough to get close to someone like him who'd brought her more of the same. One way or another, he was sure that she'd disappeared because of him, and he couldn't let that stand. The delicate part was how to explain the situation in a way Angel would understand. And he couldn't mention Cracker going into her apartment. Angel would freak out if he heard that a hit man was after him. He cleared his throat, deciding to just lay out why he couldn't get her out of his head and let the situation speak for itself.

"You ever know someone who was good?" he said.

Angel nodded.

"Not just regular good. I mean *real* good."

"Maybe one or two," said Angel. "Probably one."

"Well, she's number two then. Grew up hard. Like me. Like you. And still didn't go bad. Like me. Or you."

"Speak for yourself."

"I'm speaking for her," said Conor. "She plays everything straight. Does the right thing. And you know what that got her? Raped and beaten by her last boyfriend."

"I know a few women like that, and yet, you don't see me putting your head on a chopping block for them, do you?"

"No. But what if she was your girl?"

"Unless she's getting raped right now, what's the hurry? Why don't you just—"

Conor's gaze hardened. "Her ex showed up at her apartment right before this whole shitshow started. Somehow she got the better of him. I tuned him up a little bit and tossed him out, but I think he came back. It's the only thing that makes sense. She wouldn't go back to that town unless he dragged her there."

"Really?"

"Yeah. Really," said Conor.

Angel sucked in a long inhale through clenched teeth and muttered, "Fuck it." He shook his head as he dug in his pocket and pulled out the keys.

Conor held out his hand. "How about I leave when it gets dark? Nobody will see me."

"Where'd you park?"

"Down the street. Nowhere near the garage."

Angel dropped the keys in Conor's hand. "You're a pain in the ass. No crying if you get caught and Duck's guys skin you alive."

Conor slipped the keys in his pocket. "Thanks. I owe you." He watched Angel walk out of the office and close the door, then turned to see his dad grinning at him.

"Nice performance," said his dad.

"It's the truth," said Conor.

His dad raised his eyebrows. "Except for conveniently leaving out that you do have a hard-on for this girl."

"Angel said that was a no go, so why bring it up?" said Conor. "Plus, it's more than just her looks. It's, uh—"

His dad shrugged. "What?"

Conor rolled his eyes. "It's how she makes me feel. You know? Happy?"

"I get it," said his dad with a huge smile. "But what were you going to do if Angel didn't give you the keys?"

"I would've fought him I guess," said Conor, walking over to the desk and taking a seat. He looked at his dad. "You would've had my back, right?"

His dad walked toward the door and opened it. He looked back and winked, saying, "Always, Conor. Always," just before shutting the door.

CHAPTER TWENTY-FIVE

Julia ate a bowl of corn flakes while she watched Angela straighten her hair with a flat iron. "What time we working tonight?" she said, crinkling her nose at the smell of burnt hair.

Angela put down the flat iron. She looked in the mirror, throwing her long blonde hair over her shoulder. "Eleven."

"Will you have time to show me how to do lap dances?"

Angela picked up a pair of tweezers, examined her eyebrows in the mirror, put the tweezers down, and sighed. "Maybe. But I gotta make my own money. I'm not your dance coach."

"Sorry. I'm just nervous," said Julia.

She stepped back as Angela pushed by her and walked into her bedroom, mumbling, "Get over yourself."

Julia ate the last of her corn flakes and walked downstairs. She felt bad about last night, but she couldn't be with Angela like that. Not while she still had Conor in her head. She washed her cereal bowl in the sink.

"You better get your makeup on and stop dragging ass," yelled Angela from upstairs.

Julia rolled her eyes. As dark as Sweeties was, and as drunk as the guys were, she doubted that much makeup was needed, but she trotted upstairs and went into the bathroom, putting her face together. Anything to shut Angela up. By the time she was done, Angela was standing in the doorway, holding a pair of stilettos.

"Here's your shoes for tonight," Angela said, handing them over.

Julia slipped the stilettos into her purse. She watched Angela dig through her purse, a deep crease between her eyebrows, her jaw set tight. "You know, you don't have to dance with me tonight," said Julia.

"What are you talking about?" said Angela, still rooting around in her purse.

"Just saying," said Julia. "Like you said, you gotta make your own money."

"Will you stop it?" said Angela, pulling a crumpled pack of cigarettes out of her purse. "I have no problem dancing with you." Angela lit a cigarette, the end glowing bright before she blew out a cloud of smoke. She looked at Julia. Her eyes softened. She took a deep breath and held it, like she was on the edge of saying something.

"What?" said Julia. "Spit it out."

"It's nothing," said Angela, turning to walk downstairs. "Let's get out of here. You got a big night ahead of you."

* * *

Julia glanced over at Angela, watching her drive. She was still acting weird—all quiet and pensive. Julia sighed. Pushing her away last night was probably the reason. Well, too bad—it was the right move. Julia knew she couldn't be with anyone until she got Conor out of her head. But this driving without talking was stupid.

Angela turned on the radio and ran through stations, stopping at the familiar chords of *Possum Kingdom* by the Toadies. She cranked it and bopped her head.

Julia grinned. "Haven't heard this one in a long time."

"Yeah," said Angela. "Guy wants his girl so bad he'll kill her to keep her."

Julia touched her scar and said, "Been there, done that." She waited for Angela to agree or say something sarcastic, like she usually did. Instead, Angela stared straight ahead, gripping the steering wheel. Julia could see the muscles in Angela's jaw flex. Then Angela glanced over, her brow tight.

"You talking about James Stockton?" she said.

Julia stared out the passenger window, watching trees and mailboxes and houses fly by. "The one and only," she said.

Angela pursed her lips, the furrow between her brows deepening. She finished her cigarette, flicked the butt out the window, lit another one, and turned off the radio.

They rode through the dark roads in silence the rest of the way.

Angela flipped on her turn signal and pulled into Sweeties' gravel parking lot. The front lot was full. It was a packed house. She drove around back, looking for an open space. A pick-up truck drove toward her. It stopped in front of her bumper, its headlights blinding her. "Asshole," she whispered, shielding her eyes to get a look at the driver. He was no looker—a pit bull jaw, flattened nose, and short haircut that stood up in various unfortunate ways. "Take a look at that guy," she said.

"I already did. Once was enough," said Julia.

Angela put her car in Reverse, threw an arm over the back of her seat, and backed her car up until she was next to a dumpster. Turning the car off, she sat in silence for a moment, biting her lip, and then turned to Julia. "If you ran into James again, do you think he would hurt you?"

Julia squinted. "Would hurt me?" She touched her scar. "He already did." She got out, looked back at Angela, and smiled. "Don't worry about it. If he comes in, I'll stay out of his way. C'mon, we're gonna be late. I can't make out with myself on stage."

Angela closed her eyes and shook her head. She pulled the keys out of the ignition, got out, walked by Julia toward the back of the club, and opened the door. The smell of sweat, alcohol, and smoke billowed out. Before Julia could step inside, Angela grabbed her wrist.

"Look, if you don't want to work tonight, you don't have to," said Angela. "We can call in sick, go home, watch a movie, and chill. I could use a night off. What do you think?"

Julia pushed Angela's hand out of the way, stepped inside, and shot Angela a look. "We're already here. Let's make some money."

Angela followed Julia inside. She closed the door, locked it, took Julia's hand, and led her toward the dressing room.

* * *

The dance with Angela went off without a hitch. The guys loved it. There were even a bunch of girls that came to watch. Money rained on the stage and Julia finally loosened up enough to have fun. At one point, she even backed Angela up against the pole and made out with her while they danced. The girls in the audience really liked that—maybe even more than the guys. The lights and the music and the crowd's energy swirled around her and became part of her. She was a sex goddess, laughing while Angela took off her bikini top and squirted baby oil all over both of them. It was a good time, but there was one weird moment.

Somewhere around the middle of their act, a big redneck with a bad haircut, cowboy boots, jeans, and a white T-shirt shoved his way through the crowd to the stage. Muscle roped his huge shoulders, arms, and chest. He stared at her for a while, then reached up, shoved a dollar in her G-string, and said her name. Not just her first name. The whole thing.

Julia Terranova.

She had stopped dancing for a split second to look at him. And when she did, he nodded and slipped back into the crowd. There was no mistaking who he was—the ugly guy from the truck in the parking lot. The question was, why did that big ugly guy know her name?

Thinking it over, she came to a logical conclusion. He must be local. She'd lived and worked in Massey for most of her life, so he was probably someone who knew her from high school. Or they had friends in common or something like that. Even so, it was weird for him to say her name like that—Julia Terranova—like he was throwing it out there just to make sure she was who he thought she was.

But now it was over, and Julia was in the dressing room with Angela, so it didn't matter who that guy was or how he knew her. He was someone else's ugly boyfriend, not hers.

Julia nodded at her inescapable logic as she took off her G-string. Then she stepped out of her stilettos and toweled the baby oil off before slipping into a robe. She watched Angela kick off her high heels and grab a clean towel from a laundry hamper.

"That was wild," said Angela. She took a seat and lit a cigarette.

Julia picked up a stack of cash, fanning herself with it. "I think I like wild."

Angela busted out laughing, dropping her head between her knees. When she came up for air, Julia dropped her money on Angela's lap.

"That's for letting me stay at your place," Julia said. "And for being a friend. Sorry if I made you feel bad last night."

Angela turned as the owner, Billy Kelley, walked in.

"You girls got lots of fans out there," he said. He handed Angela a folded piece of paper and winked. "Here's that contract you been waiting on."

"What contract?" said Julia.

"It's a private thing," said Billy, squinting at her. "None of your business."

Angela stood, holding Julia's money in one hand and the folded contract in the other. She held the contract out to Billy. "Tell him I don't want it anymore."

Billy raised his hands. "That ain't my job. Tell him yourself." He picked up Julia's G-string and bikini top, handed them to Julia, and then kicked a pair of stilettos over to her. "You ain't done yet. Get dressed. You got a private lap dance waiting on you." He grinned at Angela. "First one's always the best, isn't it, Angela?"

"But Angela hasn't shown me how to do it yet," said Julia.

"Tell him to come back tomorrow," said Angela, dropping the contract on the ground and reaching for Julia. Billy smacked her hand. "Pick that up," he said, pointing at the contract. "My dressing room ain't a dumpster."

"Julia. Don't go," said Angela, looking panicked. She grabbed Billy by the arm. "Tell him I'll give him a free lap dance instead."

Julia finished tying her top and looked at Angela. "It's fine. I watched some of the girls. It didn't look hard. Plus, I gotta do it eventually. Might as well be now."

Billy pulled his arm away from Angela, giving her a dark look, and then turned his gaze on Julia. "Ain't that sweet? Angela's worried 'bout you—this being your first time and all." He smiled, showing his gold tooth. His smile went flat as he glanced at Angela. She hung her head. "Angela's just being a good friend. Ain't you, Angela?" Then he yanked Julia out of her chair. "Now get your shoes on and move your ass. You got a paying customer waiting on you."

Julia didn't like how Billy squeezed her elbow as he led her out of the dressing room. Just before they left, he glanced back at Angela.

"You stay here until her dance is done. You'll just make her all nervous, hovering around like a mother hen. Ain't that right, Julia?"

Julia turned. Angela looked stricken—her face the color of chalk. "Relax, Angela," said Julia. "I'll see you in fifteen."

* * *

Angela watched Julia walk out. She picked up the contract from the floor, put the stack of cash Julia had given her on the table, and sat in front of her mirror. She opened the contract from James. Her new job as an executive secretary was official. Her heart pounded, and she couldn't catch her breath. She looked at the curtain Julia had just walked through.

Then she was on her feet. Stuffing her purse full of their money. Taking off her heels. Yanking on her jeans and a shirt.

She put her heels back on and started to walk after Julia, stopped, walked back, and grabbed the contract. She tore it in two and threw it in the trash. Then she walked toward the curtain that led into the club, running straight into a guy walking into the dressing room.

He was big. Solid. He knocked the breath out of her. Then he clamped his hands on her, lifted her like a rag doll, gave her a look that was none too friendly, and said, "Is Julia Terranova in there?"

* * *

Julia could barely keep up with Billy. "Could you slow down?" she asked, her stilettos clicking as she did her best to keep pace. He tightened his grip on her elbow and yanked her into the private lap dance room. She glanced around at the shadowy bodies dancing over men sitting on couches.

"The room's full," she said to Billy.

Billy pulled a key out of his pocket. "You get a special room," he said, pulling her toward the common bar against the back wall.

"What special room?" she said. "Where are we going?"

"VIP section," said Billy, pushing her behind the bar. He pulled back a white curtain on the wall, revealing a door. His gold tooth flashed. "This here's for high rollers," he said, sliding a key into the door.

His grip on her tightened painfully.

Pulling the door open, he shoved her inside and closed the door. The lock clicked. Julia turned around, taking in her surroundings.

The room was the size of a small bedroom. The floor

was white tile. A black iron bed with four posters and an ornamental headboard of scrolled metalwork dominated the middle of the room. Chains hung from the ceiling over the bed, running through eyelets welded on the top of each of the four posters. On the end of each chain was a padded handcuff. Mirrors covered the ceiling. Every wall was covered in plush white carpet. The wall straight across from her was filled with sex toys and bondage gear. James Stockton sat in a chair in front of the sex gear. He held a long black nightstick.

She reached for the doorknob, trying to turn it. It was locked.

James Stockton raised out of the chair.

Then the lights went out. She couldn't see a thing, but she heard the click of the nightstick tapping the floor. Then she heard James.

"You can't see me, but that's okay. I've been in this room a hundred times. I know every inch of it. And for what I have planned, that's all that counts."

She heard him walking toward her.

"But do you know what the best part is?" he said. "It's that your new boyfriend isn't here. We're all alone. And I have something you're really going to like." He smacked the floor with the nightstick. "You're not going to walk straight for a long time after this."

Julia recalled the layout of the room. If she could get to the bed and keep it between her and James, maybe she could keep him off her long enough for her eyes to adjust to the dark. She put her hands out and stepped forward. James quickened his steps. She did the same, moving forward blindly. Her ankle turned, but she caught herself. Damn stilettos. She pulled one off and threw it toward the sound of James moving her way. She slipped off the other stiletto. A hand grabbed her arm and a handcuff snapped over her wrist. James' hot breath was in her ear.

"Got you now," he said.

She couldn't see a thing, but she could hear perfectly

fine. She swung the stiletto, aiming for his voice. The heel stabbed into something. Hot blood spurted over her hand. She almost lost her grip on the stiletto when James gasped and pulled away, but she held on, pulling it free from his flesh. A fist, an open hand, or maybe the nightstick, clipped the side of her head. She fell onto the bed and then rolled off, landing on her feet holding the stiletto tight.

"You want me? You're gonna have to earn it," she yelled.

Then she shut her mouth and held her breath.

She needed to keep quiet. It was her only chance to hear where he was—and if he was coming closer.

The bed let out a tiny squeak from James bumping it. She gripped the stiletto, pointing it in the direction of his stifled breathing, coming closer.

And closer.

And closer.

CHAPTER TWENTY-SIX

Cracker peed in the urinal, thinking over his next move. He'd found Angela's townhouse easy enough. When he went up to the front door and peeked in a window, he'd seen two girls in there. There were more than a few cars pulling in and out of the parking lot, so, rather than attract attention by trying to pull the girls out of there, he'd gone back to his truck, sat, and waited. Then he'd followed the girls to this strip club. Nice enough place. Lots of good old boys, drinking beer while they hooted and hollered at the girls. The two girls he'd followed put on some kind of show. The tall blonde with the big boobs and the shorter, dark-haired girl with the nice behind turned the club on its ear with their girl-on-girl action. Got these country boys all riled up. It had given him a chance to make sure that the dark-haired girl was Julia. Fact was, he'd thought it was her when he'd gotten his first good look at her walking out of Angela's townhouse.

She bore a distinct resemblance to the girl in the painting back in Julia's apartment.

Yelling her name when she was up on stage was just a formality. All he had to do now was grab her, take her back to Brannigan, and then get the word out that Conor needed to show his face or his girl would soon be missing important parts. Things were coming together. As soon as he finished peeing, he'd pull her out of her dressing room, shove her in his truck, and get this party started.

A young buck walked into the restroom—beefy boy with a moustache and a curly-haired mullet. There were five open urinals, but the boy took the urinal next to Cracker and started pissing. He stood six inches taller than Cracker and was so wide that he bumped Cracker's shoulder, mumbling "Sorry" while he did his business.

"No problem, son," said Cracker. He turned and pissed on the boy's leg.

The boy jumped back. Cracker aimed for the boy's shoe, wetted it down a bit, and then zipped up while the boy huffed and puffed.

"I'm gonna kick your ass," said the boy, looking downright shocked at the hot piss on his shoe.

Cracker stepped to the sink and washed his hands.

"You hear me?" said the big country boy, following him. "You're going home with your teeth in a bag, mister."

The boy grabbed Cracker's shoulder. Cracker snatched the boy's hand and twisted it back against the joint, lowering him to his knees.

"Don't touch on me," said Cracker. "That's what got you pissed on to begin with."

"Okay, okay," said the country boy. "I give."

Cracker released the boy's hand and walked over to the paper towel dispenser. The dispenser was stainless, showing Cracker a distorted reflection of the country boy walking up behind him with a cocked fist.

"Son, hold on," said Cracker, doing an about-face. He wiped his hand and tossed the paper towel on the floor. "You look a man in the eye when you fight him. Take your best shot."

The country boy flexed his fists. He looked confused. "What are… What's the trick?"

Cracker shrugged. "No trick. Just get a move on. I got business, and you're holding me up."

The country boy reared back and threw a hard right. Cracker tucked his chin, taking the punch on top of his head. He heard the boy's hand crack on his skull. He looked up. The boy cradled his hand, his teeth gritted in pain. Cracker slashed an elbow into the boy's temple, drove a knee into his crotch, and helped his downward progress with a right to the back of his head.

The boy twitched a few times and went still.

Cracker wiped his brow. That punch opened a cut on top of his head. He bent over the sink, splashed cold water on his head, and then straightened, pressing paper towels against the cut. God damn it all. It was going to be hard to keep a low profile while he was bleeding like a stuck pig. If asked by the law, people would recall the sight of a big, bloody hillbilly traipsing through the club right before Julia disappeared. He sighed and crumbled another handful of towels, pressing them against the cut on his head.

A handful of men came in while he tended to his head. A couple pulled up short and walked out when they saw the boy on the floor. Cracker knew they'd tell the club's bouncers what they saw, and he didn't have time to mess with bouncers. He dabbed at his wound one more time, then looked in the mirror. Blood oozed, but not too awful. He ran a comb through his hair. It didn't cooperate, sticking out here and there, but it would have to do. He exited the restroom and made a beeline for the dressing room Julia and Angela had ducked into after their dance.

He glanced back at the restroom as he walked.

That boy had slowed him down, but things never went exactly the way you planned them. The key was to adapt to changes in the operational environment and keep your eye on the goal. That's how things got done in this world, like kidnapping beautiful, little Julia, and—if it came to it—taking her apart piece-by-piece until Conor came to heel.

* * *

Conor drove around the back of Sweeties and wedged the Camaro next to a Mustang by the dumpster. He got out and tried the back door of the club. It was locked. He ran around to the front, hoping that Ronnie was right, that Julia was dancing here.

He paid the cover and walked into Sweeties. It was dim inside. A big, circular bar dominated the middle of the club. Girls twirled around poles on a stage built inside the perimeter of the bar, gyrating to the music. Some of the girls walked on top of the bar, high-stepping around the beer bottles, glasses of whiskey, and shots of liquor. Conor pushed to the front of the bar and checked out the girls. They were all super-hot, but they weren't as pretty as Julia. A bartender came over.

"What can I get you?"

"Looking for a girl. Julia Terranova. She work here?" said Conor.

The bartender shook his head. "Don't know. You want a drink?"

Conor held his hand below his chin. "She's about this tall. Shoulder-length dark hair. Big eyes."

The bartender shrugged.

Conor started to step away. He touched his cheek. "Big scar? Girl with a big scar on her face?"

"Oh yeah," said the bartender. "She's something. Just finished a set with Angela. I think they're in the dressing room."

"Where's that?"

The bartender pointed at a curtain around the back side of the bar.

Conor fought through the crowd to the curtain. He went to step through the curtain and walked straight into a girl coming out. She was tan, blonde, tall, had big boobs, and looked worried.

"Is Julia Terranova in there?" he said, holding the girl by her shoulders.

"Damn," she said, studying him. "Are you Conor?"

Conor relaxed his grip on her. "How'd you know?"

Angela squeezed his biceps and slapped his shoulder.

"You're all muscle," she said, smiling. "Can you fight?"

"I'd rather not," said Conor. "Where's Julia?"

"Follow me," she said, pulling him through the crowd. "I'm her friend, Angela. A lowlife little rat took your girlfriend."

Conor followed Angela toward a curtained off section of the club. "What rat?" he said as they stopped in front of the club's private lap dance area.

Billy Kelley stepped through the curtain and stopped in front of Conor.

"That rat," said Angela, pointing at Billy. "He took her to get raped by a pervert."

Conor turned his attention to the little man. He was one hundred percent hick. Long hair and a gold front tooth twinkling in the club's strobe lights. The man looked at Conor, then at Angela.

"What's going on here?" said Billy.

Conor turned to Angela. "You sure this is the guy?"

Angela grinned. "Positive."

Conor snatched Billy's shirt and wobbled him with a backhand. "Where is she?" he said.

Billy looked around, his eyes wild. "What are you talking about? Who are you?"

Conor looked at Angela. "You know where she is?"

"Yeah," said Angela.

Conor grabbed the back of Billy's head with both hands, pulled it down, and drove his knee into the hick's mouth. Billy's gold tooth bounced on the floor and spun out of sight. Billy fell on his face, unconscious.

Angela searched Billy's pockets. She pulled out a key ring. "Follow me," she said.

Conor grabbed Billy by the hair and dragged him through the white curtain. A body on the floor would bring attention he didn't need. He threw Billy onto a white leather couch. Heavy bass music throbbed through the room. It was curtained off into four sections, and he could see the shadows of strippers giving lap dances to their clients behind the curtains. He turned to Angela. "Where is she?"

Angela grabbed Conor by a belt loop and pulled him toward the bar in front of the curtained back wall. She pushed him behind the bar and handed him the key ring.

"Pull back that curtain and unlock the door," she said. "Julia's in there."

Conor did as she asked. He stepped into darkness.

He heard rattling, like chains, and a muffled scream. He moved toward the muffled scream. His thigh bumped something. He reached out and his head exploded with pain.

He dropped to all fours. A kick caught him in the ribs. He rolled over. A foot came down on his stomach, stomping the air out of him. He curled up, waiting for the next blow.

Then he heard rattling.

And gagging.

He pushed off the floor. The overhead lights in the room popped on, blinding him. He squinted.

Angela was across the room, her hand on a light switch. An old fat guy in hot pink bikini bottoms with a hard on stood over him, holding a nightstick. The fat guy dropped the nightstick, fighting to unwrap a set of chains wrapped around his throat. Julia stood behind him on the bed. She was gagged, wearing nothing but a G-string, strangling the guy with chains she'd wrapped around his throat. Handcuffs on her wrists and ankles were attached to the chains, which ran through eyelets welded into the top of the bed's four posters and trailed up to an anchor in the ceiling.

Conor buried a punch in the guy's stomach. The man slumped, but the chains around his neck kept him upright. Julia unwrapped the chain from his neck, letting him crumple to the floor.

"Get those cuffs off her," said Angela, taking a set of keys off a hook on the wall and throwing them to Conor.

"You okay?" said Conor, unlocking the handcuffs around Julia's wrists.

As soon as her hands were free, Julia pulled off her gag.

She watched Conor unlock the handcuffs on her ankles, then she jumped off the bed, bending over the man on the ground. "You sick fuck!" she screamed, kicking him in the face.

Conor pulled Julia away. She bared her teeth and fought to land another kick.

"Take it easy," said Conor. "You're gonna break your foot."

Julia caught her breath.

"I'm gonna let you go now," said Conor. "Okay?"

She nodded.

He released her and looked at the man who was moaning and rolled up into the fetal position. A flash of recognition ran through him. "Is that your old boyfriend? The one that tried to rape you in Brannigan?"

Julia pushed by Conor and stared down at James. "Yeah, and he's gonna be dead when I'm done with him."

"We don't have time for this," said Conor. "We gotta go." He watched Julia look around, grab a set of handcuffs off the floor, and then snap one on James' wrist and the other on the frame of the bed.

James stopped moaning long enough to look at the handcuff on his wrist. He lifted his gaze to Julia, Conor, and Angela.

"What do you think you're doing? The chief of police is a friend of mine. You do anything to me and I'll make sure all of you rot in prison."

"We need to go," said Angela, grabbing Julia's hand.

"Don't worry. *We're* not going to do anything to you," said Julia, looking down on James with a smile as Angela pulled her away.

Conor turned at the sound of murmuring and shuffling behind them. People were crowded at the open door, staring at the scene. Grabbing a black stiletto from the floor and one from the bed, Conor handed them to Julia, then pulled off his white T-shirt and gave it to her.

"Get those shoes and shirt on. Let's go," he said, wiping

blood off his hand. He looked at the stiletto as Julia slipped it on her foot. Blood dripped off the heel, which looked to be a perfect match for the two bloody holes in James Stockton's face—one in his cheek and another in the side of his neck. Conor shook his head. That was twice this sack of shit had tried to have his way with Julia. Both times he ended up bleeding on the floor. It was enough to make Conor believe in a higher power. Not that life was fair, or anything like that. Just that sometimes, just when things reached their bleakest point, unknown powers seemed to intervene. He grabbed Julia's hand, hoping her guardian angel was still in the vicinity. They might need a little more help tonight.

The people clustered around the doorway backed up as Conor led Julia and Angela out of the room. Julia pulled away from Conor in the middle of the crowd, still smiling. She pointed back at James, sitting on the floor with his belly overlapping his pink bikini underwear. "Take a good look at James Stockton, superintendent of the Woodlands School District. The man who looks after your children. The man who raped me. You should hear what he says about your little girls." She stopped and scanned the crowd of bikers, laborers, and other hard men who worked in the underbelly of the economy. "And what he says about your little boys."

Conor grabbed her wrist and yanked her out of the crowd surging through the door. James strangled cry rose above the shouts of the people as he pulled her away.

Conor walked Julia through the club toward the front door and pulled to a stop. The guy at the front door was a typical three-hundred-pound bouncer. His eyes were pinned on them. Conor whispered, "Stay behind me," to Angela and Julia. He approached the door man. The giant got off his stool and eyeballed the two women behind Conor. He folded his arms over his chest, lifted his chin, and shook his head.

"Sorry. Can't let the dancers leave the club until we're

closed."

There wasn't time for this. Whatever was happening to James back in that room was certain to alert the bouncers, and there were more in this club than he could deal with. They needed to get out. Now.

Conor gestured for the girls to stay put. He walked up to the door man and looked up at him. The man grinned. He wasn't going to move, not without a fight. But all Conor wanted him to do was back up. To give them room to pass. So, still staring up at the giant, he dropped a boot heel on his foot. That backed him up, but he was still in the way. Conor drove a kick into the side of his knee. The man's leg folded. He screamed and toppled like a tree struck by lightning. Conor stepped over him and ushered the girls past him into the parking lot.

Conor jumped into his Camaro and cranked the engine.

Angela got into her bumblebee-yellow Mustang parked alongside the Camaro. It roared to life.

Julia stopped and looked at one car, and then the other.

"Get in," yelled Angela through her open window.

Julia ran around to the passenger side of the Camaro. "We'll follow you," she yelled, waving for Angela to go.

Conor watched Angela stare at Julia for a long moment before she backed up and spun out of the lot, spitting gravel. He stayed right on her tail as she tore down the country roads. He had to floor it in the straightaways to keep up with her.

If he didn't know any better, he would've guessed she was trying to lose him.

CHAPTER TWENTY-SEVEN

Angela followed Julia into the town house.

"Tell Conor to come in," said Angela. "You guys can stay the night. After what you've been through, you need to rest."

"No," said Julia. "We're leaving. I just need to grab my stuff."

Julia ran upstairs into Angela's bedroom. She slipped into a pair of jeans and Chuck Taylor low-tops. She thought about putting on a clean shirt but decided to keep Conor's shirt on. It smelled too good to take off. She zipped up her suitcase as Angela walked in.

"So that's it, huh?" said Angela. "You're leaving with him."

"I gotta go," said Julia, pulling her suitcase toward the door.

Angela reached in her purse and pulled out a stack of money.

"Here," said Angela, holding out the money. "You're gonna need it."

Julia ignored the money and tried to step around her, but Angela grabbed her arm.

""I tried to tell you not to go with Billy," Angela said, shoving the money into Julia's pocket. She hugged Julia.

Julia stood stiff and frozen.

Angela finished her hug and pulled away, her eyes

welling with tears. "I'm sorry," she said.

"You should be," said Julia. "I would've never done that to you."

Angela hung her head.

Julia pushed by her and pulled her suitcase down the stairs.

* * *

The trunk of the Camaro closed with a bang. Conor jumped in the driver's seat. "What about your car?" said Conor. "You just gonna leave it here?"

Julia turned her gaze to the townhouse where Angela watched them from her bedroom window. She reached over and laid her hand on Conor's leg. "Just get me out of here."

The cool night air ruffled Julia's hair as Conor drove down the interstate. She closed her eyes and sat back. Conor held her hand.

"Did James do anything to you?" he asked.

She smiled. "No. But he got what he deserved."

Conor squeezed her hand. "Yeah. That was kinda… uh, hardcore how you got that crowd all riled up. Not that there was anything wrong with it."

She pulled Conor's T-shirt against her face, breathing in his scent. "Whatever they did to him is fine by me. Just wish I could've watched. You got there just in time. He'd just got that last cuff on me and could've done anything he wanted. I was freaking out."

"Don't thank me," said Conor. "Thank Angela. I would've never found you without her."

"She's the reason I was in there," said Julia.

Conor glanced over. "What?"

"Just drive," said Julia.

They were out of town and on the highway when Julia finally calmed down. She shouldn't have been surprised that

Angela sold her out. People always found a way to let her down. Even Conor. The only difference was that Conor came looking for her. He did something bad for sure, but he followed that up with something good. Was he good or was he bad? She watched the wind blow his long hair. His face was tan. She could see a scar that ran through his eyebrow. He hadn't shaved in a few days. Every muscle on his bare torso stood out in the moonlight, his ribs flexing with each breath. Maybe he was both. And for right now, she had to say that if it was a race, good was in the lead. He glanced over and smiled.

"I can't believe I found you," he said.

"Neither can I."

"Some bikers told me you were dancing at that club. If I got there one minute later—I don't even want to think what could've happened."

She put her hand on his thigh, sliding her finger through a rip in the knee of his jeans. "Why did you come looking for me? " She watched him stare straight ahead, driving into the darkness.

He glanced over. "I had to." He shrugged. "I don't know, I just kept thinking about you."

She pointed at a green sign appearing out of the darkness. "Take that exit."

It was a country road. Nothing for miles. Fields that stretched like oceans bordered the road, painted silver by the moonlight. A towering stand of trees lifted from the horizon. Julia slid her hand over Conor's bare chest and stomach. She pointed at the trees. "Pull over there."

Conor pulled onto the shoulder in front of the trees. A dirt road led into the trees. He eased down the road, stopping in a field circled by towering trees. He put the car in Park and cut the ignition. Julia ran her hands over his bare arms. His chest. His stomach. He lifted her onto his lap.

She buried her face in his neck. Smelling him. Kissing him. The leaves in the trees rustled, hushing everything around them.

He pulled her shirt off. Her skin felt hot. He kissed her neck and ran his hands up her back. "Hold on," he said, reaching under the front of his seat. He slid the seat back and then pushed the back of his seat down until he was flat on his back. He looked up at Julia.

She straddled him and stared into his eyes. He unbuttoned her jeans. She slid out of them while he pulled his off. The warm summer air swirled around Julia as she repositioned herself on top of him. She felt him harden under her. His hands slid up her thighs, up her back, then cupped her breasts. He licked one nipple, then the other. She reached between her legs and grabbed him. She spread her legs and rubbed against him.

"I want you," she said, feeling his mouth on her breast.

She guided him in. She ran her hands over his muscled back and shoulders. She laid back and pulled him on top of her, feeling him push in deep. She felt him tightening, every muscle hardening. Waves rolled through her, lifting her. She lost herself, falling into his rhythm. She gasped and rocked under him. A primal release exploded through her, covering everything she felt and smelled and saw and tasted and breathed in shimmering gold. Then it faded, leaving her in its warm glow.

She went slack, breathing hard. Everything seemed brighter. Conor looked down with a smile. The moon framed his head. Her heart swelled as he kissed her.

"You're beautiful," he said.

He laid next to her. She trailed her fingernails over his chest as she looked at the moon shining through the trees. He played with her hair, circling a finger around her ear.

She laid her head on his shoulder, looking into the sky with him.

"I'm sorry I didn't show up the other night," he said. "Somebody chased me. I had to jump off a bridge to get away. Went by your place the next day, but you were gone. But I don't blame you for leaving. If someone left me hanging like that, I would've left too."

Julia sighed. "I left before you came to pick me up."

He turned to stare at her.

She laid her head on his bare chest, listening to his heartbeat. "I saw you and your friends breaking into Sacred Heart Cathedral."

"You what?" he said, sitting up.

"I went to drop off my resignation letter at the rectory. I heard someone breaking into the church. I went in and saw you and your friends by the safe. You were trying to steal from the church."

"That safe was empty," said Conor, grabbing his jeans off the floorboard. "And these guys jumped us. Sully ended up in a coma. Fitz took off—I don't even know where he is. And now I have guys looking for me."

"I don't know who Fitz and Sully are," said Julia, sitting up to slip into her G-string. "But I'm guessing that whatever happened to them is karma for trying to steal from a church."

Conor looked at her. "There was supposed to be gold in that safe. I did it for us."

"What are you talking about? What gold?"

"Like a chalice and, you know, other Catholic stuff."

Julia shook her head. "If anything was in that safe, it wasn't yours to take. You work a job to make money. You don't steal it from a church."

"You're a stripper and I fix cars," he said, then huffed. "I was doing it for us."

"Not for me. Stealing is wrong."

Conor pulled on his jeans. "Really? Everyone with money is doing something wrong. Lying politicians. Crooked businessmen. And these churches aren't any better. You should know that by now."

"I do," said Julia. "But there are limits. You don't steal from your family. Old people—"

"And churches. I know."

"Forget about the church thing. You don't steal from people trying to do the right thing," said Julia.

His eyes flashed. "I'm tired of doing the right thing and still ending up on the bottom."

He ducked down to tie his shoes. Julia slid her hand up his back, tangling her fingers in his long hair. She watched his shoulder muscles flex, then shifted her gaze to the moon and whispered, "A man who's pure of heart and says his prayers by night may still become a wolf when the autumn moon is bright."

Conor straightened. "What?"

"Nothing." She twirled her finger around a lock of his hair. "So, what do we do now?"

He looked at the moon, then lowered his gaze to her. She smiled. He took a deep breath. "We're going to stay with a friend of mine. We have something planned. And it's not a church. It's what they call 'a victimless crime.' After I finish and get paid, we'll start a new life. Find someplace to grow old together."

"I have a question," she said, tugging his hair.

"Ow," he said.

"Who's your friend?"

"His name's Angel," said Conor. "He owns the garage where I work."

"Why aren't we staying in your apartment?"

"Don't you listen? People are looking for me."

Julia bit her bottom lip and nodded. "So, we're hiding out?"

"Yeah. Any more questions?"

"There's always more."

"Go on."

"What's this 'something' you have planned?"

Conor took a moment, then said, "I can't get into it. Maybe later, after I talk to Angel. But for now, you're gonna have to trust me."

"I don't know if I can."

"Well, you either trust me, or you don't. If you don't, I'll take you wherever you want, drop you off, and never bother you again."

Conor stared at her. He could see her thinking it over, struggling with her answer. He knew the answer he wanted, and he stared at her, willing her to say it.

She took a deep breath and said, "Okay. I trust you, but I have one more question before I go with you."

He smiled, feeling good about his chances.

"After you finish your 'victimless crime…'"

"Yeah."

"And get the money…"

"Yeah."

"Where are we going to grow old together?"

Conor grabbed her face and touched his forehead to hers. "Wherever you want."

Julia felt his soft kiss, then watched him start the car, drive out of the forest, and pull onto the road. She watched the wind whip his hair. She looked over his scarred face and muscled body. She closed her eyes, leaned back, and smiled.

It was going to be fun watching Conor grow old. He was going to be a good-looking old guy.

CHAPTER TWENTY-EIGHT

Things were not going as planned. Not at all.

Cracker spun on his heels and walked out of Sweeties' dressing room. There were two girls in there, neither of which was Julia Terranova. One of the girls got lippy when he'd asked her where Julia was, but she'd settled down after a smack in the mouth. She talked and made a lot of sense after that. If Julia wasn't on the stage and she wasn't in the dressing room, there was only one other place she could be. Cracker stalked across the club toward the curtained-off lap dance area. A crowd was gathered outside the area, and everyone was in a tizzy. He bulled his way to the front and was met by a line of bouncers.

He walked up to a bouncer and said, "I got somebody I need to see in there."

The bouncer crossed his arms. "Not tonight you don't."

Cracker sized up the bouncer. He looked around and counted four more. Getting through all of them would be all kinds of trouble. And even if he managed it, there was no way he'd be able to pull Julia out of there without bringing the whole club down on his head. He waded back through the crowd, walked over to the bar, and took a seat. He'd wait for Julia to come out. Patience had always been kind to him in the past, no matter what problem stood before him. Maybe it would give him a helping hand tonight.

Thirty minutes later, the lap dance area opened for

business. Cracker paid close attention. Lots of strippers and country boys walked out, but no Julia. The only point of interest was a wiry hillbilly holding a bloody rag against his mouth with one hand and a pair of bloody handcuffs in the other. The hillbilly appeared to be none too pleased with the situation. He threw the bloody handcuffs across the room, then stalked toward the bar, holding the rag against his mouth while he yelled, "Angela!" over and over.

It only took a minute of the hillbilly's yelling for Cracker to see that Angela was not on the premises. And that got him thinking.

Angela was the girl that Julia listed as a reference.

She was the one who'd driven Julia here.

She was the girl who'd danced with Julia.

If Angela was gone, chances were Julia was with her. Cracker hissed. He'd been concentrating all his energy on Julia when he should've been watching both girls. He finished the soda water and lime he'd been nursing, put a dollar on the bar, and walked toward the exit.

The girls had slipped out, quiet as smoke, and their exit probably had something to do with the bloody-mouthed hillbilly flailing around. But hell, it didn't matter. He knew where Angela lived.

He hopped in his truck.

He and Angela were gonna have themselves a chat.

* * *

Cracker cursed his luck as he closed Angela's front door, cutting off the sounds of her sobbing. He shook his head and walked to his truck. The crying, for once, wasn't due to him. The moment he brought up the name 'Julia,' Angela had broken down. She wasn't able to help a lick with telling him where Julia was headed, but Lord that girl could cry.

He got in his truck and dug a protein bar out of a grocery bag. He chewed and swallowed, breathing through his nose, feeling angry for the first time in a long time. He started his truck, backed out of Angela's parking lot, and drove away.

This current string of events was troubling. But Angela did give one useful piece of information. She'd said Julia had left with Conor Monroe. That meant Conor had been in the strip club. Conor had been in his reach, and he'd missed him. Cracker punched the dash.

"Probably when I was playing games with that boy in the bathroom," he said.

He touched the cut in the top of his head. Tonight had been nothing but a big waste of time. He jammed half the protein bar in his mouth and chewed with his mouth open. Worst of all was how the situation had changed. If Conor Monroe had Julia, she couldn't be used as leverage.

Cracker slowed as he saw a sign for the interstate.

So, what should he do? Drive away? Or continue the search for Conor?

He clucked his tongue and eased into the exit lane toward Brannigan.

There was a chance Conor was right now driving to some no-name town with Julia, but something told Cracker that wasn't the deal. He'd learned long ago to trust his intuition, and right now it told him that Conor was going home. But there was no telling how long he'd stay there, knowing that Duck wanted him dead. Chances were, if he was heading home, he wouldn't be there long. It was time to either catch him or forget about him.

Cracker turned on the radio. Once he got back to Brannigan, Conor's world was going to bear the brunt of a search and destroy campaign. Every individual the man knew was going to enjoy the pleasure of Cracker's company until he showed his face.

Cracker picked a piece of protein bar from between his teeth. He stomped on the gas.

And once Conor did show his face, it was getting smashed bloody.

* * *

"Shhhh."

Conor waited for Julia to nod before lowering his finger from his lips. It was doubtful that one of Duck's men was watching Angel's garage past two in the morning, but now wasn't the time to be lazy.

He held Julia's hand, guided her around to the back of the garage, unlocked the door, and pulled her inside.

Julia looked around. Two small emergency exit lights cast a dim light through the two car bays. One of the bays had a car up on a lift. She turned to Conor. "Where are we?"

"Follow me," he whispered. He led her into Angel's office and turned on a desk lamp.

"We can sleep there," he said, pointing at the couch.

"Where's the bathroom?" she said.

"Through the door to the right."

She slipped out the door. He could hear the muffled sound of her pissing. The toilet flushed. She walked through the office door. He took her by the hand, led her to the couch, and sat, pulling her into his lap. He kissed her neck. She slipped her hand under his shirt.

"My dad or boss could walk in any second," he said.

"I don't care," she whispered.

He undressed her. He explored, touching every inch of her. They made love slowly this time. Carefully. It was just as passionate as the car, but there was no rush. Just the feel of each other's body. The taste of each other. He had no idea what time it was when they were done, but he was spent. He fell back on the couch, catching his breath. Julia laid her head on his shoulder, her body slippery with sweat.

He rubbed her leg, listening to her breathe. He and Angel and his dad were stealing those paintings the day after tomorrow, which meant that he could relax and catch up on his sleep tomorrow. He wiped sweat off his face. Good thing—he needed the rest.

Julia sighed and pulled tight against him.

Conor smiled and closed his eyes.

* * *

Sunlight shone through the block glass windows set high in Angel's cinderblock walls. Conor looked at his jeans hanging over the back of the couch. His shoes and underwear were on the floor. Sliding his arm out from under Julia's head, he picked up his clothes and got dressed. The door to the office opened.

Angel took a step into the room and froze.

Julia sat up, holding a blanket around her chest.

"You must be Angel," she said. She dropped the blanket and grabbed Conor's white T-shirt off the floor, pulling it over her head. Looking around the room, she walked over to her jeans lying in a crumpled ball on the floor by Angel's desk. "I'm Julia," she said, picking up her jeans.

Conor stepped in front of Julia while she pulled on her jeans. He raised an eyebrow at Angel. "You mind?"

Angel backed out of the room. "Nice meeting you, Julia," he said, then wagged a finger at Conor, saying, "You're a bad boy," as he closed the door.

Conor turned to Julia. Angel's voice boomed from the garage. "You're paying to have that couch cleaned Conor."

"He's funny," said Julia.

Conor put on his shoes. He walked over to Julia and hugged her from behind.

"There's a shower downstairs," he said. "Angel has donuts, coffee, and orange juice out in the garage."

"Save me a donut," she said. "I'll see you in ten minutes."

He enjoyed the view as she walked out.

* * *

Conor ate breakfast with Julia in the customer waiting area. A glass wall provided a view of the garage. Conor watched Angel walk around with a clipboard, taking inventory. Conor knew the drill.

After inventory, Angel would close the garage to pick up parts in his truck, which would probably take the whole morning. Conor touched his pocket holding the keys to the Camaro. That would give him time to drive Julia to the hospital. Even though Sully was in a coma, he wanted her to meet him. He looked her over. Jeans and a tight black muscle shirt looked good on her. If anything would wake Sully up, it would be a hot girl like Julia.

A tap on the glass caught Conor's attention.

"Going out for parts," said Angel, waving the clipboard. "Keep everything locked up. I'll be back around noon."

"Bring back lunch," said Conor.

"What do you want?" said Angel.

Julia banged on the glass. "I want barbecue ribs," she said. "And coleslaw and potato salad. And beer—lots of beer."

The look on Angel's face was priceless. He stared at Julia, then shifted his gaze to Conor, who smiled. Angel lifted his pen, licked the end of it, and pointed it at Conor. "This is coming out of your end of the job," he shouted, writing down Julia's order.

Five minutes after Angel left, Conor was in the Camaro with Julia. He parked on the side of the hospital and walked in the emergency entrance, not wanting to take a chance of bumping into the wrong person.

He told Julia about Sully as they rode the elevator up—how they'd been friends since they were kids. He laid off on their criminal background but did fill her in on what happened at the church. How Barry's crew surprised them and put Sully in a coma. And how Sully was still in that coma.

Conor noticed that Julia hung back a bit as they went in Sully's room. He sat next to the bed, holding Sully's hand. Sully's tan had faded, but he was still handsome with his long, wavy, black hair. Even better, he was breathing on his own. Not talking yet, but breathing was a start. Julia would like him if he could talk. He was like a little kid—all energy and no filters, which girls seemed to find attractive. Conor patted Sully's hand, hoping he'd be talking soon.

"Did the doctors say what's wrong with him?" Julia whispered, still standing near the door.

"He doesn't bite," said Conor. He stood and lifted Sully's hand. "Hold his hand."

She walked over and reached for Sully's hand.

Conor wasn't positive, but he thought it happened at the exact moment Julia touched him. A mumble.

Julia gasped, backing away. "Did I do something wrong?"

"Sully," said Conor. "You awake?"

Sully opened his eyes. Then he closed them.

"Open your eyes," said Conor, grabbing Sully's face.

Sully opened his eyes again. He pushed Conor's hands away and rasped, "My head hurts."

Julia ran out of the room and yelled for a doctor. Conor squeezed Sully's hand. His heart was pounding so hard it felt like it was going to burst.

"Where am I?" said Sully.

Conor wiped away a tear and smiled. "You're here, buddy. With me. Just take it easy. Everything's fine."

The doctors chased Conor out of Sully's room. On his way to the elevators, Sully's mom and sister, Mona, rushed by. Conor kept his head down and ducked into the elevator with Julia. If Mona saw him, she would've gone ballistic, blaming him for Sully's coma. But it didn't matter now. He grinned. Sully was back.

The sky seemed sunnier as he drove back to Angel's garage. Sneaking back into Angel's garage, he felt happy for the first time in a long time. He found Julia. A big payday was coming his way for those paintings. Sully was out of his coma. His dad had even stopped drinking.

He couldn't believe it.

Everything was coming together.

His lucky streak continued as he walked into Angel's garage with Julia. Just as he pocketed his keys, he heard the front door of the shop open, followed by Angel yelling, "Little help." He looked at a clock hanging in the garage and whistled under his breath.

"What?" said Julia.

He walked toward the front of the shop. "We got back just in time," he whispered. "Angel would kill me if he knew I took the car out."

"Why?"

"Because the guys looking for me would torch this place if they knew I was here. Just don't tell Angel we went out, okay?"

In the lobby there was a white cardboard box on the front counter next to a bag of charcoal and a grocery bag. The front door swung open. Angel pushed his way in carrying two more grocery bags.

"Move everything into the garage by the grill," said Angel. "I'll meet you over there—I gotta get the beer out of my truck."

Conor took the grocery bags from Angel and handed them to Julia. Then he stacked the charcoal and other groceries on top of the cardboard box on the counter, lifted the whole shebang, and walked by Julia. "Follow me," he said. "It's time to party."

Conor stacked all the supplies on a metal tool bench next to a barbecue grill, leaving room for the two cases of beer Angel carried over. The bottles rattled as Angel set the cases down. Angel ripped one of the cases open, took out a bottle, and opened it, foam spilling over his hand as he took a drink.

"Get 'em while they're cold, people," Angel said, beer dripping over his hand on to the cement floor. "Angel's garage is officially closed." He pointed at Julia. "You wanted ribs? Well, you got 'em. I make the best ribs in town."

"Way to go, Julia," said Conor, grabbing a bottle of beer. He shook it and popped the cap, spraying Julia. She shrieked, covering her face. "Look what you did," he said, wiping beer off her face. He kissed her. "Now we have to eat Angel's lousy ribs."

"And that's not all, brother," said Angel. "We also have a special guest joining us."

Conor turned toward the sound of a door opening.

"Am I late?" said a man, holding two grocery bags.

Conor looked at Angel. "Who the hell—" he said, then put his beer down to walk across the garage. He stopped in front of the man. "Dad?"

The grocery bags rustled as his father repositioned his grip on them.

Conor stared. The man in front of him wasn't his dad. His dad was the homeless bum with long gray matted hair and a tangled beard. His dad slept in back alleys, wore filthy clothes, and pissed himself. This was a man from a long time ago, someone Conor had idolized as a kid. Conor walked around his father, checking him out.

His hair was cut and combed. He was clean shaven. His eyes were clear.

Conor turned to Angel. "What happened?"

"After he got off the booze, he asked if I could take him clothes shopping," said Angel. "We got him some jeans, a new shirt, shoes, haircut, shave—the works." Angel smiled. "Looks good, right?"

Conor couldn't speak. He turned toward his dad.

"Is this the girl you were telling me about?" his dad said, walking toward Julia.

"Yeah," said Conor. "This is Julia."

Conor watched his dad stop in front of Julia and put down the grocery bags to hug her.

"Hi, Mr. Monroe," she said.

Conor's dad held her by the shoulders as he stepped back, smiled, and said, "Call me Mickey."

Conor walked over. As clean and shaved and well dressed as his father was, Conor noticed that his hands were trembling. This was day three of cold turkey. Conor gripped his dad's hand.

"How you doing?" he said.

His dad pulled his hand away. He picked up his grocery bags. "Better than ever," he said, handing a bag to Julia. "Help me shuck this corn, Julia. I want to hear all about you."

Conor watched his dad and Julia walk into the lobby, set the grocery bags on the counter, and then sit on stools next to each other. Julia tilted her head back, laughing at something his father said as he dumped sweet corn on the counter. Conor watched in rapt amazement. His chest felt like it was going to bust.

"Doesn't look too bad, huh?" said Angel.

"I can't believe it," said Conor. Angel's hand clapped the back of his neck and squeezed.

"Let's fire up the grill," said Angel.

Conor watched Angel lift the back bay door facing the alley. He pointed at the open bay door. "Is that a good idea?" he said in a loud whisper.

Angel rolled the grill over to the open bay door and poured the charcoal in. "If you're worried about Duck and Artie's guys, don't. I drove around the block and didn't see anybody. And I parked my parts van at one end of the alley, and my truck at the other." He shoved newspaper under the charcoal, lit it, and looked at Conor. "We're good."

Angel then turned on an old boom box. Music filled the garage. Conor drank a beer while he watched Angel cover the tool bench with brown butcher paper, cut the ribs, and pat them with his homemade barbecue rub. It wasn't long before the first slabs were on the grill, sweating under low heat. Conor finished his beer and grabbed another while Angel fiddled with the flue on the grill. The man was a perfectionist when it came to cooking. Hell, he was a perfectionist when it came to anything. The smell of cooking meat wafted through the garage. Conor sipped his beer. This was going to be good.

Finally satisfied that everything was set just right, Angel

closed the grill. He looked at Julia and Mickey shucking corn in the lobby before settling his gaze on Conor.

"You ready for the job tomorrow?" he said.

Conor nodded. "Yeah."

"Good," said Angel, walking over to the boom box. He turned off the radio, flipped through a box of CDs and loaded a few. The first riff of Lynyrd Skynyrd's *Saturday Night Special* kicked in.

"Here we go," said Conor. "Somebody get my rocking chair."

"Have some respect for your elders," said Angel, dragging a cooler over to the cases of beer.

Conor laughed. Angel was old school to the bone. Fun guy when you knew him, but not to be messed with. Conor watched him put beers in the cooler. A shaft of sunlight fell across Angel's face while he worked. A few gray hairs stood out in his shiny black hair that was pulled back into a ponytail—pale threads of silver announcing that time was working its magic. Angel had always been—and would always be—an icon. Biker. Businessman. Thief. Fighter. He was even supposed to have been in some special unit back when he was in the Army—Special Ops or something like that. Conor watched him walk out of the garage and disappear in the back office. He returned with a bag of ice and poured it into the cooler. Angel was a man's man. Conor sipped his beer as Angel kicked the cooler lid closed. But the gray in Angel's hair reminded Conor that if he wanted to do something with his life, he had to do it fast. Getting old happened to everyone.

Angel opened a fresh beer as he walked over.

"So," said Angel. "You have any questions about the job?" He sipped his beer, keeping an eye on the grill. "Anything that could be a problem?"

"Nothing I can think of," said Conor.

"You sure?" said Angel, studying Conor.

Conor picked at the label on his beer bottle. "Those ribs okay for a couple minutes?"

"Sure," said Angel.

Conor waved for Angel to follow. "Let me show you something."

Five minutes later Conor turned away from the computer and looked at Angel.

"Duck hired this guy to kill me," said Conor, nodding at the monitor. "Fortunately, he has no idea where I am, so I'm safe. But you asked if there's anything that could be a problem. I'm guessing this guy could be a big one."

Angel tapped the frozen image of Joe Cracker Jones on the screen. Cracker was bent over an opponent, his mouth wide open, his tattooed tongue sticking out as he screamed his rebel yell. His fist was coming down in a blur, on its way to breaking the jaw of ex-light heavyweight champ, Andy Volcano Vata.

"This isn't good," said Angel.

"I know."

Angel shook his head. "Turn it off," he said, walking out of his office.

Conor followed Angel into the garage. He watched Angel open the grill and flip the ribs. Each flip conjured a sizzle and a plume of smoke. Mick Jagger grunted from the boom box along with the tribal beat of *Sympathy for the Devil.* Angel glanced at the boom box, then back at Conor.

"So, how do you know this Joe Cracker Jones guy is after you?" said Angel.

"He wrote me a note saying so," said Conor.

A wrinkle creased Angel's brow. "A note? How'd he get a note to you?"

"I stopped by my apartment when I went out to find Julia," said Conor. "He wrecked my place and taped a note to my television. Said Duck hired him to kill me. Said he wants to fight me to the death. The guy's mental."

Angel sighed. "I told you not to go anywhere but Julia's."

"I know. I just—"

"You could've brought everybody down on me," said Angel, narrowing his eyes.

"Sorry."

Angel stared at him.

Conor waited him out. It took a while. Angel finally turned away, tending to the ribs.

"What else did the note say?" said Angel.

"Not much," said Conor. "Stuff about me coming to him or he'd kill my family and friends."

"Which would be who?" said Angel.

"I don't know. After the church job went south, Fitz disappeared. Sully is in the hospital. And me and my dad haven't talked in years—at least as far as Cracker or anyone else knows."

Angel looked at Conor. "Well, good. Then this guy can't touch you. We'll knock the job out tomorrow and you'll take your money and run. Once Duck figures out you're gone, he'll call off the hit and everything goes back to normal."

"That's what I figured," said Conor. He finished his beer and walked over to the cooler, glancing into the lobby. His dad and Julia had finished shucking the corn but were deep in conversation. He opened the cooler and grabbed a beer. It was good to see his dad clean, sober, and happy. The butcher paper on the tool bench crinkled as he leaned against it. Angel closed the grill with a clang and wiped his hand on his jeans.

"I have a question for you," said Angel. "What if this guy did grab your dad? Or Julia? What would you do?"

"I'd find him and kick his ass."

"Really? You watch the same video I did? I'm not sure you or anyone else can kick his ass."

Conor thought about it. He'd seen more than a few videos of Cracker beating other fighters to a pulp. The man was insanely violent. Unbelievably strong. And he knew how to fight. Conor glanced over at Julia and his dad, took a deep breath, and exhaled.

"What choice would I have?" he said.

Angel shrugged. He tapped the side of his beer bottle and walked over. "Hey, I ever tell you about when I was stationed in Africa?"

"No," said Conor.

"Crazy story," said Angel. "There was this village in Somalia where these kids were disappearing. It happened at night, about once a week. Then a couple women disappeared. And finally, a full-grown man vanished, right in the middle of the day. The villagers thought it was some kind of evil spirit or maybe a warlord's gang, but a local missionary convinced them to hire a big game hunter. This British guy shows up and recons, looking for tracks, blood, whatever. It's hot. You know, the sun's nailed in the sky, blazing down. So, he walks into this field with nothing but a pistol strapped to his leg and a leopard jumps him. The guy's flat on his back, and this cat is strong. It's got fangs long as rulers. It is not fucking around. It hooks its front paws around his shoulders, opens its mouth, and tries to tear his throat out. So, what does the guy do?"

"He shoots it," said Conor.

"Can't. He needs both hands to hold it off."

"Then I guess he's dead," said Conor.

Angel nodded. "You'd think so. But the guy's a survivor. He's not going down without a fight. So, just as this maneater is about to tear his face off, he rams his fist down its throat."

"No way," said Conor.

"Swear," said Angel, holding up a hand.

"What happened?

Angel took a pull from his beer and wiped his mouth. "Damn thing went berserk. He told me he grabbed its tongue way down in its throat and held on for dear life until it died from asphyxiation or shock. Then he tracked down its lair. There were half-eaten human and animal carcasses all over the place. After he saw that, the hunter said he knew he'd met a predator that had lost its fear of everything. It scared him. According to him, that leopard was outside the flow of the universe."

Conor mulled over Angel's comments. "So, what are

you trying to tell me?" he said. "That this Cracker guy is like that?"

"Exactly," said Angel. "Based on the video we watched that guy does not care about anyone or anything. He's toxic. He's outside the flow."

"So what am I supposed to do?" asked Conor.

Angel turned at the sound of Julia and Conor's dad walking out of the lobby, carrying a bag of shucked sweet corn ready to be grilled. Angel smiled and waved them over, then turned back to Conor. "Listen. If that guy gets your dad, Julia, or anybody, you do not fight him. You do not talk to him. You do not engage with him in any way. That's the law, starting right now."

"I can't do that. He'd hurt them."

"Possibly," said Angel. "But getting yourself killed won't help."

"So, I do nothing?" said Conor.

"No," said Angel. "You most definitely do something. If you want to stay alive, you run. Without you around, he might release whoever he's got and just leave. It's your best move. At the very least, it's the only move that makes sense."

Angel turned his back, taking the bag of shucked corn from Julia. Conor sipped his beer and tried to relax, but it was impossible after hearing Angel's advice. Maybe it made sense to run, but could he do that if Cracker had Julia? Or his dad, or Fitz, or Sully, or even Angel? What if he had all of them and was making them suffer? Conor tilted his bottle back and drained it in four long swallows, feeling the beer burn down his throat. There was no way to be sure until it happened, but he was certain he couldn't step away. He'd walk straight into a dragon's mouth before he'd turn his back on anyone who meant something to him. Losing his mother and his father had taught him that. Both had run away. One for real and the other through a bottle. And to the best of this knowledge they'd survived—although he couldn't be sure when it came to his mom since he never saw her again. Even so, their running had taught him that it didn't matter *if* you survived. It mattered *how* you survived. Being broken like his father was no way to live. So, if it came down to it, he'd face Cracker. At the very least, the people who meant the most to him would know that he'd fought for them. And if by some strange roll of the dice he survived, he'd live unbroken. He glanced over at his dad, focusing on his hands that held a garbage bag of corn husks. Even gripping the bag tight, his dad couldn't hide the fact that his hands shook like he had some kind of palsy. Yeah, living unbroken had to be better than the alternative.

But, with all that said, he didn't want to test his theory.

The best outcome would be to get out without ever having to fight, talk, or even lay eyes on Joe Cracker Jones. He needed to forget about him and keep his thoughts on the here and now. Having Julia come over and put her arm around him helped. Seeing his dad clean and sober helped. The music and the smell of the ribs and the cold beer going down all helped. But if he wanted to put Cracker behind him for good, he needed to get the paintings, get his money, and get out of town with Julia. He smiled and listened to his dad tell him what a great girl Julia was. He took a drink of his beer and pulled her close, his mind buzzing.

One more day and they'd be gone for good.

Angel put corn on the grill and yelled for someone to get plates and silverware out of his office. His dad took cans of baked beans out of the grocery bags. Julia grabbed Angel's empty beer bottle, digging a fresh one out of the cooler. Springsteen drifted out of the boom box, singing about busting out of his crummy town with his girl, jumping on his motorcycle, and riding to a better place. Conor turned it up. He stepped back and smiled, watching Angel take Julia's hand and dance through the garage. They danced by and he cut in, feeling the music pound through him. He pulled her against him, kissing her.

He held the kiss for a long time. Tomorrow couldn't come fast enough.

CHAPTER TWENTY-NINE

Julia bumped around in the dark, finding the lamp on Angel's desk. It cast a dim light through the room. She wiggled out of her jeans and walked to the couch. The beer made her unsteady on her feet. She laid on the couch next to Conor. He grunted and shifted to his side, smelling like smoke from the grill. She pushed her nose into the crook of his neck.

"Conor? You up?"

"Yeah," he mumbled. He grabbed a blanket off the back of the couch and pulled it over them.

Julia turned nose-to-nose with him, watching his lips separate as he breathed slow and even.

"Today was fun," she said.

"Uh-huh."

She traced a finger around his face, then touched the scar that ran over his eyebrow. He pushed her hand away.

"Your dad is great," she said.

"Yep. Great."

"You look like him," she said, running her hands over his face. She stroked his cheek. "Hey, do you remember when you asked me if I had any dreams about my life?"

Conor turned away.

Julia rolled to her back and looked at the ceiling.

"I think I have one. Instead of Maine, let's go somewhere warm. Maybe a Caribbean island." She reached under the blanket to hold Conor's hand. "You could fix cars or something. And I could get a job as a bartender." She rubbed her thumb over Conor's palm, feeling his calluses. "We'll use the money you'll get tomorrow to set us up. It'll be a whole new life." She pulled Conor's hand to her chest and smiled. "Your dad can come down and join us. Even Angel if he wants to. One big family, you know? Maybe we'll even have kids." She turned toward Conor. "What do you think?"

When he didn't respond, she kissed his hand and snuggled against him. "We're going to do it. It'll be the best time of our lives."

* * *

Cracker woke up in the front seat of his pickup. He could've slept in a hotel last night, but why? Sleeping was sleeping, even if it was in the front seat of his truck in a strip mall parking lot. He rummaged through a plastic bag on the passenger seat, pulled out his last protein bar and chewed his way through it while he watched the sun lift from the horizon, illuminating the crumbling parking lot. This strip mall was like everything in this town—old, tired, and broken. He'd had his fill of it. But he'd finish his business today. It was time to bring out the sledgehammer. Everyone Conor Monroe had any connection to, however slim, was going to be smashed. If that boy was in Brannigan, he'd stick his head out of his hidey hole and get what was coming to him.

Cracker opened his glove box and took out paper and a pen. He chewed his protein bar thoughtfully, tapping his pen on the back of a wrinkled Chinese restaurant menu. He smoothed the menu on his thigh and started writing.

Family—Mickey Monroe
Friends—Sully Bomba and Jackie Fitzsimmons—Fitz
Current Poontang—Julia Terranova
Old Tang—Mona Bomba

He stopped writing and looked over the list. From what Derek Ryder had told him, these were all the people on God's green earth that had a relationship with Conor. And based on what he'd learned from picking through Monroe's apartment, the boy was a spook. He didn't mind spending time with himself, which was rare. Most people needed all kinds of ruckus and distraction to keep their mind occupied. Monroe was different. He was disciplined. He'd taken fourth place in the state high school wrestling tournament based on a trophy buried in his closet, and he was a pretty damn good street fighter based on Derek Ryder's broken ribs. And he didn't fear much. The beating he'd given Duck, a man who other criminals catered to, proved that. Based on the preponderance of evidence, Cracker was sure Monroe would be fun to tangle with. But somebody's pain and dying had to garner his attention first.

Cracker scanned the list of names. This was gonna be a tall order.

He scratched out Julia's name. She was out of reach, hiding out with Monroe. He ate his last piece of protein bar and sucked chocolate off the end of a finger. He scratched out Jackie Fitzsimmons. Derek Ryder told him Fitz disappeared after he, Conor, and Sully got caught trying to steal from Duck. No help there. So that left Sully Bomba, Mona Bomba, and Mickey Monroe—Conor's daddy. According to Derek, Monroe hated his daddy and hadn't talked to him in years because he was a drunk. And although Conor and Mona Bomba—Sully's sister—had once been in a relationship, Mona had a fairly strong dislike for Conor now. Taking all that into consideration, it made sense to start with Sully.

He called Derek. After a brief conversation, he started his truck and got moving, rolling through the crumbled ruin of parking lot. Sully was at the hospital. He'd been in a coma, but according to Derek, he'd pulled out of it. If Conor was back in town, he'd have surely heard about Sully being on the mend. And that would undoubtedly have made him happy. It was time to dump a big load of crappy on Conor's happy.

Cracker pulled into a drug store to get a couple things for his visit with Sully. He jumped out of his truck, walked into Walgreens, and roamed the aisles until he found what he was looking for.

Back in his truck, he dug a roll of reinforced elastic bandage out of the plastic bag that held his purchases. Wrapping his right wrist and hand took a while. When he was done, he looked over his handiwork. With his hand all wrapped up, it looked like he'd broken it. He turned it this way and that, admiring it for a bit before resting it in his lap.

Using his unwrapped hand, he reached in the Walgreens grocery bag, feeling around the shrink-wrapped legal pad and pack of ballpoint pens to grab a box of protein bars. Mmmm. Blueberry and strawberry yogurt flavor, just the thing for a shot of energy before he visited Sully. He wolfed down two of the bars and stared out the windshield, watching people walk in and out of the drugstore. Visiting hours weren't until noon. Best bet was to get there an hour or so before. He'd kill a couple hours people watching, then he'd go see Sully. It was gonna be a productive morning.

* * *

Cracker stood in the doorway to Sully's room, watching Sully eat orange Jell-O from a plastic cup. He walked in, shut the door, and dragged a chair to the side of Sully's bed.

Sully ran his spoon around the bottom of the plastic cup, ate the last of the Jell-O, and put the spoon down. He eyed Cracker.

"Who are you?"

Cracker laid a legal pad and pen on his lap.

"I'm from down the hall. Checking out today. Wondering if you could help me with something."

"What happened to your hand?"

Cracker held up his bandaged hand. "My old lady closed

the car door on it. Wish I could say it was an accident, but, well, you know how women can be. " He lowered his hand to his lap and nodded at Sully. "What you in for?"

Sully didn't say a word. He just stared at Cracker. Cracker held Sully's dark-eyed gaze and waited, but he had to give it to Sully, the boy was stone cold. He didn't flinch. Cracker tilted his head.

"Something about my face interest you?"

Sully shook his head. "Nah. Just looking." He tossed his Jell-O cup in a trash can. His bedsheet rustled as he sat up and smoothed the sheet over his legs. "They tell me some guys jumped me and put me in a coma. I don't know—I don't remember a thing."

"Is that right?" said Cracker, fiddling with the bandage on his hand.

"What's your name?" said Sully.

Cracker settled back in his chair. "It don't matter."

"Don't matter, huh?" said Sully. "Well, my mom and sister are coming to visit, so what do you need, 'don't matter?'"

Cracker lifted the legal pad and pen from his lap. "Can you write something for me? I need to leave my old lady a note."

Sully held out his hand. "Sure. But make it fast. I got shit to do."

Cracker handed over the legal pad and pen.

Cracker slowly unwrapped his bandage from his hand, winding the loose end around the palm of his free hand. "You ready?"

"Yeah," said Sully, uncapping the pen. "Go ahead."

Cracker stretched the foot-long length of bandage between his hands until it was as tight as a guitar string. "Let's start with this, 'As you can see, I'm gone.'"

"Got it," said Sully.

"And if you want to know why, ask Conor Monroe."

"Conor Monroe?" asked Sully.

Cracker continued. "One thing's for sure—if Conor had

fought Joe Cracker Jones instead of hiding like a bitch, I'd still be here."

Sully wrote it down, and then looked up. "'How do you know Conor? And who's this Joe Cracker Jones guy?"

Cracker leaned forward, tightening his grip on the bandage wound around his fists, and said quietly, "I'm recently acquainted with Conor." He watched Sully put the pen down. "And I've known Joe Cracker Jones since he was born. There's no better man on earth than good old Joe."

"Is Conor involved with your old lady or something?" said Sully.

Cracker shook his head. "No."

Sully squinted his eyes and furrowed his brow. "Well, why does Conor have to fight this Cracker dude?"

"That's between them."

"Here's your letter," said Sully, holding out the piece of paper. "Now get the fuck out. I got better things to do than worry about Conor getting into a fight. Plus, you're a fucking weirdo, and I don't want you in my room anymore." Sully lifted a hand, forced a smile, and waved. "See you later. Good luck with whatever you're doing but do it someplace else."

Cracker pointed across the room. "What the hell is that?"

Sully turned. Cracker lunged, pulling the bandage around Sully's neck from behind. Sully clutched at it, then began to kick and twist. But the bandage was too tight. He couldn't breathe. Cracker shook with the strain. This Sully was a hard-ass customer. Felt like a steel cable come to life. Cracker pulled the bandage tighter, cutting it deeper into Sully's neck. Sully bucked and fought, unable to utter a sound. His movements slowed. He convulsed a few times. Then he went limp.

"There you go," said Cracker, easing his grip, resting his chin on Sully's shoulder from behind as he caught his breath. "Just relax. Everything's gonna be all right. I'll send Conor to keep you company real soon."

Cracker grunted as Sully's elbow connected with the bridge of his nose. Cracker's grip on the bandage slipped, giving Sully a chance to pull it away from his neck and breathe. But that was as far as Sully got before Cracker stood, holding on while Sully spun this way and that, trying to get loose. Dancing with this boy was strenuous. Sully did not want to go quietly, but Cracker was certain of one thing.

He was going.

Cracker shoved a knee between Sully's shoulder blades. He arched back, pulling the bandage with all he had. Small, desperate sounds came out of Sully. The bandage cut into the carotid arteries on the sides of Sully's neck. Cracker pulled with all his weight and muscle, cutting off the blood flow to Sully's brain. Sully weakened with each pulse of blood that didn't reach his brain. His movements stilled. Cracker kept up the pressure for a full minute after Sully stopped fighting. When he finally let go, Sully flopped on the bed.

Cracker panted. He looked down. Sully's tongue hung out. His face was blue. Cracker unwrapped the bandage from his hands. He got himself a handful of tissues and blew blood out of his nose. It hurt like hell. He shoved the bloody tissues in his pocket.

"You surprised me. I give you that," he said, grabbing Sully under the arms and sitting him up on the bed. He worked fast, doubling up the bandage and tying it around Sully's neck. The toughest part was finding something to tie him off on. A water pipe running above the ceiling tiles did the trick. Sully's size helped things along. The boy wasn't tall and didn't weigh but one-eighty. Hanging him by his neck wasn't all that hard.

Cracker was almost out the door when he stopped. Damn. He almost forgot about the note. He went back in Sully's room. It took a moment to find the legal pad. It had somehow made its way under the bed during all the commotion with Sully. He tore the note Sully wrote off the legal pad and laid it on the bed. Then he pushed Sully, making him swing as he read the note.

As you can see, I'm gone. And if you want to know why, ask Conor Monroe. One thing's for sure—if Conor had fought Joe Cracker Jones instead of hiding like a bitch, I'd still be here.

He gave Sully a final push and walked out of the room, closing the door behind him. The idea that his nose must look bad struck him as he walked down the hall. He pulled the tissue out of his pocket and blew his nose, looking at the blood. Sully was a tough customer. He walked down the stairwell to the ground floor, his footsteps echoing.

Now it was time to find Conor's dad, Mickey Monroe, and give him the same treatment. One way or another, Conor would be showing his face today. And if he didn't, it would be clear that he didn't care about anybody. He'd be out of reach, and it would be time to leave and find something else to do. Cracker ran some possibilities through his mind. Maybe he'd visit that Mexican cartel boss who said he wanted the balls cut off a rival drug lord. After he pulled that off, his name would undoubtedly get circulated to the right people. It would jack up his client list something fierce. So that was the plan. If Conor didn't show after he got done working over his dad, he'd go visit Gomez and see what that piece of work would pay. It would be a shame to quit on this job, but a man had to know when it was time to move on.

He walked out into the hospital parking lot, got in his truck, and took out his cell. Derek answered with a hoarse, "What's up now?"

"That friend of Monroe's, Sully. He's up," said Cracker.

"Huh?"

"Where can I find Monroe's daddy?" said Cracker.

"I don't know," said Derek. "The guy lives on the street. He's an alky. But gimme a sec—I'll ask."

Cracker listened to people murmur. Derek got back on the phone.

"Last anyone saw, he was hanging around Angel Silva's garage. You know where that is?"

Cracker asked what Conor's dad looked like. Then he asked for the location of Angel's garage. He hung up, grabbed a legal pad, and wrote the address. Blood dripped from his nose onto the page. He wiped his nose, feeling a lance of pain. Sully probably broke it—the cost of doing business. He drove out of the hospital parking lot, glancing down at the address for the garage.

He made one stop at a liquor store on his way over to Angel's. There was no telling what kind of drunk Conor's dad was, but Cracker was feeling generous. A bottle of rotgut vodka and some radiator whiskey would give Mickey Monroe a chance to pick his poison. This could be fun for the old drunk.

Cracker parked against the curb outside Angel's garage and ripped the wrapper off a protein bar.

He ate, watched, and waited, tapping a fingernail against the whiskey bottle, then the vodka bottle. Back and forth. Back and forth. He swallowed a lump of protein bar.

Mickey Monroe had no idea of the good time waiting on him.

CHAPTER THIRTY

It was a little past noon. They were right on schedule. The car climbed a rise, heading straight into the sun. Conor shaded his eyes and looked out the window. They'd been driving for fifteen minutes. Ten more and they'd be at Malabar Farm. The landscape was beautiful this far out of Brannigan. The ground rolled away from the road on both sides, thickly wooded in some spots, fenced-off and well-manicured in others. Farming wasn't big here, because of the uneven, hilly terrain, but after they passed the padlocked gates of a shuttered ski resort, the land evened out, bordering the road with fields of corn. They slipped through the fields, banked around a curve, and then shot into a straight-away of paved road blazing with sunlight.

Conor looked at his dad's hands. They were trembling, but he drove straight and steady. He was smiling and his eyes were as clear as the sky. Yesterday they'd partied. Beer. Music. And food. So much good food. They'd danced and played cards and through it all his dad had never touched a drop of alcohol. He'd watched everyone else get drunk and stupid, knowing that no one was in any shape to give him trouble if he decided to join in. But he stuck with ginger ale. Conor snuck another look at his dad. His hair was combed, and he'd even shaved again. Someone had fired up a time machine, sending his father back in time. Conor half expected to see his mother materialize in the backseat, reach up, and hug his dad around the neck. After his father's seemingly overnight change, it felt like anything was possible. Conor sat back, feeling lightheaded with joy. This was the day he'd been praying for since his father got drunk and shot his partner. The day when his real father returned and threw that alcoholic, pathetic version of himself out of his life forever. It was the day the man Conor had looked up to since he was a child—the man who was his hero—came back from the dead.

His dad turned on the radio and fiddled with it. Music and commercials and weather reports and talk radio blurred as he scanned the dial. He clicked it off. Only the hush of the road beneath the car wheels broke the silence. Then his dad glanced over. "You know what's crazy?" he said.

Conor leaned back, feeling the sun on his face. "What?"

"That I forgot what this felt like."

Conor looked over. His dad's eyes were shiny. He looked straight ahead as he talked.

"Life is so strange. Years go by. You wonder where the time went. You just want to die and get it over with. Then you see a chance. So, you grab it, and the sun shines again." He stopped to wipe his eyes and shifted a quick glance at Conor before continuing. "I'm not sure if we'll ever do anything together again, but today, Conor, you can count on me. Today, I'm a rock."

He reached over and patted Conor on the shoulder.

"Glad to hear it," said Conor. "I missed you."

His dad settled back in his seat. "I missed me too."

Ten minutes later, they pulled into Malabar Farm. It was a perfect summer day. High seventies. Low humidity. A few puffy white clouds floated in a light blue sky. The parking lot was nearly full, which was good. The more people, the better. As his dad searched for a parking spot, Conor looked over the grounds. Open fields spread away from the parking lot, eventually turning into thickly wooded forests. A walking trail from the parking lot led to a barn where cows, goats, and sheep milled around in outdoor pens. The prize was past the barn at the top of the hill. A big white house with a green tin roof. That was Louis Bromfield's house, where the Grandma Moses paintings waited. His dad backed into an end spot, underneath a tree. Conor opened his backpack and checked his equipment. Everything was there. He zipped it back up.

"Let's do it," said Conor.

His dad nodded. "Remember, I'm going to pick you up across the road at Mount Commons. I'll be there no matter what. Nine at the latest."

"Ok," said Conor.

He walked to the house and bought two tickets. The tour group was big. Conor followed his dad inside into a huge, open foyer with a grand piano. Two staircases curled along the far right and left sides of the foyer, meeting in the middle of an upstairs landing. The tour guide talked about the history of the house. Conor hung back as the guide led the group upstairs. His dad—the last person in line—turned and nodded. Conor moved quickly, slipping into a hallway on the left and ducking under a velvet rope that cordoned off a bedroom. He took off his backpack, slid it under the giant four-poster bed, and looked at his watch. It would be hours before the park closed. He crawled under the bed, curled up, and went to sleep.

* * *

It was dark when Conor woke. He slid out from under the bed, pulled out the backpack, and listened. Crickets chirped from the fields surrounding the house.

He took a penlight from his pocket, clicked it on, and pulled a blueprint from his backpack. The wooden floor creaked as he walked through the house. It took him a few minutes to find the first painting. Another ten and he'd marked off where he needed to cut. The saw barely made a sound. It cut through the plaster, then the lathes. Conor stopped cutting and pulled out the last of the lathes. The backside of the painting was now fully exposed. He rummaged through the backpack, finding a razor knife. He carefully cut the canvas from the frame, rolled it up, pulled a reproduction from a tube, slid the original canvas in the tube, and taped the paper reproduction into the frame. A quick patch job covered the giant hole in the wall. If anyone looked at it for more than a few seconds, they'd see something was wrong, but they didn't need more than a day or so to sell the painting. Hopefully, no one would see the patched wall before they had their money. He cleaned up, sweeping the dust and debris under a couch, then he moved on to the second painting, repeating the process.

The whole job took just over an hour. He never broke a sweat.

Making sure the two tubes holding the paintings were tightly capped, Conor tied one tube on the left and one tube on the right side of his backpack. He then followed Angel's blueprint to the attic, which was dark and full of spider webs. The penlight helped him find the spot on the roof under the cupola. He cut through the roof, climbed into the cupola, pushed out a vent, slipped through, replaced the vent, and then crept across the roof with his backpack hooked over one shoulder. At the edge of the roof, he slid on his belly feet-first until he was hanging by his fingertips, and then dropped ten-feet to the gravel driveway. No problem.

He ran across the road toward the silhouette of Mount Commons. All he had to do now was get in the car with his dad and drive back to Angel's.

He stopped at the bottom of the road that led up to the top of Mount Commons.

There was no car. No sign of his dad anywhere.

Maybe his dad parked at the top to stay out of sight. He trudged up the road, feeling his calves burn. It was a straight uphill climb.

At the top of the hill, he took in the view. The summer night spread out under him, fireflies winking over the fields around Malabar Farm. A cool breeze touched his face. But there was no sign of a car anywhere. He looked at his watch. Twenty-five after nine.

Damn it.

It was a long way back into town, but since Angel had taken his cell, there was only one way to get there. He walked down to the road, hiked the straps of the backpack up on his shoulders, and started jogging. There was a chance that something held his dad up. He might come barreling through the night, making up for lost time. Conor hoped he would. He prayed he would.

But he knew he wouldn't.

A sweat born of anger and frustration broke over his face as he ran.

In the first two miles of jogging, headlights came his way twice. The first car was a big SUV. The second was a police cruiser. The cop car scared him. He slipped behind a tree, hoping he'd gotten off the road before he was seen. He was sure the cruiser was going to squeal to a stop and spin its bubblegum lights. Maybe he'd tripped an alarm back at Malabar—or his dad or Angel had done something. That would explain things. For all he knew, his dad was sitting in an interrogation room being grilled by detectives. Maybe the whole job was blowing up and he was the last to know, hiding behind a tree on the side of a country road, waiting for the hammer of the law to come down on his head. The brake lights on that cruiser would signal the end of everything. The money from selling the paintings—gone. He and Julia leaving town and starting a new life—poof. Everything would be wiped away in a blink if the cop stopped.

But the cop's brake lights never came on.

Walking out from behind the tree, Conor tightened the straps on his backpack and watched the cruiser dip out of sight around a curve. He started jogging again, then he started running.

When he finally stopped, he looked at his watch. He'd

been running for a half hour. He wiped his face with the front of his shirt, catching his breath. There was a shopping plaza a couple miles ahead, on the Route 13 exit off the interstate. A long-haired hitchhiker with a backpack like himself wouldn't draw any attention. He could hitch a ride to Angel's garage.

With no other option coming to mind, he started jogging toward the lights of the shopping plaza glowing out beyond the horizon.

CHAPTER THIRTY-ONE

Julia raised on tiptoe to kiss Conor.

"You be careful," she said.

"I'll take care of him. No worries," Mickey said, smiling and looking at his watch. "C'mon, Conor. Those paintings are waiting for us."

Julia closed her eyes, enjoying Conor's soft kiss. His rough hands held her face. He whispered, "I'll be back in no time, babe. No worries."

Then he was gone. She watched the door close and turned to Angel, standing in the middle of the garage with his arms crossed.

"They're going to be okay, right?" she said.

Angel nodded. He walked over and hugged her. He smelled good. His chest rumbled as he talked.

"By tonight, you and Conor will be a hundred grand richer. And if something goes wrong, Conor will drop everything and get out. The worst outcome is him coming back empty-handed."

"I'm holding you to that," she said.

"Fair enough," said Angel. He grabbed her hand. "But you have to do something for me."

She followed him to his office and watched him log on to his computer.

"I've taken care of everything for the paintings. Transport to Europe. Certificates of authenticity.

Provenance. It's all squared away," he said, opening his browser.

Julia shook her head. "Are you talking English?"

He laughed, typing in a web address. The login page for a bank appeared. He grabbed a pen and wrote on a notepad. He ripped the paper out of the pad, folded it, and handed it to her. "I've taken care of everything. But I need you to be my backup on this bank account. It's where the buyer is going to deposit our money."

Julia unfolded the paper Angel had given her.

"That's the login and password. Memorize it, just in case," Angel said.

"In case what?"

"In case something happens. If I'm not here, you'll need to give the buyer the account numbers and confirm the deposit. I learned a long time ago that it's better to be prepared for anything."

She looked at the paper and smiled. "This is your username and password? You're kidding, right?"

Angel looked at her and raised his eyebrows. "Do you have it memorized?"

"I'll never forget it," she said laughing.

He grabbed the paper, pulled out a lighter, and put flame to paper.

Julia stood and kissed Angel's cheek. He dropped the burning paper in an ashtray.

"You're such a good guy," she said.

Angel pointed at her, eyes narrowing. "No one ever knows that username or password."

Julia drew an X on her chest. "Cross my heart."

Angel shut down his computer and stood. "All the money—not half or three-quarters or almost all—*all of it* has to be deposited before the paintings are handed over to the dealer's associate tomorrow morning. He'll be here at six a.m." He stared at her. "If I'm not here, I'm trusting you to make sure he doesn't get the paintings until every cent of our money is in the account. Got it?"

She nodded and then followed him out of the office into the garage. Angel walked around the garage, picking up tools and putting them away. Then he grabbed a broom and started sweeping a floor that looked as clean as polished marble. He was an interesting guy. Looked mean as a pit bull but had a big heart. She walked over and grabbed his hand.

"What are you doing today?" she said.

Angel shrugged. "You're looking at it. We're staying put and waiting for Conor and Mickey."

"Do you know Conor's friend, Sully?"

"Absolutely. He worked for me," said Angel. "Good kid. Too bad he ended up in a coma."

Julia took the broom out of his hand, propped it against the wall, and then walked toward the motorcycle parked in the garage. She sat on the bike and patted the seat. "Get on. I need you to take me somewhere."

Angel raised his eyebrows. "If you say so." He opened a bay door and straddled the seat in front of Julia, letting her wrap her arms around him. He rolled through the open door and kickstarted the bike.

"Which way?" he yelled.

"The hospital," Julia yelled back, tucking her face against Angel's back.

Angel rode out into the street and punched through the gears. The wind blasted Julia's face. She grinned. This was gonna be good. Angel was going to bust when he saw Sully was awake.

***

They parked in the hospital's front lot. Julia jumped off the bike and led the way into the hospital. She grabbed Angel's hand and pulled him along. She couldn't stop smiling. The ride over had been a blast. Everyone had stared at them. Angel was a bad ass, riding his bike with a curvy young girl hanging onto him. And everyone, except for some big weirdo with a bloody nose who shouldered past them at the nurses' station, looked at Angel with equal amounts of fear and respect. The nurse shook her head in disgust as the weirdo shoved by a woman helping an elderly man onto the elevator, and then waved Julia and Angel through, even though visitor hours hadn't started yet. Yeah, Angel was a bad ass. But she knew there was another side to him. She reached for the door to Sully's room and pulled it open. After seeing Angel's username and password, she knew he—

Angel pushed by her. All her strength vanished. She gripped the doorknob to stay upright. Angel jumped on the bed. He grabbed Sully around the waist, lifting him.

"Help me," he yelled. "Untie him."

Julia stepped up onto the bed, working to untie the bandage around Sully's neck. His face was blue. His tongue was blue. She struggled with the knot. A shiver ran through her. His skin was cool like clay. The knot came loose. She pulled the bandage off Sully's neck. Angel lowered him to the bed and began doing mouth-to-mouth, then started chest compressions.

"Get a doctor or a nurse," Angel said between pushes on Sully's chest.

She stepped off the bed, watching.

"I said get somebody," said Angel, his eyes darkening.

Julia shook her head. "It won't help."

Angel pushed on Sully's chest again.

Julia grabbed Angel's hands. "He's gone, Angel. He's dead."

Angel stared at Sully. He got off the bed and backed up, bumping into a chair. He turned and kicked the chair over. The elastic band holding his ponytail came loose. His long black hair fell over his shoulders and shimmered around his face. His eyes were wet, but he didn't cry. Julia could see his anger building.

"Why did he do this?" he said, looking at Julia.

Julia was dumbstruck. "It doesn't make any sense," she

said, bending down to pick up Angel's hair band. "He was fine yesterday."

"Yesterday?" said Angel.

"He came out of his coma. Me and Conor talked to him."

"Conor brought you here?" said Angel. "I told him not to... ah hell." He stomped over to the bed and looked down at Sully. "Why'd you do this?"

"What's that?" said Julia, walking over. "There's something under him." She grabbed Sully by his shoulders and hoisted him into a sitting position. "Grab it," she said.

Angel pulled a yellow sheet of legal paper out from under Sully.

Julia lowered Sully back onto the bed. She watched a change come over Angel as he read the paper. A light of realization filled his eyes. Then he folded the paper, stuck it in his pocket, laid his hand on Sully's head, and said, "Sorry." He closed Sully's eyes. "You rest in peace, brother."

"What did that note say?" Julia asked.

Angel walked around the bed. He pushed the call button for the nurse and grabbed Julia's arm, pulling her out of the room. He whispered, "Just keep walking," as he led Julia to the elevator. A doctor rode down in the elevator with them, keeping Julia quiet, but once they got to the ground floor, she talked as she followed Angel.

"Are you going to tell me what the note said?" she asked breathlessly, breaking into a half jog to keep up with him.

"Sully didn't hang himself," said Angel, his face a blank mask. "Someone else did."

"Who?" asked Julia, barely getting on the motorcycle before Angel fired it up. She clasped her hands around his stomach. He put the bike in gear, tearing out of the parking lot.

"Doesn't matter," said Angel over the roar of the motorcycle. "I'll take care of it."

Julia hung on. Angel moved like a statue brought to life.

Turning the handlebars when they needed turning. Putting his feet down when they stopped. Shifting through the gears as he raced through the streets. But something inside him was frozen. Julia could tell he was on autopilot.

He pulled around to the back of his garage and eased the bike to a stop. It would be a stretch to say Angel was scared, but whatever was on his mind, Julia could see it had him freaked.

"Get off," he said. "I have to take care of something."

"I'll go with you," she said, locking her hands around his chest.

"You can't. Get off."

She got off. "Wait," she said, grabbing Angel's arm. She reached in her pocket and pulled out his elastic hair tie. She pulled his hair back into a ponytail, banded it, and backed away. "When are you coming back?" she asked.

"Soon," said Angel. "Just wait inside, and don't open the door for anyone but Conor or his dad." He held out his hand. She grabbed it.

"Conor is lucky he found you," he said. Then his hand slipped away, his motorcycle roared, and he was gone.

Julia went inside the garage, made sure every door was locked, and then went into the lobby. She sat on a stool. Slivers of sunlight squeezed through the slats of the window blinds. She stared at the blinds and waited.

Hours crawled by. She never took her eyes off the window. Her stomach was growling and she had to pee when she heard someone drive into the parking lot.

Whoever it was, he came in too fast, rubber squealing, followed by the sound of a metal-on-metal collision. Pieces and parts rattled over asphalt. Julia ran over to the blinds, peering through to the parking lot. She unlocked the front door and ran toward Conor's father, lying half in and half out of Angel's wrecked Camaro. The car was still idling with its bumper wrapped around a streetlamp. Steam billowed from under the hood.

She knelt next to him. "Are you okay?" she said. Not

getting a reply, she reached in the car to pull his legs out. Mickey mumbled gibberish. She looked around. The street and sidewalk were empty. Grabbing him by the shoulders, she dragged him out of the car and laid him on the asphalt. Then she stepped over him toward the car. An empty vodka bottle lay in the seat. She tossed it out, slid into the driver's seat of the wrecked car, and put it in reverse. There was a terrible screeching sound as she backed up with one end of the bumper scraping the asphalt. It made a horrible racket as she pulled into a parking space.

She got out of the car and looked at Mickey. He turned on his side and puked. His hand touched the empty bottle of vodka she threw out of the car. It rolled away from him, clinking across the parking lot. If he drank all that, he needed to be in the hospital. But she couldn't take him. She had to wait for Conor and Angel. The best he'd get was the couch inside Angel's office.

She walked toward Mickey, not sure if he could stand, let alone walk. If not, she would need help carrying him inside. But, like most things in her life, she knew there would be no help.

She touched Mickey's shoulder. He let out a full-throated moan. The smell of alcohol and vomit hit Julia in a blinding wave, making her eyes water. She stepped back and covered her nose to block the smell. Yeah, this was familiar. She'd seen this too many times in her life. Something bad had happened. Things had taken a turn. And even though she was trying her level best to keep bad thoughts at bay, she knew.

She looked at the smashed car, steam rising from under its hood.

The vodka bottle lying in a puddle of vomit.

Mickey moaning, his eyes rolled back in their sockets.

She kneeled next to Mickey and hung her head. She knew.

Her dreams of building a new life with Conor were somewhere out there in the night, drawing their last shuddering breath.

CHAPTER THIRTY-TWO

Cracker watched the car approach Angel Silva's garage. One of them old muscle cars. Camaro. GTO. Javelin. Who the hell knew? Some motorhead boys back home got all jazzed up about that kind of thing. Didn't make much sense to him. Cars got you where you were going, just like a roof kept the rain off your head, food filled your belly, and clothes kept you warm. All necessary things, except for wearing clothes. If he had it his way, people would walk around naked when it was hot. It just made common sense.

He crumbled the wrapper of the protein bar he was eating and watched the car park on the curb half a block back. A man got out and looked up and down the street before locking the door and walking toward Angel's garage. Cracker waited until the man was near his truck before he threw the wrapper into the footwell, opened the door on his truck, and stepped out.

"You cut your hair and shave your beard?" he said, stepping toward the man.

The man stopped and squinted. "You talking to me?"

"Just asking a simple question," said Cracker, closing the distance between them in three long strides. He tilted his head. "Yeah. You're him. I can tell from the picture of your son. You bear a resemblance. Why'd you get all cleaned up?"

Mickey tried to step back. Cracker grabbed his arm.

"Whoa, whoa. Where you going?" Cracker said. He

ducked under Mickey's punch and slid behind him, slipping a forearm under Mickey's chin. "You need to relax," he said, choking him.

Sully, who'd just came out of a coma, had put up a better fight. This was pathetic. The grunting and shuffling went on for ten seconds at most. Then the old drunk, Mickey Monroe, gave up the ghost. Cracker held the pressure long enough to put him in twilight, then carried him over to his truck and jammed him into the passenger seat. The old man came out of it pretty quick, but the shuttered GM plant wasn't that far away. Old Mickey barely had time to form a coherent thought before they were inside the factory gate.

"Who are you? Where we going?" said Mickey, straightening in his seat.

Cracker parked next to the factory. He cut the engine and nodded at Mickey. "This is your lucky day. Look what I got for you. Right there by your feet."

The sound Mickey made when he picked up the whiskey bottle was less than enthusiastic. Mickey's attempt to open his door was, however, very lively. Cracker watched Mickey fumble with the lock, pull the handle, and kick the door open. Cracker didn't move a muscle. There was no one in earshot of this factory. The old boozer could get out, run a bit, and burn off some adrenaline, which would probably make him more amenable to a discussion about the whereabouts of his pain-in-the-ass ghost of a son. He'd drink his booze, whether he wanted to or not, get his tongue all greased up, and spill everything he knew about where his son might be hiding. But Mickey surprised Cracker. He didn't run. What he did do, however, was uncalled for.

That old drunken bum got out, lifted that bottle of whiskey over his head—that brand-new, unopened bottle—and smashed it on the pavement.

"Now why'd you go and do that?" said Cracker. Getting a defiant stare for an answer, Cracker got out, grabbed hold of Mickey, and pushed him up against the truck.

"I can see where your son gets his stupid from," said

Cracker. He shoved Mickey to the pavement and went back to the truck, feeling around under the passenger seat. "Do not get off that ground or I will break every goddamn one of your fingers," he said, grabbing the bottle of vodka. It made a glugging sound as he got out of the truck and raised it high. "Well, looky here," he said. "A backup bottle. How 'bout that? It's your lucky day. Now get up and walk toward that door over there. We're going inside. You can walk or I can drag you by your ear. Don't matter none to me."

Mickey walked into the old GM plant without a complaint. But he wasn't nearly as happy about drinking. For some as yet to be determined reason, he didn't cotton to it today. But it wasn't altogether hard to get him drunk either. Pinning him flat on his back, Cracker knelt on his arms and held a hand over his nose and mouth. Eventually, Mickey's eyes bugged out, and then he began grunting for air. That's when he got a chance to drink between his frenzied gasps for air. It was the only way to get the vodka in him. It took ten minutes to get the whole bottle in his belly, but in the end, Mickey reached a relaxed state of mind. Old drunks were highly tolerant of their alcohol. Problem was, that much booze cut the timeline to talk down to nothing, so Cracker worked fast. He walked around Mickey and toed him with his boot.

"I'll keep it simple," he said. "Only want to know if you've seen your son, Conor."

Drenched in vodka, Mickey tried to sit up. Cracker put a heel in his face and pushed him down.

"No sir," he said. "You stay right where you are. Don't want you throwing up. That bottle cost me seven dollars and eighty-nine cents. You stay down and you keep it down, or I'll go to work on you. Now what about Conor? Where is he?"

"Conor?" said Mickey. "I, uh, what?"

Cracker lowered to one knee and jabbed a finger between Mickey's eyes.

"You best start using your faculties while you still have

them," said Cracker. He gave Mickey a short, hard punch in the forehead and stood. Mickey held his head and rolled back and forth.

"He hasn't talked to me in years," yelled Mickey. "I'm a drunk. I'm nothing to him."

Cracker stepped on Mickey's shoulder and put his weight down. "I know you're a nothing. Everybody in town knows that. What I don't know is where that son of yours might be holed up. Can you provide any insight into that?"

"He, uhhh, shwait a minute. Lesh me tink," slurred Mickey.

Cracker stomped on his shoulder. Mickey screamed. "You ain't that drunk yet," Cracker said. "I better hear something fast, or I will pop one of your eyes out your skull. Now tell me what you know and don't lie, or it will go bad for you and one of your eyeballs."

"I swear," yelled Mickey. "I haven't talked to him. Last I heard, he had an apartment at Sunset Boulevard. It's been like seven years since I've even seen him."

Cracker bent over Mickey. He poked a finger under Mickey's right eye. Mickey tried to push his hand away. Cracker slapped Mickey in the face, and then kneeled, whispering in Mickey's ear as he ran his finger around Mickey's eye.

"Touch my hand again and I will surely pop your eye out. Now straighten up, cowboy. I'm just gonna ask a couple more questions, you hear?"

Mickey nodded.

"Does Conor have any friends in town?"

Mickey shook his head.

"Oh, that's not being honest," said Cracker, kneeling on Mickey's chest and jamming his finger under Mickey's eye.

"None are around anymore," screamed Mickey. "Jackie Fitzsimmons and Sully Bomba were his only real friends. I heard Fitz—I mean Jackie—disappeared after their last heist. Sully is in the hospital in a coma."

Cracker took the pressure off his finger and looked

down on Mickey. That eye was a hair away from coming out before the old drunk spouted the truth. Most likely, Mickey now knew playtime was over. One more test, however, to make sure. That girl next door to Conor, Julia Terranova—no one in town knew about her. He ran his finger around Mickey's red eye, listening to him breathe all shaky, vodka fumes pouring out of him with every breath. There was one way to determine if the old drunk was telling the truth.

He'd ask him if Conor had a girlfriend. If he said yes, he'd ask her name.

If Mickey knew Conor's girl was Julia, then the old drunk was trying to pull the wool over his eyes. He'd been in touch with Conor. And he'd lose an eye for not fessing up to that. Lying would not be tolerated. Cracker pressed his finger under Mickey's eyelid, watching his eye bulge.

"Now don't think too much with this next question," said Cracker. "I ask, you answer. You try to spin it, your eye's out, and I'll step on it for good measure. Get me?"

"Yeah," whimpered Mickey.

"Does Conor have a girlfriend?"

Mickey hesitated.

Cracker pressed down. "I told you what I'd do if you didn't answer right off."

"But I don't know how to answer that," yelled Mickey. "He had a girlfriend, but I don't know if they go out anymore."

"What's her name?" said Cracker, pushing harder.

"Sully's sister!" shrieked Mickey. "Mona!"

"Would he hide at her place?'

"No! Yes! I don't know. There's no telling with Mona. She might either screw him or kill him if he showed up—maybe both."

Cracker clenched his teeth. "You swear you haven't heard one word from him or anything about where he's hiding?"

"No. I'd tell you. I don't owe Conor nothing. He hates me. I'm nothing to him. I'm a waste of life."

Cracker hissed and slowly backed the pressure off Mickey's eye. He stood, brushed his pants off, and held out his hand.

"What are you doing?" said Mickey, looking at Cracker's hand.

"I'm helping you up. What's it look like?"

Cracker pulled Mickey to his feet. He put an arm around him, holding him steady while he half carried him toward the door. "Hold your water," he said, propping Mickey against the door and running back into the factory. He came back holding the empty bottle of vodka. He handed it to Mickey. "This is yours," said Cracker. "I don't like people that litter."

By the time he'd driven Mickey back to his car, Cracker could see that the bottle of rotgut vodka was punishing the old drunk. Mickey couldn't sit up straight. He swayed back and forth in his seat. When Cracker stopped his truck and pulled Mickey out, it was as if the man had no bones. He wobbled all over the place. It took a lot to keep him upright while Cracker rummaged through his pockets for the keys to his muscle car. Pouring Mickey into the front seat of that car was an adventure. The boozer kept sliding down the seat and mumbling something, but Cracker knew deciphering it would take a better man than him. Cracker leaned into the car over Mickey, wrinkling his nose at the smell of alcohol. It burned the hair out of his nostrils. He turned the key in the ignition, and the engine caught with a throaty rumble.

"Drive careful now," said Cracker, mussing Mickey's hair. He spun on his heels and looked at his truck. "Wait a second. You forgot something." He ran over to grab the empty vodka bottle off the truck's floorboard. Mickey's head snapped up as he shoved the bottle between his thighs.

"I dint ay nuffin," said Mickey.

Cracker patted him on the cheek. He reached over, put the car in Drive and stepped back to watch the Camaro lurch toward Angel's garage. He got in his truck and was driving away when he heard the crash.

Mickey hadn't put him any closer to Conor, but sharing time with the old drunk was enjoyable. It would probably be a good time to check in with Duck to let him know how things were progressing. He might even tell him the details of his meeting with Mickey Monroe. It was always good to let an employer know what they were getting for their money.

* * *

Cracker parked in front of Duck's. He walked up the driveway. Some inconsiderate son-of-a-bitch had parked his motorcycle on the walkway leading to the front door. Cracker thought about pushing the bike over, but he walked across the front lawn instead. Whoever parked there didn't care that he was interfering with other people's ingress and egress. Selfish bastard. After talking with Duck, it would be appropriate to inquire about the owner of the motorcycle. Whoever the boy was, he was gonna be rubbing a knot on his head.

He opened the front door and heard Duck in a heated conversation. Stepping into the house, he studied the situation. Duck sat at the head of his dining room table. Some big old boy with a ponytail was bent over, hands on the table, getting in Duck's face. When Duck looked over and caught sight of Cracker, his eyes lit up.

"Here's the gentleman you need to talk to," said Duck, pushing out of his chair to stand and point at Cracker.

Cracker watched the big boy with the ponytail turn around.

"Joe Cracker Jones, meet Angel Silva," said Duck, smiling.

"You an Indian?" said Cracker, eyeing Angel.

"Angel is upset," said Duck, rubbing his hands together as if he was washing them under a faucet. "A friend of his, Sully Bomba, hanged himself in the hospital."

"Is that right?" said Cracker. He tilted his head and

stared at Angel. The big boy returned his stare. He wasn't happy. Not at all.

"And Angel thinks I have something to do with it," said Duck. "Some crazy notion about me putting a hit out on Conor Monroe and having his friends killed until Conor turns himself over to me. I've explained that I have no idea what he's talking about, but he won't listen."

"You the guy Duck hired to kill Conor?" said Angel.

"Uh-huh," said Cracker. He pointed toward the front door. "That your motorcycle out there?"

"Yeah."

"It was in my way and anyone else's that's trying to get to the front door," said Cracker. "That was very selfish of you."

Angel turned to Duck. "You gonna call him off, or do I have to get involved?"

Duck held up his hands. "This is between you and Mr. Jones. Talk it over with him."

The first thing Angel did was interesting. Cracker liked it. Angel was a big boy. The big ones usually stepped right in and started swinging punches. But Angel just stretched his left hand way out there, showing his palm like he was giving a blessing, and then edged closer. And when his hand got in near to touching distance, Angel stopped. The boy was measuring him. Getting a feel for where he could throw punches and still be able to jump back and avoid counters. It was a pleasure watching him do it. Cracker stepped forward and watched Angel slide back a step, maintaining his safe distance. Definitely a fighter. Problem was, although he looked to be a fighter with skills, Injun Joe probably had no conception of what he was getting into.

Then Angel stepped in and started. Nothing fast. Nothing hard. But everything hit. Two jabs to the face. A right to the kidney. A left hook to the jaw. Two rights to the body. The punches seemed slow to Cracker. Like every one of them could've been ducked or sidestepped, but for some reason he couldn't get out of the way. And he felt every one of them. His broken nose flared with pain from the first two punches to the face. The wind got knocked out of him with the last two shots to the body. The pace hypnotized him. Bang, bang, bang, bang—

Enough.

Cracker ripped a right hook at Angel's head. But nothing was there. Another volley of punches rained down from every direction. Every shot found a home. The shots to the face blinded him. The shots to the body turned his legs to rubber. He covered up and tried to weather the storm. None of the punches were hard. But they were deadly accurate. This Angel was a devil. And he was walking him down. Beating him to a pulp.

Cracker backed up and took the blows, waiting. A man had to get close to finish things off. And Cracker could feel Angel, moving in a little closer with every punch.

A punch to the jaw.

A little closer.

A punch to the temple.

A little closer.

A punch to the kidney.

A little too close.

Cracker came out of his shell, reached up and grabbed Angel's head with both hands. He heard Angel curse as he pulled Angel's head down and jumped, driving his right knee into Angel's chin. This big ole Indian-looking fella knew he'd gotten too close. He knew he'd screwed up. But that's the way it went when you got to fighting. You got your blood up and started wading in, thinking you were king of the hill.

The crack of knee against chin—bone on bone—was harsh. Angel staggered. The lights in his eyes went out for a moment. Then he was back, struggling with everything he had to stay on his feet.

Cracker kicked him in the balls. He'd once heard a trainer call a groin shot 'old-school Kung Fu,' and for his money, it worked better than just about anything. Like now, for instance. Angel crumpled like a piano had been dropped on his back.

Cracker grabbed Angel's ponytail, lifting his head off the floor.

"No, no, no," he said. "Don't go to sleep on me yet. I ain't finished. Not by a long shot."

He pulled Angel to his feet and pushed him against a wall. Angel pawed at him. Swung powder-puff punches. Cracker stuck his chin out, let a couple shots land, then got in Angel's face, opened his mouth wide, and screamed his rebel yell.

CHAPTER THIRTY-THREE

The streetlamps gave Conor a clear view of Angel's garage. He stood in the bed of the truck and surveyed the street, thinking he should bang on the back window of the cab and yell for the kid to stop and drop him off in the alley, but the whole street was empty. None of Barry's or Duck's guys were hanging around. No strange cars were in sight. The only thing out of place was Angel's Camaro parked by the front door. He looked at his watch. His dad was supposed to pick him up two hours ago, but there sat the Camaro. What was it doing here? And where was his dad? He knocked on the pickup's back window.

"This is good," he said. The truck rolled to a halt. He jumped out of the pickup bed, walked to the driver's window, and gave the teenage boy a fist bump. "Thanks for the ride," he said.

The kid nodded. "Sure. Have a good night."

Conor watched the truck drive away. He hiked the backpack up on his shoulders and walked toward Angel's garage with his head on a swivel. His gaze kept getting pulled back to the Camaro. If his dad had gone on a bender, it would be parked at a bar, not here. Halfway through the parking lot, he stopped and reached in his pocket. He pulled out the set of keys that Angel had given him when he drove to Massey to find Julia.

He had the paintings. He had the keys to the Camaro.

And the car was right here, waiting for him. Something was telling him to drive away, to put distance between himself and everyone else. Once he was clear, he could call Angel to make sure nothing had gone wrong. It made the best sense. It was too quiet. Too many things were lining up wrong.

He put his head down and walked toward the Camaro, stepping around a puddle in the parking lot. The sweet, metallic smell of radiator fluid wafted over him. He walked to the driver's side and stopped.

The whole front end of the Camaro was wrecked. This car was going nowhere.

Conor fumed. So that's what happened. His dad had gotten wasted and cracked up the car. He was probably inside right now, sleeping it off.

And Angel's probably driving around looking for me, thought Conor, shaking his head as he walked to the front door. He tried to turn the doorknob. It was locked. He knocked, waited, and knocked again. Footsteps thumped toward him. The door flew open.

"Get in here," Julia said, pulling him inside.

He didn't get a chance to say a word as she dragged him to the restroom. His dad hugged the toilet bowl, retching. It smelled like someone poured a case of cheap vodka on the floor. Conor took off his backpack.

"How long's he been like this?" he asked.

"I don't know," said Julia. "He crashed Angel's car out front a couple hours after you left. There was an empty bottle of vodka with him. He's been doing nothing but passing out and throwing up since. I tried to get some aspirin in him, but he can't hold anything down. I don't know what to do."

Conor stood over his dad. "Little sick, huh?"

His dad raised his head out of the toilet. "I didin say nuffin."

"And he keeps saying that," said Julia. "'I didn't say nothing.' Took me an hour to figure it out. What does that mean?"

Conor backed out of the bathroom. "It means he's drunk." He shook his head. "Go make some coffee while I throw him in the shower."

His dad could walk. Not perfectly, but he managed. Conor put him in the shower, found a clean pair of Angel's coveralls, hung them on the towel rack, and then sat on the toilet, watching to make sure his dad didn't slip and kill himself. Once he got the money from Angel, he was leaving with Julia for good. This bullshit was over.

After his dad was cleaned up and dressed, he led him into Angel's office and shoved a hot cup of coffee in his hands. Then he went out in the hall, grabbed his backpack, and went back into the office, closing the door. Julia eyed him from her seat on the front of Angel's desk, sipping coffee. His dad sat on the couch.

"So, where's Angel? Driving around looking for me because you're a drunk?" he said, looking at his dad.

His dad took a big gulp of his coffee. "I din't…say anything," he said, slowly and deliberately, his hands shaking.

Julia put her coffee cup on the desk. "You should sit down, Conor."

Conor set the backpack on the floor. "Just tell me where I can find Angel. We need to get our money and get out of here."

"I did nah tell him anyfing," said his dad.

Conor scowled at his dad. "Shut up."

"Sully's dead," said Julia.

Conor straightened. "What?"

"Me and Angel went to see him. He hanged himself."

Mickey lowered his head. "No," he moaned.

"We just saw him yesterday," said Conor. "He was fine."

Julia walked over to Conor. She put her hands on his shoulders. "I know. And I'm sorry."

"It doesn't make any sense," said Conor. "Why would he do that?"

"He left a note," said Julia.

"I did nah tell him," said Conor's dad. "Nuffffing."

"Stop it," yelled Conor, pointing at his father. He walked over and smacked the coffee mug out of his father's hands. It flew across the room and shattered against a wall.

"I didn't," said his father.

Conor turned his back on him. "What did the note say?" he asked.

Julia looked at the broken coffee cup. "I don't know," she said. "Angel has it. He read it, then he dropped me off and said he had to take care of something."

"Where did he go?"

She shook her head. "He didn't say. But he seemed different."

"What do you mean, 'different?'"

She took a deep breath, thinking hard, and then exhaled. "Like…worried…or scared."

Tires squealed out front. An engine revved in the parking lot. Conor looked at Julia. He whispered, "Stay here," and slipped out the office door, closing it behind him.

He crept through the garage. The engine revving stopped, but he could hear someone yell, "Now get the hell off my truck," followed by the sound of a thud. He peeked through the blinds. His blood went cold.

Angel was lying in a heap on the asphalt behind a pickup truck. A man was in the bed of the pickup, pushing Angel's motorcycle out. The motorcycle tipped over the opened tailgate. It fell on its side in the parking lot, right next to Angel. One more foot and it would've crushed Angel's head. The man in the truck straightened, looking over his handiwork.

It was Joe Cracker Jones. Conor had seen enough of him on the Internet to know. All muscle and vein and sharp bone and bad haircut wrapped up in a squinty-eyed package. His nose was swollen, and his face was bruised, but he didn't move like he was hurt. He brimmed with power as he raised his gaze and stared at the garage, seemingly straight through the blinds at Conor.

When Cracker finally looked away, Conor realized he hadn't taken a breath. He pulled in a lungful of air, watching Cracker jump off the bed, get in his truck, and drive away.

Conor looked at his hands. They were trembling. He walked outside, peering down the street. The brake lights on Cracker's truck brightened three blocks away, then disappeared as the truck took a right. Conor stared at the empty street. Maybe Cracker saw him. Maybe he was circling back right now. Conor looked at Angel, then back down the street.

Let him come.

He went to Angel, sat on the pavement next to him, and cradled Angel's head in his lap. It could've been seconds or hours later when Julia showed up. Conor had no concept of time. All he could do was hold Angel and marvel at the damage Joe Cracker Jones had done. Angel's face was smashed, his hands broken, his eyes swollen shut. Blood was splattered over every part of him. Julia touched Conor's shoulder.

"I called an ambulance," she said.

Conor stroked Angel's forehead. "Hang in there, Angel. It's gonna be okay."

Angel stirred. He opened one eye into a slit and reached for a piece of paper hanging halfway out of his pocket, trying to push it back in with broken fingers. Conor grabbed Angel's wrist. "I'll get it," he said, pulling the paper out.

"No," Angel mumbled through swollen lips. "Don't read it."

Conor opened the note. When he got to the part that read, "*One thing's for sure—if Conor had fought Joe Cracker Jones instead of hiding like a bitch, I'd still be here*," he knew. This was the note from Sully's room. Cracker had killed Sully. He was doing what he said he would do, destroying the people Conor cared about to make him fight.

"He mayme drink. Tried to make me tell'm where you are. I said nuffin."

Conor looked up at his father, wavering on his feet.

"Cracker made you drink?" said Conor.

"I don't know. Sum hillwilly guy."

"Take Julia and run, Conor," mumbled Angel.

A black mist dropped over Conor. It sifted through his pores, filling him until he was heavy with it. It felt like cold lead ran through his veins as he turned to Julia.

"I gotta go. Watch over Angel," he said. He waited for her to sit and hold Angel's head in her lap before he stood. She grabbed his hand.

"Where are you going?"

Conor tried to pull away, but her grip tightened.

"Tell me what you're going to do," she said.

"I know the guy that did this," he said. "I have to find him."

"Why?"

"Because if I don't, you're gonna be next. He left a note in my apartment saying he would kill everyone that mattered to me unless I fought him." Conor shifted his gaze from Julia to Angel, and then back to her. "After we broke into the church, I went after the guys who put Sully in a coma. I hurt them pretty bad. One of them hired someone to kill me. I thought it wasn't a big deal, until now."

The whine of an ambulance rose out of the night. Angel coughed, starting a trickle of blood from a nostril. Julia let go of Conor's hand to wipe the blood off Angel's face.

"Then Angel's right," she said. "We should run."

Conor looked down on her. "He'll still come after me—and you. He won't stop."

He watched her face tighten. She looked down at Angel's ruined face.

Conor sighed and stepped over to his father. "You did good, Dad," he said, taking his father's hand. His dad smiled, then lost his balance. Conor caught him and held him. The smell of vomit was stifling, but Conor hugged him tightly, and then lowered him to the ground next to Julia.

He walked over to Angel's motorcycle, pushed it upright, and heeled out the kickstand. Straddling it, he looked at Julia. The ambulance siren whooped, drawing closer.

"Take my dad and follow Angel to the hospital," he said. "Stay in the lobby where other people can keep an eye on you for the night. No matter what, don't you or my dad leave."

Julia looked up. "What about you?"

Conor started the motorcycle and rolled it next to her. He brushed his hand through her hair. "I'll meet you here in the morning."

Her eyes darkened. "Make sure he never bothers us again."

He leaned down and kissed her. "I'll try," he said. "I promise."

As he rode out of the lot, Conor thought back to the note Cracker had left in his apartment. He'd said to go to any bar in town and to ask for him. The Red Fox was as good as any. He parked Angel's bike in front, walked in, and pushed between a couple guys sitting at the bar. One of them turned.

"Watch what you're—"

Conor glanced at the man. The guy turned his attention back to his beer. The bartender approached. Conor recognized him from the night he'd beaten Duck and Artie bloody. It was Mike, the bartender.

"What do you want?" said Mike.

"Joe Cracker Jones said I could ask for him here."

Mike's smile was not pretty. "Oh, yeah. That guy." He grabbed the landline phone and dialed. Conor noticed that big, ham-faced Mike never lost his smile as he talked and then hung up.

"He's on his way," said Mike, wiping the bar top with a dishtowel. The dishtowel went over his shoulder as he stepped in front of Conor. "I'm gonna love hearing about what he does to you."

Conor punched him in the mouth. Bottles and glasses

shattered as Mike reeled and fell. Conor walked over to a booth. The bar was packed, and everyone stared at him, but no one moved. He swept his gaze down the length of the bar. Everyone looked into their beer like it was turning to gold. He focused on the front door. Cracker showed up in under two minutes.

Conor watched him walk in. The squinty-eyed hillbilly was rangy. His arms and legs were long. He had the neck of a bulldog. He had huge shoulders, a deep chest, and a narrow midsection. His block head belonged on a bigger man. Easy to hit, but it would be a bitch to break without a sledgehammer. Last and definitely least was his face. Flat and wide, with eyes set far back under a prominent brow. He sat across from Conor and nodded. Conor nodded back. The only part of Cracker that didn't look dangerous was his terrible haircut. It stuck out all over and looked patchy. He needed a better barber.

"So, Sully boy got your attention, huh?" said Cracker, cracking his knuckles. "Or was it the old rummy you call daddy?"

Conor looked at his hands. Long, thick fingers. White scars crisscrossed knuckles as big as jawbreakers. "Where do you want to do this?" said Conor.

Cracker's eyes widened. "You're fast to the trigger, ain't you?"

"Let's just get this over with," said Conor.

Cracker stood. "Well, I'll tell you what, I can't wait. You follow me, a'right? It ain't far. We'll be dancing in no time."

Conor stood and followed Cracker outside. He got on Angel's motorcycle, started it, and trailed Cracker through neighborhoods into the shopping district. Just beyond the mall, Cracker took a left on Fourth Street, heading toward the outskirts of Brannigan. A little farther up the road, Cracker pulled up to the old GM plant's front gate, unlocked it, and waved him through. Conor motored inside the gate, stopped to scan the desolate parking lot, and then followed Cracker toward the main building.

Conor pulled into a parking space next to Cracker. Emergency lights glowed over the doors of the abandoned factory. Conor looked at the sky. A few clouds floated by a full moon—the same moon he and Julia had been naked under a couple nights ago. They should've never come back to this town.

"Come on then," said Cracker. "Ain't no rest for the wicked. Let's get this show on the road."

Conor dropped his gaze to Cracker, who stood in front of an open door. He walked by Cracker into the dark interior of the factory. The door boomed shut, enveloping Conor in total darkness. A click was followed by light flooding the factory.

"This way," said Cracker, walking past him.

Conor followed Cracker, getting his bearings. The interior of the abandoned factory was super clean. The concrete floor had blue, black, and red lines painted over it, outlining the routes of old production lines. A few pieces of machinery, old drill presses, hydraulic vises, and the like, stood silent. The ceiling was three stories up. Huge windowpanes were set high on the walls. During the day, the sun would have no trouble finding its way inside. Conor looked ahead. Dead square in the middle of the floor was a big structure. A tool crib. Two stories tall and encased in rubber-coated black chain link. It was the size of a small house. Empty except for two steel staircases set in opposite corners that ran up to a second level with a metal grate floor.

"Should make for a good place to tangle, don't you think?"

Conor looked at Cracker, who was walking backward, staring at him.

"That's where we're fighting?" said Conor, nodding at the cage.

Cracker bounced on his toes as he walked backward. "No place to run once that door closes."

The comment started an echo in Conor's head—of Angel, saying he should take Julia and run. Butterflies fluttered through his stomach. He thought about Angel's busted face. His broken fingers.

As they reached the cage, Cracker stopped and pulled out a cell phone. Conor surveyed the cage while Cracker made a call. When Cracker was finished, he sat on the floor and pulled off his shoes, saying, "Get ready. Our audience will be here in short order."

Conor sat and untied his shoes.

"You ever cage fight?" said Cracker.

Conor took off his shoes and socks. "No."

"It's for pussies," said Cracker, lying flat on his back to unbutton his jeans. "Best fighting's what we're gonna do. Takes as long as it takes and only one person walks out." He stood and stripped to black Lycra fighting shorts.

Conor looked over Cracker. His body was a landscape of muscle and scar tissue, but something was missing. Conor caught Cracker's gaze. "How come you don't have tattoos like other fighters?"

Cracker snorted. "You mean all that barbed wire, tigers, and lions, and bears? I *am* barbed wire, tigers, and lions, and bears. Don't need it drawn on me like a two-year-old, do I?" He thumped a fist on his chest and wagged the Confederate flag tattooed on his tongue before saying, "It's what's inside you that counts." Spitting in his hands, he rubbed them together. "Now get a move on. They'll be here any time now."

Conor stripped to his gray fighting shorts.

"And remember," said Cracker. "We fight until one of us is ushered through the pearly gates of our Lord and Savior or is cast down into the black pits of Old Scratch. Understand?"

"Do I look like I'm stupid?" said Conor.

"Don't know," said Cracker, eyeing Conor. "You came here to fight me, didn't ya?" He let out a long sigh, and his eyes glazed over. "You know, I once ran into this Chinese fella. A defrocked, hard core, Kung Fu priest straight from one of them secret temples. You never think there is such a thing until you run flat into it. But it's true, I guaran-fuckin-tee you that. That boy did all kinds of things to mess with me. Went on for hours and hours. But here's the thing. Nobody ever thinks it'll last that long. They think one way or another, someone has to give up. 'Oh, please stop. It hurts,'—you know? They can't comprehend the possibility that someone may actually like the pain. But that's me, see? I love pain. The worse, the better. So, here's a hint that'll put you one step ahead of that Chinaman. Whether you want to go long or short with this, I'm okay. Either way, eventually, you'll wonder what in the hell you ever did to God to end up in a locked cage with me. I know that'll happen because that's what they told me Mister Kung Fu said right before I rebel yelled in his face, ripped off his ears, shoved 'em down his throat, and choked him to death." Cracker tapped the side of his nose and nodded at Conor. "Words to the wise."

Conor cocked his head and stared at Cracker. "I don't know Kung Fu, but I do know you're about to have a real bad night." He tapped the side of his nose. "Words to the fucking crazy hillbilly."

Cracker flinched. But he covered it up quickly, drilling holes in Conor with his beady eyes. "Guess I got myself a fight then," he said.

The front door of the factory banged open. Duck and Barry came in and walked toward the cage.

"It's showtime," said Cracker. He opened the cage door and extended his arm. "After you."

Conor walked into the cage. Cracker didn't follow. He walked across the empty factory floor toward Duck and Barry. When Cracker got close, Duck held up a red gym bag. Cracker lifted a stack of money out of the bag, put the money back, and then led the way back toward the cage, rambling on about how Duck and Barry were here to enjoy the show but not to interfere, and what he would do to them if they did. Conor tuned it out. He thought back to everything he knew about fighting. All the years he wrestled.

The street fights he got into with Sully and Fitz. The sparring sessions with Angel. All the dirty boxing his dad taught him. And out of all of it, one thing stuck out. Angel eyeing him after their last sparring session, saying, "A fight doesn't have rules. Better you learn that here than when it matters."

Duck, Barry, and Cracker stopped outside the cage. Cracker started toward the door to the cage, and then turned around and walked up to Barry. He cocked his head, looking at Barry for a long moment. He reached into Barry's coat and pulled out a pistol. He smacked Barry in the mouth with it. As Barry bent over and moaned, Cracker frisked Duck, and then he disassembled Barry's gun and smashed it on the concrete floor. He kicked the broken pieces every which way as he walked toward the cage door. Conor emptied his lungs and shook his arms. It was time to fight with no rules.

Cracker opened the door and stepped in the cage, his hand on the door. "When this door closes, we dance," he said. "You ready?"

Conor shook his arms and rolled his neck.

Cracker turned to close the door.

Conor ran and smashed an elbow behind the hillbilly's ear before he could turn. Cracker went down on all fours. He kicked him in the face. Blood poured from Cracker's nose. Conor jumped on Cracker's back and wrapped a forearm around his throat.

Cracker's blood made everything slippery. Conor struggled to slip his arm under Cracker's chin. Cracker grabbed his arm, holding him off. He was slippery as an eel, buying time to shake the cobwebs. And Conor could feel him getting stronger with every passing second.

Being on the floor with this hillbilly when he regained his marbles seemed like a supremely bad idea. Conor eased up on his chokehold, readying himself to jump to his feet. Cracker grabbed his arm and pulled it under his chin.

"Where you going? Choke me out," said Cracker.

It didn't matter who you were. Big. Strong. Crazy. Didn't

matter. Once that chokehold was locked in, you were going to sleep. But Cracker was inviting him to choke him out. Why would he do that?

Conor slipped the chokehold in. Then he felt Cracker's hips shift.

It was the blood that did it, making Cracker slick and greasy. In one quick motion, Cracker spun until they were face-to-face. He locked his legs around Conor's midsection, blood streaming from his nose. He looked calm to Conor. Almost pleased.

"You're in a world a hurt," said Cracker, looking up at him as he began banging punches into Conor's kidneys.

Conor gripped the back of Cracker's neck and tucked his face against Cracker's chest, feeling the punches dig in.

There was no upside to this position. But there was a way out.

Conor let go of Cracker's neck. Before Cracker had a chance to move his punches up from his midsection to his face, he leaned back, braced his hands on the floor, and sat back, pulling Cracker into his lap. It took every ounce of his strength, but he stood, holding Cracker tight. Then he threw himself to the floor, slamming Cracker's back on the concrete.

The jolt stunned Cracker for a moment. Conor pushed off and rolled away. He came to his feet, adrenaline pumping.

Cracker stood slowly. The man's nose was dripping blood, but he wasn't even breathing hard as he lifted his fists and moved forward. Conor didn't back away, but he didn't meet him either. He circled to one side, then the other, staying on his toes. As he circled, Duck and Barry came into view, hanging on the outside of the cage. Duck pointed through the chain link at Cracker.

"Get him, you damn hillbilly," yelled Duck. "You're supposed to be killing him, not the other way around."

Cracker reached back, grabbed Duck's finger, and snapped it. He kept his eyes on Conor as he pressed forward.

"How you doing?" he said, looking at Conor while Duck wailed. "You look tired."

Conor inhaled deep through his nose and breathed out through his mouth, bouncing away as Cracker feinted forward. "You're not looking too good yourself."

Cracker wiped his nose and licked the blood off his fingers. "Just getting warmed up."

Conor smiled. He darted in, threw a head and body combination, and slipped Cracker's lunging counterpunch. And he kept it up, falling into a rhythm. For all the bluster of this backwoods maniac, he found that Cracker couldn't contend with speed.

So, Conor obliged.

He worked him over, pounding him with jabs, crosses, hooks, and leg kicks. He put on a clinic, showing Cracker the devastating effects of speed. But the pace was withering. Sure, the damage to Cracker's face, legs, and body piled up, but Conor's hands throbbed. His lungs burned. And although bloodied and bruised, Cracker never slowed. He stayed right in front of Conor, taking his punishment just to land a body shot here and there.

Trying to back Cracker up and get some breathing room, Conor stuck two jabs in his face. Fatigue slowed his reaction to Cracker's counter to the body. It caught him flush under the ribs, bending him double. Conor stumbled back, sidestepping Cracker's bullrush. He managed it, but just barely. He backed away from Cracker to stretch a cramp out of his calf. Sweat stung his eyes as he started to bounce and circle again. He wiped a forearm across his face, watching Cracker plod forward. This was getting ridiculous. It felt like he was dancing in sand. A memory floated through his consciousness.

He was fifteen, practicing combinations on the heavy bag in the garage, following his dad's instructions. Jab, jab, kick. Jab, jab, knee. Hook to the body, hook to the head. Denting the bag with a vicious elbow. He was fast. A whirlwind. Then his dad threw a towel at him and told him that he fought like Jersey Joe Walcott. Not a ton of power, but fast. His dad explained how people who fought Jersey Joe got picked apart until they crumbled. That is until Joe met Rocky Marciano. Jersey Joe dropped Marciano in the first round, then stayed out of Marciano's range and tattooed him for thirteen rounds. He was too slick for Marciano. But Marciano was a bull, taking three punches to deliver one to Jersey Joe's body. And the punishment eventually slowed Jersey Joe until the thirteenth round, when Marciano landed a right that put Joe on his knees. And that was where Joe stayed, one arm draped over the ropes while the ref counted him out. He didn't get up for a long time after that punch.

Conor remembered his dad slapping him on the back and saying, "So here's the deal. If you're gonna fight like Jersey Joe, remember one thing—don't ever fight Marciano." Conor looked across the cage at Cracker, still plodding relentlessly forward.

Shit.

Cracker rushed in, feinting a left to Conor's head. Conor looped an overhand right to Cracker's jaw. It connected with a crack, but Cracker's uppercut to his midsection came out of nowhere. Conor felt a spear of pain deep inside. Cracker dove in to grab his legs. Conor sprawled, using his weight to drive Cracker to the ground, then jumped clear. He circled away, coughing. That punch hurt. He coughed again and wiped his mouth. Blood shone on his hand.

"And it begins," said Cracker, rising to his feet, nodding at the blood.

Conor ran scenarios through his head. Cracker had nearly finished him on the ground. Standing with him was no better. Punches bloodied him but didn't seem to hurt him. The only option seemed to be Angel's advice. Run. And try to outlast this thing that looked like a man but fought like a machine.

He almost got caught twice over the next half hour. The

first time he was jabbing and moving, trying to stay away from Cracker's body shots. But he was so tired he didn't realize Cracker was steering him into a corner. Cracker dove in, wrapped his arms around his legs, and lifted. Conor was off the ground, bracing for a slam on the concrete when Cracker slipped in a smear of blood. He lost his grip and Conor wriggled free.

The second time was bad. Cracker's body shots had taken their toll. Blood rattled in Conor's lungs. Every time Cracker got close, Conor threw a combination then dropped his guard to block the inevitable body shot. Then Cracker got cute. He faked to the body and went to the head. The punch rocked Conor. Warning lights flashed. Conor went into overdrive and stood toe-to-toe with Cracker, trading punches. The first head shot by Cracker was the hardest punch of the flurry, but he caught three for every one he landed after that. The crazy hillbilly even backed up under the barrage, but Conor couldn't keep up the effort.

He was so tired.

And Cracker kept pressing him, never giving him a moment's rest.

The dance in Conor's step faded to nothing. He slid flat-footed around the cage, watching Cracker, searching for something that would make a difference. He'd used everything he'd ever learned. Kicked him in the balls. Chopped him in the throat. Even poked him in the eye. Nothing stopped him. Cracker's face was a mess, with his left eye all puffed up, but it was a fool's bargain to go for that eye. To get to it, Conor had to step in close enough for Cracker to land a body shot, and he wasn't sure he could take one more. Conor spat blood on the cold concrete. One more to his body would finish him. He searched through all he knew about fighting. He'd used every last bit. Nothing was left but a memory of Angel comparing Cracker to the man-eating jaguar in Somalia, advising Conor to run. He licked his lips, tasting blood as Cracker closed on him.

Cracker lunged. Conor dropped his arms to cover his ribs. Something hard and heavy clubbed the side of his head.

As he was falling, Conor saw the blur of Cracker's foot sweep past. Cracker caught him with a head kick. Conor's skull bounced off the concrete. Then he saw two Crackers, both bloody-faced and dripping with sweat, standing over him. He tried to move, but every part of him was short-circuited. A high-pitched ringing filled his head. He watched Cracker straddle him, placing his knees on either side of his face.

Conor closed one eye, turning Cracker's two faces into one, watching as Cracker opened his mouth. Conor flexed his fingers, feeling the air vibrate with Cracker's rebel yell.

Conor wondered if this was what the hunter felt like when the jaguar opened its mouth for the kill.

CHAPTER THIRTY-FOUR

Julia rolled up both paintings and slid them back in their tubes. She looked at the young, unshaven man in the suit and tie. He was handsome beyond belief, but he'd been eyeing her up and down like he owned her since he'd walked in. And now he'd shifted that same look to the tubes holding the paintings.

"As promised, two Grandma Moses paintings," she said, taking a seat in front of Angel's computer. She logged into Angel's bank account and looked up. "They're all yours after you transfer the money."

"Where's Angel?" the man said. "I thought I was doing business with him." He smiled and walked over to the tubes on Angel's desk.

"Don't touch those," said Julia.

The man tucked the tubes under his arm. "Tell you what. I'll settle up with Angel later."

Julia stood. She was a foot shorter than the man, but she grabbed his tie and pulled until he was face to face with her. She talked through clenched teeth.

"Put those down until you pay what you owe."

She let go of his tie, her eyes blazing. The man straightened his tie. He eyed her. Julia's stomach knotted, but she stared daggers right back. The man chewed the inside of his lip. He put down the tubes. Julia grabbed them.

He took out his phone, pressed a button, and put the phone to his ear.

"I have them," he said, sneering at Julia. "Do the transfer."

She turned toward the computer. It took a tense minute, but the numbers finally appeared. Three hundred grand. She handed the tubes to the man.

"Have a nice day," she said, smiling. She followed him through the garage to the parking lot and watched him get into his glossy black Rolls Royce. Cinders crunched under its tires as he drove into the street toward the brightening horizon signaling the approach of dawn.

Julia leaned against the door, exhausted. She had been up all night at the hospital, waiting to hear about Angel, watching over Conor's dad, and worrying about Conor. That was the worst, worrying about Conor. She went back inside the garage. Angel had been nip and tuck for a while last night. Something about a clot. But he'd survived. Conor's dad was hungover to the point of death, but after they got back, he'd fallen into a fitful sleep in the back seat of an old yellow Monte Carlo in the garage. Conor said he'd be back by sunrise. It wouldn't be long before she'd know if he'd come through on that promise. Just enough time to take a shower, brush her teeth, and get ready to leave, because one thing was certain.

If Conor didn't show, she had to run.

Before he'd lost consciousness, Angel had made her promise to leave if Conor didn't make it back. To take a hundred grand out of the account, take the work truck, and drive so far away no one would ever find her. She walked downstairs to the bathroom, turned on the shower, stripped, and stepped under the hot water, knowing that if Conor didn't show, that was exactly what she'd do.

Leave and never look back.

***

Her hair dripped as she walked out of the garage into the parking lot, holding a cup of coffee. She was barefoot, wearing jeans and an oil-stained work shirt she'd found in Angel's office. The coffee steamed, matching the fog rising from the scrub grass across the street. A slice of molten orange sun peeked over the horizon. She couldn't hold off anymore. It was time to go. She sipped her coffee, dumped the rest on the ground, and went inside, grabbing the keys to Angel's work truck.

It took a few minutes to transfer the hundred grand into her bank account, then she logged out, slipped on tennis shoes, and walked to Angel's truck parked on the side of the garage. It started right up. She pulled out, stopping at the edge of the parking lot. A pair of sunglasses were stuck in the passenger visor. She slipped them on, the truck idling while she stared at the sun. She looked both ways down the street. Empty, except for a cat darting into a field across the street. She pulled into the street and started driving.

Then stopped.

She backed the truck into the parking lot. She put it in Park and ran inside, leaning into the open window of the Monte Carlo.

"Mickey, wake up," she said.

He sat up. Pasty-eyed, hair sticking straight up, and with breath that could kill, but he was awake. He moaned, holding his head.

Julia opened the door and helped him out. "I just wanted to say goodbye," she said, hugging him.

Mickey stepped back. "Hang on," he said. "Let me get cleaned up and get some aspirin and coffee in me before you leave."

"I can't," she said. "I have to go. I promised Angel."

Mickey nodded. He held out his arms.

She hugged him. Tears welled as she walked away, but she didn't look back, even though she could hear Mickey following her. She got in the truck, put on her sunglasses, and pulled into the street.

"Take care of yourself," shouted Mickey.

She looked in the rearview mirror as she drove. Mickey walked into the street and waved. She lifted her hand to return the wave.

She stomped the brakes.

The truck screeched to a standstill. Her gaze locked on the rearview mirror.

She put the truck in Reverse, draped an arm over the back of her seat, and sped backward, zipping by Mickey, the engine whining as she backed up toward the figure in jeans and a white T-shirt. He was blocks away, walking down the street with a red gym bag slung over his shoulder. Waves of heat shimmered off the blacktop, giving him the wiggle of an illusion. He turned into hard reality as she got closer.

The truck squealed to a stop. She threw the door open and jumped out, her feet pounding the street. She leaped into Conor's chest and hugged him. He dropped the gym bag and grunted in pain, but he didn't stop her. He held her with one arm, lifted her, and gave her a weak twirl. She kissed his neck, tasting blood and sweat.

"You did it," she said, burying her face against him.

"Can't believe I made it," he croaked, setting her down. "The chain on Angel's bike snapped five blocks back. I can barely walk, but I promised you I'd be here."

She stopped hugging him but couldn't take her hands off him. She had to touch him. His arms. His shoulders. His bruised and bloody face. She kissed him and looked him over. He looked terrible. Beat to hell. Her breath caught in her throat as she saw his hand and said, "Oh my god. What happened?"

His right hand was covered in blood. A thick, wet drop dripped from his closed fist to the street, followed by another. He lifted his bloody hand and opened it. Something dark and wet with blood dropped from his grip. It slapped the blacktop.

Julia looked at it, then shifted her gaze to Conor. "Is that—"

"Someone opened his big mouth at the wrong time," he said.

Julia swallowed. "Is he still—"

"He'll never bother us again," said Conor.

She helped him into the truck and then walked around to the driver's side. Conor put the gym bag on the seat between them as she slid behind the steering wheel.

"Did the money for the paintings come through?" he asked.

She nodded.

"Are Angel and my dad okay?"

She nodded again.

"Good. Did you tell my dad about the money?"

Julia smiled, the rising sun painting her face in a warm, yellow glow. "No. Let's go tell him right now."

Conor nodded, then said, "I got something else he'll want to hear. It took a little work, but I got Duck to fill me in on how he and my dad used to work together. Turns out the thing that turned my dad into a bum wasn't his fault—it was Duck. He killed my dad's partner." He patted the gym bag. "So, I took this, as, you know, payback."

Eyes narrowing with a grin, he looked at Julia.

"Open it," he said.

She unzipped the bag. A pair of busted glasses lay on top of stacks of money spattered with blood.

Conor picked up the glasses. "Wonder how these got in here—they look like Duck's."

He tossed them out the window, leaned toward Julia, and kissed her. Then he settled back and pointed at his father standing in the parking lot of Angel's garage. "Let's go see my dad."

Julia slipped the truck into gear and drove into the blinding glare of the rising sun. She felt like she was floating. Weightless. As if she could rise out of her seat, fly through the window, and lift into the sky until the clouds were at her feet. Only one thing tethered her to the ground.

Conor's hand holding hers.

AUTHOR'S NOTE

If you want to know some background and thoughts I have about this story, keep reading. If that doesn't interest you, but you enjoyed the read, I recommend that you check out my novel TWO DAYS TO DIE. It was written in the same fashion as this story, with a classic battle of good versus evil. Theres a synopsis and a short excerpt you can check out right after this note.

How and why I wrote NEST OF THIEVES:

This story is straight from my bucket list. I've always been a big fan of thrillers, crime fiction, and romance. THE PRINCE OF THIEVES, written by Chuck Hogan, (and made into the great movie, THE TOWN, directed by Ben Affleck) was the spark that first hooked me on the idea of mashing up these genres. Writing a first draft took me years. When I finished, it was nearly twice as long as this final version. It was huge. A door stopper. I'd never written such a long novel—over 150,000 words—but I loved the characters so much that I couldn't help myself. And it taught me a huge lesson. I'd heard the quote, "Writing is rewriting," many times, but I'd never really had to test the theory until NEST OF THIEVES. In the end I cut almost half the words, but I discovered that the backstory I'd created for Conor, Julia, Cracker, Angel, Mickey and all the other characters was still there, giving each of them life as they walked, talked, loved, and fought their way through these pages. My hope is that they entertained you as much as they did me. I'm not sure if I'll revisit them again, but I can tell you this—I wouldn't mind spending more time with them. In fact, I've started an outline for another novel—but that's a story for another day. As always, thank you for reading my work. My goal as a writer is to give you my best, and I did everything in my power to deliver that with NEST OF THIEVES. I hope the effort paid off.

The unknown stranger motif:

I didn't realize the connection of this story to the unknown stranger motif until I was finished. Let me explain. I wrote this story with a vague idea of where it was going, as I do much of my work. My focus was the characters. Their backgrounds. Their friendships. Their obstacles. And most importantly, their desires. But, as any fiction writer will tell you, the worth of a character is only as great as the power of their enemy. This is the role Joe Cracker Jones plays. I was halfway through the manuscript when Cracker appeared. And that, as they say, was that. The story suddenly condensed and hardened into a straight line battle of good versus evil. Cracker was a joy to write. He entered the narrative fully formed. He comes from nowhere. His skillset is terrifying. And he has a certain, shall we say, je ne sais quoi, which, for the purposes of this story, means he's one unique, bat-shit-crazy individual. The man just gets things done. And, strangely enough, he's one of the most honest characters I've ever written. There is not one shred of bullshit in Cracker. But it took me a long time to recognize his roots. He is a product of a long-standing theme in literature and movies, the unknown stranger. If you've ever watched an old Clint Eastwood spaghetti western, or read one of Lee Child's Jack Reacher novels, you know what I'm talking about. Cracker is a mysterious, unfamiliar character who represents the danger of life. He is outside everyone's experience, and as such, wrecks all their conventions about how life is supposed to work. The unexpected result for this story, however, was that, unlike Clint Eastwood's spaghetti western loner, or Lee Child's traveling, one-man, wrecking crew, Jack Reacher, Cracker is pure, unadulterated bad. Except for his honesty, he has no redeeming qualities. As such, he occupies a special place in the unknown stranger lexicon. He never helps, as most unknown strangers do. He only hurts. As a fan of unknown strangers who change the dynamics of a narrative, I'm grateful that Cracker walked into this story. His appearance made everything better in the worst, and hopefully, best of ways.

One last note. I do have another novel in the works. Not sure when it will be done, but I hope you'll do me the honor of reading it when it's complete. Talk to you later.

Jules Adrienn
December 5, 2024

DON'T MISS ANOTHER ROMANTIC MYSTERY BY JULES ADRIENN

Two Days to Die

Detective Gabriel Emory has muscle, smarts, and survivalist skills. Even better, he has gorgeous detective Anita Wolfe flying with him to an all-expenses-paid island vacation. Too bad it's really an escaped convict's game to punish those who put him in prison.

Now Gabriel must use all his skills to survive a race through a dangerous wilderness. But how does he save himself and Anita in a contest where only the winner lives? It's a race for their lives, and it ends in two-days. Tick, tick, tick…

EXCERPT

Martinez walked over to the bar. He picked up his cigarette, took a drag, and blew smoke toward the ceiling.

"You have forty-eight hours. If no one wins, everyone and their family will be killed." He pointed his cigarette at the Colombian. "This man will hunt you down and skin you alive. My men will do the same to your families." He took another drag on his cigarette, walked over to the table, and tapped a finger on the map in front of Davis. "You have to cross twenty miles of wilderness in forty-eight hours or everyone dies. If you try to get off the island, you will be shot. If someone does escape, his or her family will be killed. There are no options. You'll all experience the same hell you put me through when you made sure I had no place to turn—no one to trust."

Martinez looked at his watch. He snapped his fingers, directing his men out of the lodge. The Colombian stayed put next to him as he looked over the group. "For now, enjoy yourselves," he said, tapping his watch. "You're my guests until seven a.m. tomorrow. After your long trip, I wanted to make sure you got some rest before the game and the killing begins." He turned toward the door then stopped and looked back over his shoulder. "One more thing. I am the only person who can save your families. If something happens to me, all your families die. Have a good night."

ABOUT THE AUTHOR

Jules Adrienn is an award-winning author from Ohio. Her novels include the YA Legends of Ava series ("Ava the Brave" and "Ava the Hunted"), and the thrillers "Two Days to Die" and "Nest of Thieves." Ava the Brave was a finalist in the 2021 Independent Audiobook Awards, a finalist in the 2020 Launch Pad manuscript competition, and reached the ranking of "#1 YA Action Suspense audiobook" on Kobo. The follow up in the series, Ava the Hunted, reached #1 on Amazon's Hot New Releases. With Amazon ratings above four stars for all her novels, Jules is quickly becoming the go-to author for heart pounding stories that, according to readers, are "Everything You Want In A Thriller," "Can't Put It Down Suspense," and "Action Filled To The End!"

https://www.instagram.com/julesadrienn/
https://www.facebook.com/JulesAdrienn/

Made in United States
Cleveland, OH
23 January 2025